SHADOW PLAYS

Special Thanks to: The Lemarr family (far and near), Robin Parrish, Ryan Jennings, Jason Webb, Michael Garrett, Chip Smitson, April Nicole of *Nicole Paradigm Media*, Bob Raymond, Heather Holmes, John Jennings, Starbucks at Tom Thumb #1786 (Karen, Danielle, Shantel, Sierra, Bobby, and Sam), The Village Church Flower Mound.

Extra Special Thanks Patreon Supporters:

Mandy Schumacher
Tom Lemarr

COVER DESIGN BY YOUNESS EL HINDAMI
AUTHOR PHOTO BY PATTY WEBB

SHADOW PLAYS

15 Stories of Darkness and Light

WWW.WRITECROWDPUBLISHING.COM

For Lee and Patty

Sail again the darkened sea
with hope, the lighthouse guiding thee,
set course for that eternal shore
where truth was found, and trust once more
the grace sent down to fallen men,
embracing now, as we did then,
the faded glory of our days
and dreams beyond these shadow plays.

JPL

CONTENTS

FOREWORD

DARK AND LIGHT. THE TWO OPPOSING FORCES that define the universe.

Superman once said, "There is a right and a wrong in the universe, and that distinction is not hard to make." The absolutes on either end of that spectrum are constant and unchanging, but most of us live our lives in the tension between them.

My friend J. Patrick Lemarr juggles that tension with dexterity and aplomb in the dangerous, beautiful book you hold in your hands. In each of his short stories, Lemarr puts humanity's darkest impulses under the microscope, but this is not an examination of evil for evil's sake. Nor is it a psychological or forensic exploration of the making of evil. Rather, I believe it to be an invitation to question your own impulses and decisions. Difficult choices, alternate paths that might have been taken, and most importantly, the consequences one must live with. Will these characters take the easy, fast road, or will they be more deliberate and intentional with their decisions,

A

investing time in getting it right?

There is always more to the world around us than what our five senses can determine—a notion near and dear to my own heart. Lemarr plays with this idea brilliantly, yet it's ultimately just another color on his paintbrush, another tool with which he can build his shadow plays. He has far deeper concerns, mostly about what a proud, deceitful thing the human heart can be.

In J. Patrick Lemarr's world, the darkness is always fascinating, but it's never venerated. It stands eternally in sharp contrast to the light—even if the light isn't overtly visible. The hint of that bright, piercing hope is always there; sometimes it's just "off screen," but it's never far away. The characters in these stories sometimes do terrible things, but they still know the difference between right and wrong. They may not always care about doing the right thing, but Lemarr does, and he makes sure we're creeped out or disgusted at all the proper times.

As unsettling as many of these stories are—and make no mistake, this is not "light reading material"; keep it away from the youngsters—you're going to find this book impossible to put down. Don't be surprised if you keep impulsively turning its pages long into the night.

These are tales that sneak up behind you and shock you—not with a jump-scare, but with a meticulously placed twist you will never see coming. Never have I seen a writer accomplish an edge-of-your-seat thriller composed of nothing but two men chatting in a booth at a diner, but I held my breath, chest clenched tight during each shocking twist in "Bootstrap." It's original, audacious, and delicious.

B

I was haunted by the twisted "The Man Who Came to Help," while the bone-chilling "Hubert H. Hargrove" stayed with me for days. "The Cinder Man" is the kind of horror/morality tale Stephen King would dig. Don't even get me started about creep-out fests like "On the Nape of Her Neck," "Can You See Me?," or the truly twisted "In the Orchard," with its shocking final twist. The less you know about any of these going in, the better.

Yet for every few descents into the yang of darkness, there's a refreshing flip to the yin of hope and faith. The poetic, almost lyrical "Bob and Julia" is one of these, as is the surprisingly touching "An Impromptu Chat." And definitely don't skip the closing title, the lovely and affecting "Tolly."

My personal favorite of the lot, not that you asked, has to be the compelling world building and fascinating characters of "Monster/Hunter," and I desperately want to experience more of that world and its adventures. I have a feeling you will feel the same.

(Pay close enough attention, and you might spot a few subtle canonical connections between some of these stories, but you didn't hear that from me...)

Shadow Plays is not for the faint of heart. If you're squeamish or puritanical about language and violence, you may have come to the wrong place. There's some extremely graphic stuff within these pages, because Lemarr is brave enough to examine the tropes of horror, science fiction, and the supernatural with an uncompromising vision. That's not a terribly common thing in this day and age, and should be applauded.

If *The Twilight Zone* ever makes a comeback, they need

Foreword

to give J. Patrick Lemarr a call immediately. The man knows how to do creepy, hair-standing-on-end fiction, yet always with a deep moral core that will leave you pondering life's greatest questions. Be sure to share this book with someone you care about, because you're really going to want to talk to someone after reading these stories.

Just remember, as frightening as the night may be—and there are plenty of dark and scary nights in *Shadow Plays*—darkness may be able to temporarily blot out the light.

But nothing can erase it.

Robin Parrish

D

BOOTSTRAP

I WAS FINISHING MY SECOND SLICE OF CHERRY pie when the bell attached to the entrance of the Breaker One Diner announced a new arrival with a gleeful jingle that would make Ol' Saint Nick jealous. The mercury in the thermometer had dropped to 29 degrees Fahrenheit that blustery February morning, but the air inside the diner was nice and toasty and the scent of French fries and grilled onions hung in it limply like a balloon losing its helium.

Along with the sticky plate that had once held my second piece of pie, my booth and table were littered with manuscript pages and sticky notes scribbled on in such a way only I would be able to decipher them…and then only after sliding my reading glasses down to rest on the tip of my nose like some schoolmarm from an old movie.

I'd been at the diner for three hours already, but my corner booth was the closest thing I had to an honest-to-God office and Gus Von Tranzer, the owner and sometime griddle man, had known me since he taught my gym class back in elementary school. He wasn't about to give me the boot so long as I ordered food occasionally. Besides, being on the ass-end of an old four-lane stretch of macadam made obsolete by a spiffy new turnpike, meant any paying customer was a good customer no matter how tired you grew of looking at their face day after day.

The new arrival was quite the puzzle. A thin, sinewy fellow in a trucker cap and a raincoat, he seemed ill-prepared for the harsh wind and frigid temperatures outside. He scanned the counter and booths with a keen eye before taking a seat at the counter near the rotating pastry case. His eyes never stopped roaming, though, as if he expected a threat to emerge.

Curious, I left my booth and took a seat at the counter with only a single stool between us. He eyed me suspiciously for a moment before continuing his visual assessment of the diner.

"Ruthie," I said to the only waitress on duty, a 40-something divorcee who often flirted with me despite my usual obliviousness to anything outside my own manuscript, "Can you get my friend here a warm cup o' joe and a slice of baked nirvana? He looks like he could use some warming. Throw it on my tab and I'll settle up before I leave."

"Sure thing, Davey," she mumbled, shuffling off to carry a meat and three to the elderly gentleman seated at the other end of the counter.

"Thank you," the stranger said, not bothering to look my way again. "You didn't have to pay, though. I have money."

"Didn't assume otherwise," I assured him. "It was just my way of welcoming you. Don't think I've seen you around. Get lost on your way to the turnpike?"

"Nah," he said, blowing into his cupped hands to warm them. "I'm right where I need to be. My name's Kaden. Kaden James."

"Dave," I offered. "Wannabe writer and breaker of hearts. Good to meet you."

Kaden nodded his thanks to Ruthie as she placed a steaming cup of coffee in front of him along with a small bowl filled with creamers.

"What kind o' pie did ya want, sugar?" she asked.

"What's good?" he countered.

"Go with the Chess," I suggested. "It's sweet, but not too. Goes down smooth with a bottomless mug of jitter juice."

"Chess then," he said, which sent Ruthie off to the pastry cabinet. "You're a writer, you say?"

"Depends on who you ask," I replied. "I say yes, the critics say no. It's anyone's guess really."

"What kind of stuff do you write?"

"Fiction, mostly—the sort critics tend to turn their noses up at."

"So, write something true," he said, cautiously sipping at his cauldron of coffee. "Maybe that'll be your ticket to fame and fortune."

"Bah! Reality is boring," I offered.

"Not always."

Ruthie brought the pie. The stranger picked at it cautiously as though it might be caustic and then, after his first real taste, scarfed the remainder down with all the decorum of a pig in mud.

"I told you it was good," I gloated. "The proprietor, Gus, got the recipe from his grandmother and, try as they may—and other establishments certainly have—no other diner has been able to match it. I suspect some sort of voodoo."

"I might believe it," Kaden said before taking another hesitant sip of java. "Thanks, mister. For the pie and cuppa."

"My pleasure," I said with a smile. I left the counter and returned to my perch in the corner booth, assuming Mr. James would like to be alone with his coffee. To my surprise, he followed me and sat across from me in the booth.

"You mind the company?" he asked.

"Not if you don't mind the mess," I said. "I'm trying to get these notes into some sort of sensible order before I dive into the next draft."

He picked up a sheet of grid paper and examined my scribbling.

"You write it all out by hand?" he asked.

"Not usually, no," I admitted. "But this one has come to me in fits and starts...and out of order like a bad Tarantino flick."

"Or a *good* Tarantino flick."

"Sure. But this order is making it feel more like Death Proof than Pulp Fiction."

"Hey, I liked Death Proof."

"To each his own," I replied. "My point is simply, in its current state, this baby isn't sellable. Forget convincing a publisher to buy it. I'm not buying it."

"So, what do you do?" Kaden asked and, to his credit, seemed genuinely engaged. "I mean, if you've worked as hard as you know how to achieve the outcome you want, and it still doesn't seem to be in the cards, what do you do? Give it up? Press on? Scrap everything and start over?"

I gave a loud whistle, which drew Ruthie's attention.

"Two more slices of Chess, if you please, Ruthie, and top off the bean squeezin's. My new friend here is seeking the wisdom of the sage and I'm a pint low on brain brew."

"You ain't just whistlin' Dixie, sugar," Ruthie said with a yawn. "Better have a nice tip for me, Davey."

"Just the tip?" I asked with a grin, prompting Ruthie to give me a wink.

"Didn't realize I was asking such a big question," Kaden said, sliding my papers back to me.

"I just wanted some pie," I admitted. "The second slice is yours—my way of saying gracias for the human interaction. I get surprisingly little of it these days. As for your question, I suppose the answer depends on the sort of person you are. Lots of people think they have a novel inside them waiting to come out."

"Yeah?"

"Yes. And most of those people are wrong. Writing, like all worthwhile pursuits, requires work, skill, patience, and—here's the bit most newb writers don't want to hear—perseverance. Getting the first draft done is work. Hell, sometimes even the outline is work. Skill comes into play once I'm in editing mode. My first draft is the block of granite and I need to chisel away at it."

"Which takes patience," Kaden said as Ruthie refilled our mugs and set two nicely chilled slices of Chess pie between us.

"And perseverance. There's no guarantee the second pass will get the job done either. If the finish line ever becomes more important than the quality of the story, no es bueno. If I get more attached to my own way of saying something than servicing the story…"

"No es bueno," Kaden snickered.

"In the words of Saint Arthur Fonzarelli, correcta-mundo."

"But let's say you've tried time and again to make the story better," Kaden said, "and the harder you tried to right the ship the faster it seemed to sink. There has to be a point where you're so damned tired of the struggle you scrap the book altogether, right?"

"No. Even the worst manuscript can be saved with enough work, skill, patience, and perseverance applied. Problems—even narrative problems—are a lot like people. Even the gruffest man alive can be smooth-talked by the right person. Maybe I wouldn't have a shot at friendship. Maybe you wouldn't. Maybe Maurice back there on the grill tonight would only piss him off something fierce, but Ruthie tosses him a wink or calls him "sweetie" and she's in like Flynn."

"You lost me," the stranger admitted.

"No bother," I said. "Hell, sometimes I confuse myself when I really get going. Why the interest, Mr. James? You got a story you're aiming to take a crack at?"

"It's already written," he said before taking a slow sip from his steaming mug. Once he set his cup down, his slid his pie plate closer. "And it's Kaden. No need to be formal, Mr. Collins."

"Dave," I said, not realizing until much later I hadn't given him my last name.

"See, Dave, my problem is in the edit. Maybe I'm running a bit low on perseverance, but I'm struggling to see a way out of the corner I've...written myself into. Every edit seems to make things worse."

"What sort of story are you writing, Kaden?" I asked around a large bite of pie.

He laughed loud enough to draw the attention of several other patrons. It wasn't a joyous laugh but a desperate one.

"It's sci-fi," he said, sniffing back another urge to laugh. "Most definitely sci-fi."

"Maybe you should tell me the basics," I said, "and I can try to give you three cents worth of free advice."

"I don't want to keep you from your work," Kaden said, raking the tines of his fork over the top of his slice of pie.

"Sometimes a distraction is exactly what I need to refocus."

"Hmm? How so?"

"Your own intention for the story tends to override your ability to spot mistakes or sloppy dialogue," I said. "When I edit, I have to spend time away from my pages before I can see them with fresh eyes. If I were to try editing a manuscript immediately after I finished the initial draft, my mind would plug in any narrative gaps or missing words because it knows the story too well. I usually step away from it for a few weeks until my mind gets a bit fuzzy on the details. Then, and only then, can I see it more critically."

Kaden jabbed at his slice of pie a time or two but didn't bother to load a bite onto his fork. I sipped my joe and awaited his next question. Instead, he threw a statement at me.

"I don't have time," he said, shaking his head as if it was the most insane thing ever to leave his mouth.

"Deadline?"

"A hell of one," he confirmed, finally giving up on the pie and pushing the plate back toward me. "I'm sure your advice is spot-on in most cases, but I don't have the time to step away from it long enough to see it with fresh eyes."

"Let me take a crack at it," I said. "Do you have it on you?"

"No," he said, scratching at the stubble on his chin. "I, uh, left my laptop at home."

"So, tell me. Be an honest-to-God storyteller, Kaden James, and present your work to your adjunct editor and pie aficionado. If there's a way of whipping your story into some salvageable state, we'll figure it out together."

He looked at me with suspicion.

"Why?" he asked.

"Why not?" I replied. "I told you I'm neck deep in my own story's mess. A break from it might give me the perspective I need to see the proper order."

"And provide some perspective for me, as well?"

"I make no promises," I said, before taking a serious gulp of mediocre coffee. "The thing is, Kaden, I genuinely like stories. It's why I do what I do. So, spill. What's this here sci-fi masterpiece in the making all about?"

"The end of everything good in the world," he said grimly.

"Sounds cheery. Who'll star in the obligatory Broadway musical?"

Kaden slammed his fist on the table so hard his coffee sloshed out onto the paper coaster it sat upon.

"This isn't a joke, dammit!"

"Sorry," I said, taken aback by his sudden mood shift. "I didn't mean to offend."

Kaden removed his trucker cap and ran his fingers through the short, greasy blonde mop atop his head. As he replaced his cap, I caught sight of an unusual tattoo near his right ear—script previously hidden by the headgear. It read: BTT-09B-719.

"I'm sorry for snapping," he offered. "It's been a long, long day."

"No offense taken," I said, "but if you scare Ruthie like that again, she's likely to throttle you with a steaming hot carafe."

Kaden turned to see Ruthie standing there waiting to refill our mugs, her face as red as a cherry tomato. He mouthed "sorry" and put his palms together as if praying for her forgiveness. Ruthie simply rolled her eyes and went back to warming our cups before shuffling on to the next booth.

"The stress is gnawing at your gut, huh?" I asked. "Sorry if my attempt at humor was misplaced. Please continue."

"My...protagonist, I guess you'd call him, grew up in an ugly future," he said.

"*Back to the Future 2* ugly or *Terminator 2* ugly?"

Kaden raised an eyebrow.

"More Skynet than Biff. Got it. This protagonist have a name?"

"I've waffled on the name a time or two. Let's call him Will for now. When Will was in high school, he read a book about time travel and convinced himself he was the main character in the story—that the tale was all about him."

"Very meta," I said.

"He doesn't tell anyone, of course, because time travel isn't a real-world thing. He just goes on living his life but that book nags at him…tugs at a thread in his thoughts and he can't seem to shake it. Then, one day a news story catches his attention."

"Someone created a time machine," I guessed, "and, suddenly, our hero has a reason to believe he's on a mission."

Kaden nodded.

"The thing is," he said, "the world began to change overnight. The company that invented the machine only had to prove it worked for the nations of the world to bend over for them. No one else was even close to a competing technology."

"So, if anyone put up a fight, the folks with all of time at their disposal could simply fiddle with the past and remove their enemy's power to retaliate," I said. "Or, I suppose, eliminate them altogether."

"Exactly," Kaden said. "Because these people were futzing with time, they were well hidden. A giant conglomerate was suddenly in power across the surface of the world and no one could get past all the shells and partners, etc. to see who was really doing what."

"What does our intrepid hero do?" I asked, leaning in toward him until the steam from my mug fogged my glasses.

"That depends on what draft of the story I go with," Kaden replied.

"I see."

"In the first draft, Will formed a group…a resistance, I suppose, to the threat and control spreading like a virus throughout the world. Things society had long taken for granted: internet privacy, confidential transactions, and the like all became things of the past. Will and his people couldn't research this conglomerate or get intel on where the time machine might be or who might own the damned thing because all such efforts led to arrest with charges of treason."

"Because, as in the present, big corporations own the government," I said. "Seems like a good foundation for a story."

"The reality of the world as it exists today is tame in comparison. Businesses try to run the government. They pressure. They grease palms. They make promises. But in Will's future, they have everything locked down. If any politician has ever spoken out against Synergis—that's the name of the conglomerate's public face—no one remembers them taking a stand."

"Because either they are too afraid to risk it, or they spoke out and were erased from the timeline like Marty McFly without his parents' first kiss," I said. "You might want to research the John Titor hoax. Or you could watch an anime called *Steins;Gate*. Fun research material to be had on the subject."

"If I had the time for that sort of thing, I would," Kaden said, closing his eyes and shaking his head as if defeat was clawing at his thoughts like a bird of prey and he was hoping to shoo it away while expending as little energy as humanly possible.

"Okay, Kaden, tell me where your drafts go turvy-topsy," I said. "With an ounce of luck and an endless supply of caffeine, maybe a solution will jump out at us like a drunken son-of-a-bitch on Halloween."

He stifled a laugh and yawned. It was the first time I noted how exhausted he looked. I'd seen a few long-haul truckers stumble into the Breaker One powered by nothing but sheer will power and energy drinks who carried more pep in their step. With his bloodshot eyes dramatically underscored by dark circles, the man who had introduced himself to me as Kaden James looked as though he hadn't seen the cool side of a pillow since Bob Hope last aired a Christmas special.

"My POV character, Will, jumps back to what he believed was the inciting incident. After years of searching and many good people lost to the cause, he and his rebels had discovered the initial research that had ultimately led to a working prototype of the World Drive, Synergis executives' catchy name for the time machine that broke the world. So, the rebels researched the scientist who developed the initial theory and discovered what had to be the spark leading to their dystopia. Someone near and dear to the scientist was killed, see, and it led them to obsession with the notion of fixing "mistakes" in the timeline. Their obsession eventually paid off and the world went to hell."

"What did Will and his rebels do?" I asked.

"They used their remaining forces on one last ditch effort: a suicide mission. It was clear the final form of the machine—the one used like a gun to the head of the entire planet—would never be found. Synergis kept it on the move from one black site to another so it couldn't be used or destroyed. But the rebels found the prototype and, though still heavily guarded, the security around it was a trifle compared to the finished World Drive. So, they threw everything they had at getting to the prototype machine and, when they did—"

"Your protagonist, Will, pulled a Sam Beckett and tried to correct the future by altering the past," I said. I cracked my knuckles, an act I always reserved for jumping into a tough edit. "Tell me about his mission."

He leaned over the table and spoke softly. There was something frantic in his eyes which frightened me even as it drew me in. It was as though he was Morpheus about to inform Neo of his choices and the deeper meaning of the world. I couldn't know then how accurate that analogy was.

"The scientist who developed the theory from which time travel was finally birthed had lost her brother years earlier," Kaden said. "He had been stabbed to death and the murderer was never found. She and her brother had been close, and the loss did something to her. She was never the same. She became a recluse. She broke contact with every other human being in her life except for her father. She obsessed over the possibility of altering the past and, because she was brilliant and no longer cared about her standing in the scientific community, tested and tweaked her theories in secret until, at last, she stumbled over something that could work. The rebels don't understand the quantum mechanics of it all. They don't even understand why the prototype was a success. But she got it to work and the world…well, it went to hell."

There was ash in my mouth and my tongue felt too thick to speak. I could feel my heartbeat thundering away so hard I worried it might crack my sternum. I felt dizzy and nauseous. All the pie in my digestive tract was booking tickets for a return trip. My vision went blurry as I tried to focus in on the stranger. I must have been doing my best Casper the Friendly Ghost impression, because Ruthie shouted at me from behind the register as she rang up a trucker in a faded Clint Black tour shirt.

"You okay over there, Davey? You look like someone pissed in your corn flakes."

I managed to look in Ruthie's direction and give her a disingenuous smile.

"You might need some sleep, sugar," she said. "Your thousand-yard-stare just broke into miles, hon."

"He'll be alright," Kaden assured her, stretching a false smile across his face. "He had a bite of pie go down the wrong way is all."

As Ruthie shrugged and went back to her routine, Kaden again leaned forward and whispered.

"I need you to keep it together, David."

"Little hope there," I mumbled.

"I'm serious. Things are in flux and I'm not sure what happens next. I need an ally and I'm choosing you. You started me on this path, now I need you to help me finish it."

"This is impossible," I managed to whisper as my mind ran through our full conversation again. "Wholly impossible."

"Welcome to the impossible," Kaden said. "I introduced myself to you as Kaden James because that's who you wrote about in 'Bootstrap' all those years ago. Well, for me it was years ago but, for you, it hasn't happened. Not yet."

"Bootstrap?" I repeated.

"The title of the story I first read about time travel. The one that convinced me it was somehow all about me. You wrote it."

I jumped up from the table and ran to the men's restroom where pie and coffee lurched out of me into a technicolor Rorschach test amorphously changing shapes in the toilet bowl. Once my stomach had been fully evacuated, I dry-heaved for several minutes until my tears overtook me and the trembling set in.

I know what you're thinking, dear reader. Why such an extreme reaction to what could have been nothing more than a prank? Why even attempt to believe in something so impossible without proof? I hear you. I do. And I'm not sure I can explain in a way that will satisfy you. I can only say that my subconscious had been assembling the puzzle pieces "Kaden James" had been placing before me and could see them connecting to pieces in my own puzzle. I knew that man, whatever his real name was, had been telling me the truth…not about some fictional story he couldn't properly edit, but about a timeline he had been unable to fix. He had come to me with a purpose. He had come to me because I knew the woman who, according to him, would eventually bring about the end of the world.

When I returned to my corner booth, the stranger still sat there ignoring his coffee. I sat and took a deep breath before speaking.

"You, uh, you're talking about Ella?" I asked.

"Ella Von Tranzer was a brilliant woman with a good heart. What little we know of her confirms as much. Her intentions were undoubtedly noble," Kaden said, "but it all went wrong, David. It all went to shit so fast no one could stop it."

"So, you're telling me you're from the future," I whispered, stunned at how readily such absurdity could cross the threshold of my teeth and lips to hang in the air as a condemnation of my own rationality.

"From 2054, yes."

"And Ella—*my* Ella—is responsible for the madness you described? All because of Karl's murder?" My brain was melting faster than a Nazi guilty of opening the Ark of the Covenant. "I knew she shut me out. Wouldn't take my calls. Wouldn't see me. Hell, I staked out her apartment for the better part of a month hoping to catch her coming or going. Nothing."

"She didn't leave for months. Didn't eat anything that wasn't delivered to her door. History revealed she sold every patent she had to fund her research, including a black site lab. It was small but well stocked with everything she needed to continue her tests."

"Ella doesn't have that kind of—"

"She did. Or, she does," Kaden explained. "She apparently played things pretty close to the vest…even with you."

"I don't believe any of this," I said, fighting the urge to throw the remnants of my pie at his face.

"You do," Kaden said, "or you wouldn't have written the story I read. You believe me and you're going to help me. I need to believe that. I—I'm at the end of this, David. I'm the only hope for the people in my time and I've failed them over and over. I need you to tell me why. I need you to help me fix it."

"I need a cigarette," I said, drumming my fingers on the table.

"You don't smoke," Kaden said, as if he was an authority on all things David Collins. But, of course, he was an authority. He wouldn't have risked his team and his own life without being prepared for anything and everything. Any man, woman, or child connected to Ella Von Tranzer would have been the subject of research and scrutiny. "You quit ten years ago," he reminded me, "because she asked you to. It's why you eat so much pie."

"Thank you, Doctor Phil."

"I get it," he said. "You're freaking out. Things you thought you knew are in question. I've been there. But my time is limited. Synergis knows what I've done. They've sent someone back."

"A friendly T-800?"

"This isn't funny," he snapped.

"I run my mouth," I said. "It's how I process. You'd better get used to it if you want my help."

He adjusted his cap and waited for me to continue.

"I need to know what you've already tried," I said. "I need to understand what changes you made that didn't provide the fix you were looking for."

"That's exactly why I came to you," Kaden replied. "I was hoping you'd be able to uncover a pattern I've been missing."

"Spill," I said, rubbing the bridge of my nose with my thumb and forefinger. "Don't leave anything out. Even something you find inconsequential could have a connection to causality."

"The obvious first step was to jump back to 2006 and prevent Karl Von Tranzer's murder," Kaden said. "Details, as you can imagine, were sketchy. There were never any suspects. No arrests."

"And none of the fingerprints they took at the scene matched anything on record," I said. "Gus and Ella stayed on top of the police. Hell, they even called in a federal agent on the premise that the killer may have crossed state lines."

"Agent Kyle Bradford," Kaden said. "I read his final report. He had served in the Navy with your friend, Gus. His grounds for being on the case were a bit of a stretch, but he went to bat for Gus and convinced his superiors to let it happen. When all was said and done, he had no better luck than the local or state boys. And now I know why."

I could feel my eyes furrowing. I didn't know exactly what was coming, but I instinctually knew I wasn't going to like it.

"From the police reports, we knew where the murder took place," Kaden said.

"Behind the Von Tranzers' house over on Bellflower," I said. "They found Karl behind the garden shed but figured he must have been killed in the alley. They found blood there, along with the knife from the Von Tranzers' kitchen. But Gus told the police Karl had been inside the house after dinner and wasn't aware he had left."

"He saw a prowler," Kaden said. "In fact, he thought he saw someone watching his sister's room and marked him for some kind of perv. He grabbed a knife and went out to confront the creep. What he couldn't have known, though, was the prowler had come there to protect him."

"Shit," I said, my nausea returning. "I was hoping to God you weren't going to say what you said. But now you've said it and…a thing like that can't be unsaid."

"He attacked me before I even saw him coming," Kaden admitted. "Some hero I am, huh? I was taken by surprise by a…a dumb kid just trying to look out for his sister."

Kaden sniffed back a tear and shook his head from side to side before continuing.

"Karl was so angry he wouldn't buy any lie or excuse I tried to sell him. He sliced my arm a time or two before I managed to wrestle him to the ground. I couldn't free the knife from his grip, but I saw an opening and kicked him square in the chest and he landed on the knife. H-he landed on the damn knife. I went from wannabe hero to murderer in less than three minutes."

"Was it always that way?" I asked. "I mean, was it a… what's it called? A paradox?"

"That's above my paygrade, David," he replied. "I was so horrified by what I'd unintentionally done that I ran all the way back to the World Drive prototype—still covered in Karl's blood—and jumped forward to 2019."

"Two years from now? Why?"

"Because our sources pinpointed 2021 as the likely breakthrough point for Von Tranzer's research. I tried to contact her discreetly, but she had become a full-fledged hermit. I'm reasonably certain her intent was never to share the device with anyone. Either she reached out to the wrong colleague for help or her secure server was breached by some facet of the conglomerate. None of that would matter, however, if I could convince her to stop her tests, wipe her hard drives, and let it go."

"You don't know Ella," I said. "She'd write you off as a looney and be more determined than ever to finish what she started."

"I couldn't even get past her security," Kaden explained. "Her lab had a single point of entry monitored by security cameras. Three armor-reinforced doors stood between the outside world and her lab and could only be opened with her thumbprint. I was nothing more than a stranger at her gate."

"So, what did you do?"

"I came here and kidnapped you."

"You…*huh*?"

"You were sitting in this same booth, nearly two years from now, eating a slice of cherry pie and proofing a horror manuscript. I struck up a conversation—acted like I recognized you from a book jacket and was a fan. We chatted about fiction and I pulled a gun under the table and let you know you'd be coming with me."

"And did I?"

"You took some convincing," Kaden said, and I'm fairly certain my gulp was loud enough for the kitchen staff to hear. "I took you to Ella," he continued. "Stood you right there at the entrance so she could see you on the camera. No surprises. She opened the door. I put the gun on her and moved us inside, but you—damn you, David. You made a play for the gun and it went off. The round ricocheted off one of the armored doors in that entry way and struck Ella in the throat. Neither of us noticed, though, as we were still scrambling to gain control of the gun. Von Tranzer bled out while we tussled."

"She's dead?" I asked, my mind instantly recalling how good things had once been with Ella before her brother was killed.

"She will be. In two years, if we don't change things," Kaden said. "Before I got the gun away from you, you managed to squeeze off a round that caught me in the side."

"And me? Or, I guess, future me?"

"Dead," he said grimly, the memory of my death clearly haunting him. "I didn't have a choice. It was me or you."

"Sure."

"I didn't want to kill anyone, David. You must believe me. I wanted to be a hero—to fix things and usher in a better future. But, no matter what I tried, I failed."

"Seems like," I agreed. "Is there more?"

"With both of you dead, I wiped her hard drives and burned the lab. I don't know what sort of redundancy Ella had in place, but the future didn't change."

"You know this how?"

"I went back," Kaden said. "I found things had changed

but not by much. The timeline had altered—Synergis had not taken over as quickly—but it was basically the same. Ella hadn't lived to finish her prototype, so my using it to travel into a timeline in which it had never existed created an anomaly. As I said, I'm not real clear on all the specifics. People are more likely to confuse me for a particle than a particle physicist, but I had this feeling in my gut that I couldn't shake. It may have just been the loss of blood from that gunshot, but this uneasy fear ripped through me. I couldn't contact any of the resistance. None of my safe houses were safe houses. Too much had changed."

"And the prototype? You mentioned an anomaly?"

"That's what I'm getting at," Kaden explained. "I had this uneasy feeling that, because the prototype didn't belong on that particular timeline, it couldn't stay. I got it into my head that it might disappear or explode or something. Somehow, the timeline was going to fix the problem. I was convinced of it. And I know how that sounds, David. I had heard my share of crackpots and conspiracy theorists ranting about how the world would end long before it all went to hell. They all missed the mark. But I was sure the prototype was either going to have to go or there might be even worse consequences… so I used it again to remove myself and it from that timeline."

"Why travel here? Why now?" I asked.

"I'm not at all certain," he confessed. "The World Drive prototype couldn't possibly work indefinitely. I'm not sure what Ella used as a power source, but I had the feeling I wasn't going to get many more chances. I remembered what kicked off this whole thing for me…reading your book. You described meeting a man named Kaden James and sharing pie and coffee with him as he talked with you about fiction. At the end of the story, Kaden James revealed himself to be a time traveler. You didn't believe it, of course, but he gave you something which managed to convince you. When you first published your story, it didn't find much traction. But a short time later, a small imprint added it to a collection of stories—science fiction and monster tales. The book itself was a dud, but your story made you low-key famous."

"So, you came here?"

"Honestly, what did I have to lose? When I first became convinced your Kaden James character was a version of me from some other time or reality, I absorbed every bit of information about you I could find. I read interviews, listened to podcasts, and found a few archived blog posts you had written. I even wrote you. First, an email and later a handwritten job."

"Luddite," I said with a smirk.

"Says the guy still working everything out on paper," Kaden said. "Anyway, over time, it felt like I knew you. I know that's not accurate, but it felt that way. And there I was, sitting in the prototype trying to decide where I could go and all I could think about was that tussle with you. I admired you. Respected you, even, and you died because of me. I could go back and try to save Karl again—"

"But since you had already tried and inadvertently caused his death," I said, "it was likely a fixed point...an abhorrent anchor in the sea of time."

"Or, I could try to undo the things which hadn't happened in my timeline—preventing you from dying that night in 2021."

"You came back to a time early enough to not run into your past self while still allowing plenty of time to cause a sea change."

"That's my goal," Kaden said. "But I don't have the first damn clue of how to get there. I came here because, as weird as this may sound, I trust you, David. I'm either going to succeed at this thing or the world is going to hell faster than any of us imagined. I needed someone on my team—someone who doesn't think like me—to help me, to steer me."

The silence which followed was surely unnerving to the time traveling stranger who had gone through so much to accomplish every opposite thing from his intentions. But I needed to think. I needed to brood on it the way I do over my plots when they get jumbled in what passes for my brain. I needed to untangle the narrative threads and rotate them up my mental fork like so much cerebral spaghetti. I needed to roll it around my palate and determine what ingredient was missing.

To his credit, Kaden remained still and quiet while my mind worked and reworked the story he had laid before me. I didn't realize until I looked back at him to speak, that he had devoured the slice of pie he had not found the stomach for mere moments earlier. Apparently, confession is as good for the appetite as it is for the soul.

"Since you studied me, feel free to stop me if you've heard this before," I said. Kaden looked up and used the sleeve of his raincoat to wipe the crumbs from his lips. "I was a comic book fan as a kid. Couldn't get enough of them. If Marvel or DC published it, I consumed it. By high school, I had moved on to King, Koontz, Crichton, and Grisham…but middle school belonged to Chris Claremont, Roger Stern, Frank Miller, Dennis O'Neil and on and on. Those four-color comic book heroes and the creative teams behind them were my obsession. In fact, the first time I ever wrote a story, it was some silly thing about Batman finally bringing the clowned prince of crime to justice. And, by justice, I mean he killed him."

"I'm not sure where you're going with this," Kaden admitted, "but go on."

"It wasn't a real story," I told him. "It was more of a scene, really, but I was proud of it. You would've thought I expected a Pulitzer or something. I showed it to all my friends and most of them, being 8th graders, thought it was awesome. But this one kid—a recent transfer from out of state—he told me I had it all wrong. The story didn't work, he said, because I missed something fundamental: a truth about heroes and villains."

"Go on."

"This kid didn't know me from Adam, but he was as passionate about writing as I was about comics. Hell, if I'm honest, my conversations with him were what prompted me to pursue this mad notion of being a writer. I should've kept up with him. By the time we got back from Christmas Break that year, he had moved on."

"What does any of this have to do with me?" Kaden asked.

"Like I said, he and I argued over my attempt at a Batman story. This kid—damn, I can't quite recall his name—said my story didn't work because Batman would never kill the Joker. I argued he should. It was dumb, in the opinion of 8th grade Davey Collins, that a methodical guy like Batman wouldn't figure out putting the Joker away in Arkham Asylum never solved the problem. The Joker always broke free. People always died. Bats always caught him again. It was a cycle and it never stopped. But Batman was way too smart to let such a thing go on, I argued. If he wasn't in a comic book where the status quo had to be restored every few years, he'd surely put an end to such a vicious and unpredictable arch nemesis."

"But this other kid felt differently, I'm guessing."

I pulled a scratch pad from the worn messenger bag I kept beside me in the booth and, with my trusty Parker 51, made two vertical columns. At the top of each was the letter D. Under the first, I wrote *Dusty, Dustin, Dylan, Darren, Dennis, Devon*, and *Derry* before running out of two-syllable names. I was sure it was a two-syllable name. Under the second column, I wrote *Dart, Douglas* (which I then, likewise, added under the first column below Derry), *Denton, Darwin, Dannon*, and *Drake*.

"Doing your own time traveling?" Kaden asked.

"Trying to remember that kid's name. He had two Ds for initials. I remember because that's a standard comic book trope…Peter Parker, Bruce Banner, Matt Murdock, Lois Lane…even Clark Kent. Different letters, of course, but a similar scheme. Anyway, the kid's name isn't important, but what he said to me was."

"Still waiting on it," Kaden said. "What did you get wrong? Why can't Batman kill the Joker?"

"Because, as soon as he did, no matter how many lives it ultimately saved, he would stop being a hero. Not simply because he murdered someone, but because he lost hope.

This kid—Dustin or Dylan or whatever the hell it was—said, and I've since come to believe him, what draws us to heroes is not superpowers or cool origin stories. It isn't the inevitable team-ups or crossovers. All those things are great, but they aren't at the root of what makes a hero a hero."

"And you're saying what? Hope is the key? I don't follow."

"Batman doesn't refrain from killing the Joker, or anyone else for that matter, because it's wrong or illegal. It's because, beneath the dark, brooding exterior we all love, Batman never turns his back on the mad hope his damaged foes can be restored. Even someone like the Joker, a chaotic madman who wants to watch the world burn, has tragedy woven into his story. We are each born with our own particular set of evil inclinations, but it takes something extra to make a Charles Manson, a Jeffrey Dahmer, or a Joker. Something broke them."

"Not every broken thing can be fixed, David," Kaden said. "I've learned this the hard way."

"No, you haven't," I argued. "You tried what was easy. See, killing the Joker would make Batman's life easier… but it would mean we, as readers, would be cheering on a murderer and villain. Batman maintains some hope that the Jokers of the world can be restored because he needs to believe Bruce Wayne can be restored. He hopes against all odds that, one day, the compulsion that drives him will end—that what is broken inside himself can be healed and the world won't need a Batman anymore. Sure, he's smart enough to know the world may not afford him that opportunity. It may not be in the cards. But he must believe. He must keep the flame of hope burning, however dimly, because once he lets it go out—once he stops believing the broken can be restored—he will find that he, too, is beyond restoration.

You jumped into your past thinking you could be the hero, Kaden, and you *were*. You wanted to save Karl's life. It was a noble, selfless move. And you, by your own account, failed. What happened that night was an accident, but the accident propelled you into far more frantic actions. Your hope was diminished. You planned to deal with Ella and make sure her hard drives were wiped clean. When that didn't work, you kidnapped me—someone, I must remind you, that you claim to admire. And I'm not exactly a threat, right? I was a means to an end. You used me to get access to Ella."

"I didn't see another choice," Kaden said.

"There's the problem," I replied. "You didn't see it, but there was one. But let's stay with the chain of events as they happened. I'm not a brave man, Kaden. I'm no action hero. I don't have any secret SEAL training or spy gadgets in my bag of holding, and no mutant powers. Hell, I get winded when I stand up to get more pie."

"Your point?"

"I know myself well enough to know I wouldn't have attacked someone with a gun if I thought there was a way out of it without getting hurt. Something about that moment must've made it clear to me that your intention wasn't to let Ella go after you got what you wanted," I said. "You always intended to kill her, right? It was your plan B?"

"It wasn't a plan," Kaden said, what little color he had

leaving his face. "I just knew I would…put an end to things if I had to."

"Say what you mean," I replied gently, though from Kaden's expression, he heard it as a demand.

He looked around the diner to make sure no one was eavesdropping and lowered his voice to barely above a whisper before speaking.

"I knew I would kill her if I had to," he said. "It would make me sick. I might not ever be able to live with it, but I'd do it. If that's what it took."

"And that's precisely where you failed," I said, pushing aside my scratch pad and my sad attempt to remember that student's name. "Once Karl died—not *despite* your efforts to save him but *because* of them—you decided all hope was lost. You gave in to your baser instincts and bought into the lie that violence was the answer."

"What choice did I have?" Kaden asked. It was clear he wasn't looking to dodge my accusation. He simply couldn't see another angle wherein his hands remained blood-free.

"When you came to me," I said, "you came gun in hand. You kidnapped me. Forced me to play along with your plan."

"I wasn't looking for you to get hurt," Kaden said, "or even to scare you. I just needed you to get to Von Tranzer."

"Did you make any attempt to convince me to go with you *before* you pulled the gun?"

"I didn't think you'd go."

"You studied me," I reminded him. "You knew more about me and who I would become than it's possible for me to know at this moment in time. You had to know I wouldn't be a threat to you."

"That's what I thought. But you attacked me."

"Because you were going to hurt Ella," I replied.

"Okay, but…I couldn't take any chances. I needed you to come with me. The gun was my way of ensuring you would," Kaden said.

"You had time on your side," I told him. "Even if this villainous conglomerate knew you had the prototype—and I don't doubt they did—they couldn't have known what you would target after what happened with Karl. In fact, they may not have sent anyone back for you at all. Why would they? If they had deciphered what originally happened that night, they wanted you to go back."

"What are you saying, David? I've had a shitty couple of days and the way I'm feeling after three time jumps laughs in the face of jet lag."

"Time travel makes my head hurt," I admitted. "I don't understand all the whys or hows, but Synergis may have messed with time much more than you thought. The timeline could have changed so much that even you aren't sure of what's real and what's not. Who's to say they didn't know you killed Karl all along? Who's to say they didn't make sure my story was published to move you into position? Maybe they leaked you the right information in such a way to make it feel like you worked for it."

"That's bullshit," Kaden said. "I told you it was a suicide run to get to the prototype. I lost good people."

"And if you had simply waltzed in," I replied, "you'd have been suspicious. It might have altered the events."

"That can't—how could they know? I don't follow."

"I'm only throwing out some possibilities," I admitted. "My real point is that you stopped being the hero of this story the minute you decided to resort to violence. Whatever she may or may not invent, Ella Von Tranzer is a kind, loving, and brilliant woman. Deciding she was expendable for the sake of the 'greater good,' caused you to switch sides. Suddenly, you were the one with the power of life and death in your hands. You were the one with enough ego to decide whose life was worthy and whose was not. You came from a future in which the murderers of the story were given free license to alter events to their own ends. You became a murderer trying to alter events for your own ends. Why would you have expected a different outcome?"

"It wasn't for my *own* ends," Kaden argued. "I was trying to make things better for everyone."

"What's better for one isn't always better for another," I said, "but I agree, given what you've said, it's for the best not to let Ella's research come to fruition. But our goal doesn't require bloodshed. That's my point. One set of people willing to kill for what they want being exchanged for a man who would kill to get what he wants doesn't provide the sort of rewrite you were hoping for in your story. You only get that sort of change with hope…and a bit of grace. You get it from being a real hero…which means keeping your hands clean and trying to see a path of redemption."

"Don't get all religious with me, David," Kaden said. "I've studied you enough to know you aren't the type."

"You're right. I'm not usually the spiritual sort. I am a writer, though, and I believe strongly in the power of stories. I'm not talking about hope and grace in some vaguely spiritual sense. I'm talking about what you put into action. Nothing you could read about me, or Ella for that matter, could lead you to believe us to be villains. You said yourself her work was stolen, or pirated, or she simply trusted the wrong people. But that's not how you approached stopping her, Kaden. You approached her the way I had Batman deal with the Joker. You decided her death would make the world a better place. And you lost. You were wrong. You made it all worse. The bad guys still won but, when you went back, your resistance was no more. What little hope remained in the world had died out…put to death years earlier by your carelessness and lack of concern for another human being whose goals happen to oppose yours."

"You're oversimplifying things a bit," Kaden said, his eyes narrowing. "One life in the balance with millions of others—"

"This was *never* a math problem, Kaden. It was a heart problem. Yours. Theirs. Ella's. We're all filthy, fallible humans beneath our social disguises. We come from different places, but we are—every last mother's son of us—beautifully and tragically human."

To his credit, Kaden took a deep breath and let my words settle. He had, of course, been through an ordeal the likes of which many of us couldn't comprehend. He was weary and frantic, and I didn't enjoy placing such a weight upon his already burdened shoulders.

"I've looked up to you my whole life, David," he said at last. "I've read everything you've ever written, hoping to find another reference to 'Kaden James,' the time traveler you once met at your favorite diner."

"I never wrote about him again, though, did I?"

Kaden shook his head. I leaned forward and spoke softly.

"You became a villain in the second draft, Kaden. That doesn't mean we can't make the next draft better. I don't doubt your good intentions, but we know all too well what road they pave, yeah?"

"I guess we do."

"So, let's make this next draft count," I said. I slid my pad and fountain pen back between us and ripped off the page containing my name brainstorming. "We know how the story of the World Drive begins. We also know how we want it to end. What we need is a narrative through line to get us from one to the other."

At the top of the blank page, I wrote: *Ella's grief leads her to plan the prototype.* I drew a double line under that sentence and, at the bottom of the page, wrote: *The working prototype never existed. The world is saved. Hooray!* Above those sentences, I drew another double line. The space between those sets of double lines was all I was concerned with. It wasn't that I didn't understand what needed to happen next. It was that I needed to convince a time-traveling stranger to trust in my plan.

"I met Ella's dad, Gus—he owns this diner, by the way, in case your research missed that little detail—when I was in elementary school," I told Kaden. "He was my first coach. I had little to no athletic prowess, but Gus treated me far better than my alcoholic dad or my other crusty teachers, so he quickly became sort of a role model and mentor to me. I didn't meet Karl or Ella until they transferred into my school a few years later in the 6th grade. Karl was a little young to be a close friend, but Ella…she was the best friend I had ever had. Later, in high school, she became a lot more."

"Karl's death did something to her," I admitted. "She ended things with me and withdrew from all her other friends. I tried a few times, over the years, to reconnect but it never took. I couldn't reach past her hurt. But I know her, Kaden. I know her as well or better than I know myself. If she thought for even a moment her work could become what you've described to me…that it could be used for such horror…she wouldn't do it."

"So, what exactly do you suggest?" he asked.

"That we tell her your story," I said. "We step into the mess of her life and bring some hope and grace into the narrative. That's what she needs. We engage the hell her emotions have trapped her in and help her see that bringing Karl back will never happen—that her noble intentions would lead only to misery. You're the living, breathing proof of that. Then, we trust her to make the right call. We believe in her. We put our hope in her."

"I can't bank on hope, David," Kaden said. "I need results."

"How's that result-driven action working out for you so far? Hmm?" I asked. "Seems to me, we already know where it will lead: to blood and regret. Nothing more."

"We just put smiles on our faces and try to get her to believe me?"

"No," I said. "We tell her. We trust her. And, when she gives up on the notion of saving her brother, I remind her that I'm her friend and, if she'll let me, I'll step into the grief with her, and Gus and everyone else who loves her can stop allowing her to shut us out. We can stand against her…for her. We can help her find hope outside of the notion of having her kid brother back."

Kaden thought on that a few seconds and sighed.

"I see why it's an appealing thought, David," he said, "but it's not solid. I appreciate that it would spare me from becoming the antihero—"

"Villain," I corrected.

"—but, there's no guarantee your solution would work. I would love it if life was so simple, but it's not. Sometimes you have no choice but to do bad things to get a good result."

"That's a lie that you've sold yourself on," I argued. "Evil begets evil. Always has, always will. Sure, sometimes violence and war are necessary because we can't step into a bad situation involving thousands upon thousands of people and always find a way to talk it out. Doesn't mean we shouldn't *try*, mind you, but this isn't that. This is one man with a mission—a good man on a good mission, no doubt—versus one kind and damaged woman who will, one day soon, make a grave mistake. Your lack of hope and the fear it feeds kept you from seeing Ella as a human being first and foremost. Instead, you saw her as a road block to a better future. Anyone—and I do mean anyone, Kaden—who treats another human being as nothing but a means to an end has already taken a step on the road to villainy."

"That means all of us are villains," Kaden said, slumping down in the booth.

"I never said otherwise."

"And we fix that by...trying to talk it out?" the time traveler asked.

"Like I said, talking and stepping into her pain. The truth of your future can only do part of the job. It can breach Ella's defenses and make her doubt the nature and result of her research. But once we have an opening, we need to flood the wound in her heart with some love and devotion. Add a touch of grace to the mix and those will eventually bring healing."

"You sound like some sort of hippy priest," Kaden said, "or a yogi."

"And here I sit without my pic-a-nic basket," I said, doing my best to mimic Daws Butler, who voiced the famous cartoon bear into the late 1980s.

Kaden laughed, shaking his head as it faded.

"Do you honestly think it could work?"

"It will," I said. "It *did*. Believe that. Hope for it."

"You make it sound like it's already guaranteed." Kaden said with a scoff.

"When you first read my story about Kaden James, the David Collins of that story didn't believe him, right? I mean, he likely thought the Kaden in his story was a few fries short of a combo meal. But you said the Kaden in the story left him something that convinced him, right?"

"Yeah," Kaden said, reaching into his pocket. "It was a quarter—"

"Dated 2042," I finished for him. Kaden had produced the quarter from his pocket. I had produced the same quarter from mine.

"What the hell?" was all he could muster.

"It's my turn to tell you a story," I said, placing my

quarter on the table. As I suspected, he picked it up and compared it to his own as I spoke.

"This morning, right before this blasted storm kicked into Bachman-Turner, I sat in my car trying to get the engine to turn over. My old beater has never liked the cold. Every winter, I go through the same bullshit. Luckily, I set my own hours so being late to work is never an issue. When I can't get her moving, I work from home. But I prefer to be here for the pie, the coffee, and the witty conversation." I raised my voice loud enough for Ruthie to hear me from her post behind the counter. "Isn't that right, my darling Ruthie?"

"Whatever you say, Davey," she called back before checking the window for her next order.

"This morning, though, as I finally got my car to turn over," I continued, "I spotted someone approaching the driver's side door. To my surprise, it was Ella Von Tranzer."

That, as you can imagine, got Kaden's attention. He placed both quarters on the table and leaned in to hear the rest of my story.

"Why didn't you tell me this before?" he asked, his voice tinged with anger.

"I wasn't sure it was safe to," I admitted, "and, honestly, I wasn't sure what to make of my encounter with Ella until after you told me your story. Now that I think I understand it, I can share it."

"Go on."

"I hadn't seen Ella in years before this morning," I said. "She looked exhausted and worn thin…like a strong gust of arctic wind might snap her in two. She was dressed for the weather but still shivering. I unlocked the passenger door and motioned for her to get in. Instinctively, I embraced her as soon as she closed the passenger door. She stiffened at first but, within 30 seconds or so, she was weeping into my shoulder. I'm man enough to admit I joined her. I wasn't even sure what we were crying about."

"What did she say?" Kaden asked.

"Not much. Before I could ask her any of the myriad questions tumbling through my noggin, she took my hand and placed this quarter in my palm. She closed my fingers around it and made me promise I would hold onto it for her.

'You're a writer, Davey,' she told me, 'And I know you'll sort it all out given enough time. Hold onto it and you'll know what to do.'

She also said she wanted me to know I was successful—a comment that prompted me to laugh because I wrongly assumed she was talking about my writing career—and that she would keep her word as soon as she got back. Then, she opened the passenger door and ran off into the falling snow and I drove here where, a few hours later, you walked into the Breaker One with your…plot issues."

"You think she time traveled," Kaden said.

"I do. I think she came from a timeline in which we convinced her of the danger her work would cause, and she promised to destroy her prototype and data. I think she had her prototype built much earlier than you ever suspected, Kaden. So, before destroying it, she tested it out…exactly one time."

"To bring you proof your plan would be the one to work?" Kaden asked. I simply nodded and retrieved my quarter from the table. Kaden retrieved his as well.

"You know where she's holed up, yes?" I asked.

"Yeah," he said, scratching under the bill of his cap.

"So, we go," I said, "and let hope lead our way."

"And that will be enough?" he asked.

"It always has been, Kaden," I said, pulling enough bills from my wallet to cover my tab plus a fat tip for Ruthie and leaving it on the table. "But hope often needs our legs and our mouths and even our hearts to get from should be to *will* be."

"Like I said," the time traveler said with a weary smile, "you're a regular yogi."

"The future ain't what it used to be," I said. "Let's just hope we can get my engine to start."

"Lots of men your age havin' that trouble, sweetie," Ruthie offered, brushing past me to refill the mug of a matronly woman who, like me, had been occupying her spot for hours. "They make little blue pills for it now."

"You see, Kaden?" I said, gathering my papers, "Hope abides."

HUBERT H. HARGROVE

HUBERT HARGROVE DUG DEEPLY INTO THE gray wood of the back porch with the pocket knife, hoping to carve his initials in the weathered pine before his mother came out with the lemonade. As he scratched out the second "h" of the three, he heard her modestly-priced flats sliding over the cracked linoleum of the kitchen followed by the witchy whine of the screen door.

"Hubie? What are you doing over there?"

Lana Hargrove had only been 17 years old for two months when Hubert's father, a merchant marine home on leave, left his DNA in her nether regions. Lana's parents, pillars of their idyllic community, sent young Lana to live with relatives and crafted a lie suitable to assuage any questions the neighbors raised about their daughter's whereabouts. Nine years later, she was June Cleaver without the pearls – the pinnacle of motherhood in 1961.

Lana's husband, the story went, had perished at sea during a military training exercise gone awry, leaving her alone to raise young Hubert. There were suspicions, of course, but most neighbors felt inclined to believe the tale, which is why Hubert considered them all to be morons.

"Hubie!" God, he hated it when she called him that. "Answer me when I'm speaking to you."

Hubert turned toward her after tucking his grandfather's Barlow back into his pocket. "I was imagining those soldiers in Cuba. The ones President Kennedy sent over to kill Castro."

Lana's frown was not the work of the sour beverage she carried. Hubert was at it again. "Our president sent those men to depose Castro, Hubie. That means they will take him out of power. Our government doesn't kill people."

"They hung that soldier—Bennett was his name. They hung him dead on account of raping some woman." He knew exactly how to get under her skin. It had become a game to him. "It said so in the newspaper."

"I told you that you aren't to read the newspaper anymore." She handed him a sweaty glass of lemonade. "Furthermore, I don't like you talking about things like rape and hanging. It isn't proper for a grown man to discuss such things, let alone a little boy."

"I'm not so little," he mumbled into his glass.

"I said I won't have it," Lana said, her prim demeanor growing more ragged by the second. "Don't talk back to me, Hubert. I don't care for it."

Hubert gulped down his lemonade and looked back to his initials. "I'll bet it's on the television. When they kill Castro, I mean. Bet they put a bullet through his head."

"Why do you insist on doing this to me?" Her voice

was less than a whisper, but he heard it.

"It's no different from hunting, mother," Hubert said. "One shot through the heart or the head—"

"Hubert!"

"—and it's all over. No more problems. Guns are loud, though, and you have to be a good shot. Knives are better."

"Hubert Humphrey Hargrove! Enough!" Lana glared at her son before scanning the neighboring yards to ensure they were alone. "If your father were here—"

"He'd have to remind you of his name." She slapped him hard. Exactly the response he was hoping for.

"You—I'm sorry, Hubert," she said, her eyes glassy with saline "You just push me too far sometimes. Now, stop with all the killing talk. Miss Preminger says your drawings and stories are not normal for a boy your age."

"Miss Preminger puts her boyfriend's tinkler in her mouth when she goes into the teachers' supply closet." He watched with delight as his mother nearly swallowed her tongue. "Jimmy Larkin saw her in there when he stayed late for detention. Is that what you used to do for my dad?"

Another slap.

"Don't you ever—"

"I'll bet if you would have done it better, he might have stayed."

Slap.

The slaps stung, of course, but they were necessary. This time, however, Hubert dropped his glass and let it shatter on the porch.

"Damn it, Hubert, that was your grandmother's set!"

Lana Hargrove bent to pick up the remnants of her inheritance when her 9-year-old son stabbed her in the neck with her own father's knife. A flick of the wrist launched a spray of red onto his sleeve and a river of blood onto the porch. It ran between the fragments of glass entrancing young Hubert for the briefest of moments.

He left the knife where it was, jutting from her freckled neck. He would run to the neighbors and tell them the tale; how his mother had beaten him frequently, how she was always yelling at him and throwing things at him. He had been scared, he would say, afraid she might kill him. He had done only what he had to in order to survive the horrifying encounter. He would explain it all with a moving performance of tears and guilt, and they would buy it. People were sheep. Brainless sheep who deserved nothing but slaughter. Hubert Humphrey Hargrove meant to bring it to them. His mother was only the first of many. He still had work to do. A whole lifetime of bright and bloody work.

THE MAN WHO CAME TO HELP

EARL "BOON" BAILEY PARTED THE CURTAINS of his hotel room window with the barrel of his Winchester XPR, squinted his left eye, and peered through the magnified AccuPoint sight with his right. At the pool below, a young woman in a white one-piece bathing suit exited the water and toweled herself off. Boon couldn't hear what she said to her companion—a young, solidly built Latino with a tattoo of the name "Rosaria" on the shoulder of his left arm—but, whatever she said, it made the young man laugh.

Boon's trigger finger remained on the guard. He was watching, not shooting, after all, and he wouldn't want any accidents.

"Enjoy your swim, gorgeous," he whispered. "It's a good day for it. Nice and warm with your honey at your side."

"Is that kindness in your heart?" the man in the corner asked. "Or some wicked joke for your own amusement?"

"Can't it be both?" Boon asked, setting the rifle down

and looking the man over. "I didn't realize you had come back, Ghost Guy. You hungry?"

"No," the man said, "but thank you all the same. And, I'm not a ghost, you know. I've explained this."

Boon shrugged, snagging his half-eaten bag of corn chips from the shoddy hotel room desk before plopping onto the king-sized mattress.

"Wasn't sure you were coming back," Boon said. "Been a day or two."

"I suppose it has," the man said. "It appears you've been busy…doing all the things we talked about you *not* doing."

"You're not the boss of me, Ghost Guy," Boon said as he smacked his chips. "Don't even know who you are."

"I told you," the man said, taking a seat in the room's only armchair, "I'm here to help. Why do you insist on thinking I'm a ghost?"

"Not a ghost, exactly. A figment."

"Ah," the man said. "You think I might be a bit of underdone potato, eh? Less grave and more gravy, to paraphrase Dickens. I assure you, I'm no hallucination. Nor am I your Clarence, Mr. Bailey."

"It's just Boon to my friends," Boon replied, grabbing the small television remote and powering the flat screen television bolted to the wall.

"Is that what you think I am?" the man asked.

Boon shook his head, distracted by the on-screen menu. "Figment," he repeated.

"You've hallucinated before, yes?" the man asked. "I'm assuming it's why Dr. Klein put you on his little antipsychotic cocktail."

"See?" Boon said. "Figment. It's only Klein and me that know that stuff."

"Everything that ever was is written in a book somewhere," the man said. "I've read your story, Mr. Bailey. I know everything about you."

"So would a figment," Boon argued. "You like horror movies, Ghost Guy?"

"Not especially," the man said.

"There's a good one on cable right now," Boon said. "It's all about a fellow what gets his ass trapped in a mine. There's only him and one other guy down there and the more they get to know each other—"

"I haven't seen the movie, but I know the story," the man said. "Like you, Mr. Bailey, neither of those men were what they appeared to be."

Boon snorted at that.

"True story, I read," he told the man in the armchair. "Happened out Pennsylvania way or some such. Place is still burning underneath. It's what they say anyhow. I think it's all just…*whaddayacallit*…a myth."

"Myths and truths are not mutually exclusive," the man replied. "Trust me. I know."

"Yeah, well, I don't believe that," Boon said. "So, neither do you."

"Again," the man insisted, "I'm not a figment of your imagination. I'm no avatar of your subconscious. I'm every bit as real as you are, Mr. Bailey."

"Sure you are," Boon said, brushing chip crumbs from his shirt. "That's why you can appear and disappear like a ghost. Every real person can do that shit."

"Not every person, no," the man agreed. "But the how

and why of it doesn't change the fact of the matter. I'm here to help, Mr. Bailey, and I sincerely hope you'll let me."

"Don't go holding your breath," Boon said. "That is, if you even *need* to breathe."

"I do, I assure you."

Boon looked the man over. He was dressed casually in jeans and a t-shirt bearing the emblem of some rock band Boon was too old to have much use for. It was the man's shoes that bothered him the most. He was wearing a pristine pair of red Chuck Taylors which made it appear as though they were part of some costume he wore rather than his actual attire. He was clean-shaven and well-coifed with the mere hint of a tattoo peeking out from the neck of his tee.

"I'd like to tell you about two people," the man said, "and then I'll leave you to your...preparations. Is that fair?"

"Shoot," Boon said, chuckling at his own joke.

"Carmen Villanueva," the man offered, "is a fourth-year med student pursuing a career in pediatric surgery. She put a few miles on her soul after high school by spending a summer in Central America working with a mission that builds schools and clinics for communities which simply cannot afford them. She plans to return once she's finished with school to live and work where too few are willing to."

"So?" Boon asked.

"She'll stay in Central America for seven years before she's killed by an addict looking to rob her of supplies but, during those seven years, she'll save the lives of 16 children between the ages of 6 months to 11 years old. And she'll improve the lives of countless others."

"You're telling me you know the future, Ghost Guy?" Boon asked.

"It's only the future from your perspective, Mr. Bailey," the man said. "I've read the whole story. Time is inconsequential to me. And, please, call me Dylan."

"And I suppose you're going to tell me she'll be in the crowd tonight?"

"Yes," Dylan said. "She's been invited to the party by her brother-in-law, who works for your firm. But it won't be your bullet that kills her. The panic will do that. The shots will cause a stampede for cover and her skull will be crushed between the pavement and the boot of a man who flirted with her earlier in the evening."

"Dying tonight or seven years from now," Boon said, turning his attention back toward the television, "I don't see much difference."

"For at least 16 children, it's all the difference in the world."

"Okay," Boon said. "That's one down."

"Eastman Sinclaire," Dylan said. "I assume the name is familiar."

"You know damn well it is, Figgy."

"Dylan," the stranger reminded him.

"Figgy," Boon insisted. "Short for figment."

Dylan sighed and leaned back in his chair. After raking his fingers through his hair, he sighed again and sat upright.

"You know Eastman, of course, because he's been your boss for some 7 years," Dylan said. "And, thanks to your hacking of his private server, you now know you're being fired."

"Fired next month," Boon corrected. "After I finish the designs I've been working on for two years, of course. They wouldn't want to be on the hook for a delay."

"He's not the one I want to talk to you about," Dylan said, "but, rather, his son."

"Didn't even know that asshat had a kid," Boon said, wadding up the empty chip bag and tossing it into the trash bin.

"He has three, in point of fact," Dylan said, "but it's the youngest, Lincoln, I want to tell you about. You see, Lincoln is the baby of the family and, despite the family's prim and proper demeanor, Lincoln loves to play in the dirt. He loves it so much that, at the tender age of eleven, he'll contract a rare strain of meningitis. The illness will nearly kill him. In fact, it will mark him forever and, by the time he enters college, he'll go pre-med with his mind set on becoming an immunologist."

"Good for him," Boon said, standing and approaching the room's mini bar. "Again, I ask…so?"

"Lincoln Sinclaire proves to be quite the genius, Mr. Bailey, and his research will draw the attention of immunologists all over the globe. Upon his death, his son, Chester, will form the Sinclaire Foundation for Immunological Study and, in addition to funding a great deal of research, will provide grants for the best and brightest med students bent toward that pursuit. One such recipient, a Miles Epstein, will use his funding to go back to one of Lincoln Sinclaire's pursuits and prove to be successful where Sinclaire had not. In the year 2127, after pursuing it for half his life, Dr. Epstein discovers the cure for Acquired Immune Deficiency Syndrome. This, of course, leads to great recognition, including the Nobel Prize. In his acceptance speech, he thanked his wife, his children, a few mentors and, lastly, Lincoln Sinclaire, without whom he believed his research would have ended in failure."

"Okay, Copernicus, you've convinced me," Boon said, opening the tiniest bottle of Jim Beam he had ever seen. "Hallelujah, I've seen the light."

"You're mocking me," Dylan lamented.

"Damn straight, Figgy," Boon said before downing the contents of the tiny bottle in a single gulp. "You can't know the future because I can't know the future."

"For the last time, Mr. Bailey, I am not a figment of your damned imagination!"

"Oh, sure. Sure."

The man moved so fast Boon didn't have time to defend himself against the right cross that collided with his chin. Boon fell back into the mini bar and landed on his rump with a thud.

"I'll kill you for that, Figgy!" he spat, lunging for one of the 12 firearms in the hotel room.

If there was any fear in him, the man called Dylan showed none as he returned to his seat in the armchair.

"Can you kill a figment?" he asked. "Even one that takes a crack at your jaw?"

"We could find out," Boon threatened.

"We could," Dylan agreed. "But I didn't come here to fight you, Mr. Bailey. I came here to help."

"So you keep on saying," Boon said, rubbing his sore mandible. "But you ain't said anything useful yet, Figgy.

Just some nonsense about the future. You're all what-ifs and coulda-beens."

"So, let's talk facts, Mr. Bailey, if that is what pleases you."

"Jump on it," Boon said, helping himself to another small bottle. After all, he had no intention of paying for it.

"Let's talk about your perceived grievances against your firm and, as you've come to see it, the world at large," Dylan said. "We can begin back in middle school if you'd like."

Boon laughed. "Wherever you like, Figgy. Nothing's gonna derail my plans."

"You were an awkward kid. Friendless for the most part, but you had a mom and dad who loved you, so… it could have been worse. You needed attention, though, and found you could get it by acting out. Whether you were setting off firecrackers in the boys' bathroom or letting the air out of teacher's tires, it gave you a thrill. If you got caught, well, even better. There's always a group of ne'er-do-wells who latch onto each other, and you eventually found yours."

"We weren't so bad," Boon insisted.

"I never said you were," Dylan replied. "I'm only setting the stage."

"Whatever makes you happy," Boon said.

"Ah, yes. Your motto," Dylan said. "Sounds like a good one on the surface, but happiness is a cheap commodity. It can be bought and sold. It can also be stolen from you in an instant. I find joy a far greater treasure as it is rare and mined somewhere beyond the confines of your own tale."

"I think all these mini bottles are affecting my brain," Boon said. "You're talking more nonsense than usual."

"My point is only that joy is a full-bodied wine of the finest vintage, whereas happiness is mere ripple."

"Whatever you say, Figgy. Why don't you steer yourself back to whatever point you were trying to make about me and my middle school friends."

Dylan chuckled.

"Something funny?"

"You think of those boys as friends," Dylan said, "yet every one of them abandoned you in high school. To them, you were only as cool as your last stunt. And since you were smart enough to not derail your entire future for school pranks, you were quickly out of fashion."

"Didn't need 'em by then," Boon said. "I had a plan for my life. I knew where I was going."

"Yes, you did. Your God-given talent for design and architecture drew quite a bit of attention before you graduated high school, Mr. Bailey. And, with that attention, you got serious about your studies and pursued a scholarship opportunity."

"Which I won," Boon added, walking back to the window to peer down at the pool.

"But, even in college, you heard the whispers," Dylan said. "For all your talent, you didn't have the vision of your contemporaries. You were ahead of the curve when it came to functional details, but your designs would never be confused for...well, art."

"What the hell did they know, huh?" Boon asked. "Buncha little hipster dipshits who wanted to be the next

Frank Gehry. Well, that's fine and great and all, but most clients are interested in function more than form. Art costs a shitload of money to maintain, but my designs had a uniformity that made maintenance and retrofitting a breeze."

"And two decades ago," Dylan said, "you were right. And while you were the flavor of the month, clients were beating down your door. In fact, your firm initially hired you into the fold because all of their resident architects were so artsy-fartsy they couldn't weather the sea change. It allowed you to quickly rise to the top, bringing more money into the firm than your more artistically inclined peers."

"And because my designs weren't pretentious bullshit, I was able to work faster than they were."

"That's right," Dylan said, "and you rode that wave as far as it would carry you. Even won a prestigious award, if I recall."

"Hell yeah, I did," Boon boasted. "Got an all-expense paid trip to New York City out of it, too."

"That you did. But those whispers came back, didn't they? Even at that lovely banquet with your crystalline trophy still warm from your touch, others in the room were questioning whether your pedestrian designs deserved such accolades. Rewarding mediocrity, after all, often encourages more of the same."

"Screw you, Figgy. Screw them, too."

"I've touched a nerve, it seems," Dylan said. "Their whispers did, too. It's why you did…what you did."

Boon approached Dylan, drawing so close as he bent to look Dylan in the eyes, their noses nearly touched.

"You better watch what you say," Boon growled. "You may not be real enough for me to throttle, but I've got a couple of pills that can quiet you down."

"But if you take them, Mr. Bailey," Dylan replied with a smile, "you might not go through with your plans for this evening. So, it would still be a win for me."

"Bah!" Boon shouted, spinning on his heels and walking into the bathroom. "Say what you want, Figgy. In a couple of hours, there won't be a thing you can say to rattle me."

"Then you don't mind me talking about *her*."

There was a pause. However lost Earl Bailey—dubbed "Boon" by his maternal grandfather—had become in the madness which had overtaken him, he still remembered what he had done on that all-expense-paid trip to New York City and didn't relish being reminded. After considering it, he found his resolve.

"Say what you need to, Figgy," he said, not bothering to exit the restroom. "Let's get this over with."

"You were angry," Dylan said. "More so, in fact, than you had ever been before. The whispers had grown louder. Your peers sneered without apology. Their growing derision—or at least all you imagined it to be—became an itch you couldn't scratch. Within an hour, the itch was a cancer eating away at your flesh. An hour later and you desperately wanted to feel something…anything other than being a joke. So, you hired an escort and paid double for the option to play a little rough. But you didn't just *play* rough, did you?"

Boon stepped into view, leaning against the door frame of the bathroom.

"What do you want from me, Figgy? What do you really want?"

"I want you to tell me what happened to Tyana Rambeau."

"Who?"

"The prostitute you hired that night," Dylan said. "That was her name. I read her sad story before I came here today. She had a mother in Houston, you know, who prayed for her every night for 3 years. Tyana had run away a few weeks shy of her 16th birthday. No one knew why...not even Tyana. She had a similar story to many who fall into that line of work. She was broken, Mr. Bailey. Men paid her for her body, but her heart and soul were wounded nearly beyond repair. Still, there remained a glimmer of hope—the thought that, if things didn't get better soon, she'd swallow her pride and run home to her momma."

"And you know all that because you've read her story?" Boon asked.

"Yes. It's my job, Mr. Bailey. To Read. To Know. To Act. Now, tell me what you did to Tyana Rambeau."

"If you read all about it, Figgy, you already know what I did."

"True," Dylan said, "but the clock is ticking, Mr. Bailey, and confession is good for the soul."

"I don't believe that junk," Boon spat, as if the thought of it made him ill.

"Nevertheless," Dylan replied.

"She was nothing but a whore," Boon said, pushing past Dylan to go back to the window. "She was getting paid for the rough stuff, so I played rough."

"Oh, I know you did," Dylan said, standing but keeping his distance from the madman. "Your attempt at sexual distraction couldn't drive out your growing feeling of inadequacy. In fact, it only exacerbated it."

"Shut it, Figgy," Boon warned.

"You couldn't get it up," Dylan said, allowing his smirk to tinge the tone of his voice. "It was a relief to her, of course, so she tried to manipulate the moment into something less dangerous."

"Stop," Boon said, reaching for the .45 Magnum he had tucked under his belt after checking into the room. He pointed it at the young man who had been appearing to him on and off for several weeks. "I'm warning you, Figgy."

"Your impotence may have been stress-induced," Dylan offered. "Likely not a permanent condition, but in Tyana's manipulation you thought you heard a hint of disgust. You decided she was mocking you, and you weren't going to take it anymore. Not from a prostitute, at least. So, you…vented."

"Last warning," Boon said, his anger causing a small, blue vein to pulse over his left brow.

"You vented until her blood soaked through the cheap mattress," Dylan replied. "When you were finally sated, there were cuts on your knuckles from her broken teeth and her young face was…something her poor mother in Houston would never be able to identify. It was one of the few times in my…well, career, I guess you'd say…that I was glad I wasn't going to see the story in person."

Click.

The gun's failure to fire prompted a perplexed Boon to look at it, which meant taking his eyes off his intended victim for the briefest of moments. That moment proved to be long enough for Dylan to cross the space between them and disarm him. A solid punch to the ribcage took the breath out of the would-be gunman and dropped him to his knees.

"I took the liberty of unloading your gun while you slept last night," Dylan said. "I don't fancy a new vent in the cranium, Mr. Bailey, and you don't get to check out of this conversation until I'm done with you."

"Fuck you," Boon spat, fighting for every breath.

"No, thank you," Dylan said. "Now, let's get back to NYC and young Tyana…or what was left of her. After your head cleared, you were in a panic, Mr. Bailey. Luckily for you, you had given the girl's pimp a false name. Trusting that a man in his business wouldn't be quick to call the police, you showered, dressed yourself, and escaped down the fire escape. Twelve hours later, you were back on the west coast, working on ways to justify your actions so you could sleep at night. It didn't take long, did it?"

Boon struggled to stand and, surprisingly, the man who had punched him offered him a hand. Still, he remained doubled over, hands on his knees, trying to get his breath under control.

"It never went away, did it?" Dylan asked.

"What didn't?"

"That feeling you felt. The god-like feeling that rushed through you as you took a life which wasn't yours to take. And you embraced it, Mr. Bailey. You nurtured it…just in case. And then, two weeks ago, you grew suspicious and hacked the email server. But what the email about your firing could never reveal, Mr. Bailey, was how your

57

own mania led your employers to that decision. All the imagined sleights and whispers had made you impossible to work with. The chip on your shoulder grew too big for them to ignore…because you kept feeding your monster. You kept building toward your next release."

"Shut up!" Boon demanded.

"So, here we are," Dylan said. "The would-be gunman and the man who came to help…only hours away from your madness making the news and ending the lives of people who came here to celebrate the company's good fortune."

"Can't catch my breath," Boon squeaked out. "Can't—"

"I'm guessing there's a bit of pain in the left arm, too, yes? All the classic symptoms of a heart attack, Mr. Bailey. Perhaps our talk has introduced too much stress."

"H-help," Boon gasped. "Said…came…to help."

"That I did," Dylan said, looking down at the horrid man. "But I never said I came to help *you*, Mr. Bailey. All the other times I came to see you, I offered to help you turn from the path you were on. I gave you every reason to turn back from this madness and get the help you needed. But you didn't want hope. You wanted the monster. And this is what becomes of every monster in the end, Mr. Bailey. They all die—alone and filled with rage—while hope lives on and on."

Earl "Boon" Bailey dropped back to his knees and tried to crawl for the room's only telephone. Halfway there, his heart stopped.

Dylan stepped over the body to the window and parted the curtains to glance at the pool. Event planners were already at work setting the stage for the night's festivities.

"Enjoy your evening," Dylan said. "I pray you all make the most of what you've been given."

He turned and made his way to the door leading out into the hotel's 3rd floor hallway. When he turned the knob, however, the door opened to somewhere else entirely. With one last glance back to the dead man on the floor, he stepped into the Evermore and closed the door. His work was done.

BY THE HORNS

IF YOU WERE TO READ MY MAIL—AND YOU shouldn't since it's a federal offense—you would find it all addressed to the name on my birth certificate: Kent Allen Crawford. If, however, you were to ask my friends what they think about their ol' pal Kent, they wouldn't know who you mean. To them, I am and always will be "Jazz." Don't ask. Ever.

Like most small-town kids, I found my fair share of trouble to get into. Shoplifting? Well, I was poor. So, if I wanted something, I took it. Vandalism? Sure. I was no artist, but I did some decent work on a few overpasses and back alley walls. Joyriding? Naturally. Who could pass up a drive down Main St. in a supercharged Challenger? Assault? Well, let's just say I gave as good as I got and never backed down from a punk with a smart mouth.

Throughout my assorted juvenile attempts at badassery, I had my cousin, Jessica, as my wingman…or, I suppose, wing woman. I didn't have any siblings, but I grew up with Jess at my side and she was like having a sister, a brother, and a crazy uncle all rolled into one. If I was ankle deep in nonsense, so was she. If she was selling fake I.D.s, I was keeping an eye out for the boys in blue. We had each other's backs. Always.

Now, I've admitted to you my interests have not always been lawful and above board, but Jess and I always had a sort of code we lived by. The basic gist was this: nobody already hurting for cash gets hooked in a scam or robbed from…and nobody gets hurt or killed on our account. Not ever. It was our code that kept us far removed from kidnappings, sex trafficking and the like…until Jess's ex came to us with a ransom job which, according to him, would mean we could leave the life behind once and for all. I said no. So did Jess.

Weeks passed, and we found ourselves behind the eight ball, owing a sizeable debt to a drug runner called "Dust." No one knew the cat's real name but we all knew his rep. The feds had been after him for years and he had proven damned near untouchable. He had people everywhere and always knew who was coming for him and when. He was also known for leaving bodies in his wake. If you were on his radar, you'd better not fail him. We learned this the hard way when Jess and our mutual friend, Alberto, brought me into a gig running payments for Dust and his crew. It was a sweet gig for the first three weeks. Then, one rainy night on the drive back from an Atlanta drop, the feds hit us hard. Lead was exchanged but Jess and I managed to slip through their fingers. Alberto wasn't so lucky. We lost him to a bullet and the cash to the feds. Dust was…displeased.

We had one shot to make things square with Dust and

that was to pay back the two mill we lost with Alberto. So, Jess brings up the ransom job again: says her ex, Grady, had it all worked out down to the second but needed a solid team to make it happen. Last she had heard, he was still trying to get the right people.

I'd love to tell you I'm above that sort of pressure—that I value my ethics over my skin. I'd love to say, even under that kind of heat, I'd never even consider snatching a kid and holding the threat of violence over them for a payday. But I knew Dust. He didn't play. His patience had an expiration date, and time was racing in that direction. So, I called Jess and she set up a meeting with Grady at some abandoned auto parts store marked for demolition. The signs on the construction fencing claimed there'd be a Starbucks springing up in its place.

"Glad you two finally came to your senses," Grady said, stomping out the remnant of the Marlboro he had tossed to the ground. "This job is cake."

"I'll double check your plans," Jess said, "and decide for myself if it's cake. What we need to know is the payday."

"Five million, easy," Grady said, his shit-eating grin the sort begging for a right hook. "That's a million each. Cash money."

"Why a five-man team?" I asked.

"Because the plan calls for a five-man team, Jazz, including you and all your tech shit that I've never understood. Jess is here for her brains. You're here for your experience with comms and your nerves of steel. But you guys leave the planning to ol' Grady. I ain't steered you wrong yet."

"'Yet' being the operative word," Jess said.

"The way I hear it told," Grady said, scratching at the concrete floor with the toe of his boot, "you two can't afford to be too picky. Dust is getting all itchy and it won't be long 'fore he scratches. For that sort of money, you know I'm the only game in town."

"That's the only reason we're here," I said.

"But seeing as how I'd as soon die as go to prison, I'll be checking over your plan," Jess said. "I know you're a detail man, Grady, but it never hurts to have a second pair of eyes on things."

"Fair enough," Grady said.

"And I have a condition," I said.

Grady sniffed and motioned for me to continue.

"We don't hurt the kid," I said. "Not when we nab her. Not when we wait for the ransom. I don't aim to have a kid on my conscience, Grady, and I don't think you or Jess does either. So, we keep our faces covered. We use codenames. We do this shit right so everyone walks away happy and healthy and the cops have no reason to get vengeful."

"You think I'm looking to hurt this kid?" Grady asked, his features growing hard as he stepped toward me. "You think that's me?"

"No, I don't," I said. "But I don't know the rest of your crew on this. I don't want to ride with you and later find out someone turned their back at the wrong time and one of these other guys had a bit of perv in him or something. You vouch for them, that's fine. But I want Jess on the girl once she's nabbed. I won't have this kid alone with men I don't know. That's the way it is, or I take my chances with Dust and you can keep looking for a team."

"Jess is on the girl," Grady repeated. "That works for me."

"Me, too," Jess added.

"So, let's do this," I said. "Jess and I will get square with Dust and the rest of your crew gets to live the high life…assuming the parents will pay."

"Oh, they'll pay," Grady said with a laugh. "These people are so rich that little girl's allowance is probably more money than we're asking. Like I said, it's cake."

"Yeah," I mumbled. "Cake."

NABBING THE KID TURNED OUT TO BE AS easy as Grady had predicted. I had to hand it to the guy, he had watched the family long enough to know their schedules and every detail of their daily routines. He knew Wednesday was the only day of the week that the kid got home to a nearly empty house. It was also the day the cleaning crew came to clean the house with only the live-in maid to supervise until the parents returned home around 6 p.m. If we got in and out within an hour, we could be 60 miles away before the parents returned to discover their maid tied to a chair and their daughter gone.

We hijacked the cleaning crew and left them tied up in the old auto parts shop. An anonymous call to the cops about kids using it as a drug den would set them loose after the job was completed. We were in and out of the Devereaux place as easily as Grady had said. The other two members of the crew—a weaselly driver called Sonny and "Brick," the team's muscle—were all business. Nothing about them gave me a bad vibe. So, I sucked back the bile in my throat and committed to life as a kidnapper for a few days in an effort to keep the boogie man known as Dust from grinding me up to feed his dogs.

The plan was to stash the kid in some ancient, rundown motel that had mostly collapsed the last time a heavy storm system had moved through. As the place had no guests at the time, no one was hurt, but the old joint had likely breathed its last. Four of the rooms on the lower floor, however, remained intact and mildew-free. Grady said they had shut the place down because of the mildew and were waiting on insurance claims and disaster relief before deciding whether or not to rebuild.

So, we had the kid and the hideout. We just needed the ransom.

Jesse did her level best to make the kid comfortable and assure her she wouldn't be hurt. To her credit, the kid—ten year-old Lucinda Devereaux, daughter of tech mogul Peter Devereaux of DevComm Systems fame and his socialite bride, Angela—seemed nonplussed by the whole deal. I chalked it up to shock and fear and figured Jess would be able to keep her calm and docile without resorting to the violence that was often the stock and trade of these sorts of jobs.

Grady and his boys were jumpy but gave me no real reason to be concerned for the kid. Grady was a sleaze and a cheat and, while I didn't doubt his word to me wasn't worth the spit he invested in giving it, I didn't think he had it in him to hurt a kid. That didn't mean, though, he hadn't brought in Sonny and Brick to do the dirty stuff if things went sideways. So, while Jess stayed with the kid and got her accustomed to the new situation, I set up the communications gear and voice scrambler for the ransom call while keeping an eye on the rest of the crew.

"You know how all this stuff works?" Sonny asked, looking over my assortment of equipment.

"Yeah," I replied. "Worked with a guy in Travis who taught me how to route and scramble comms. Used to do this shit for a fence who was under FBI surveillance. He went on doing business as usual and the feds never knew what they were missing. We'll still use a burner phone, of course, but this stuff will keep them from triangulating our location."

"Just like that, huh?"

"No. I had to visit a couple of cell towers back in town," I said, "but, once you've done it a time or two, it's no big deal. The voice scrambler is a simple doohickey we attach to the phone, but the rest of this equipment works the real magic."

"When we makin' the call?" Brick asked Grady.

"Tomorrow," Grady said. "We left the note. They know not to call the cops but, even if they do, the cops won't keep them from losing their damn minds with worry. We let them steep in it overnight and make the call tomorrow afternoon."

"And if they don't pay?" Brick asked.

"They'll pay. Devereaux's got more money than God. Ain't asking for the keys to his company. We need the 5 mill and he needs his kid. Ain't nothing for him to even think about."

"Nothing is ever that easy," I said, not realizing how prophetic my words would prove to be.

"Relax," Grady said, punching my arm. "I got this all worked out, Jazz. It's as good as done."

THE NEXT DAY, JESS FED THE GIRL SOME breakfast—some fast food shit Sonny had picked up—and stayed in the room with her while Grady and I scripted the ransom call, preparing for any potential twists and turns in the conversation. We needed to keep the call short and on point, but I also didn't want to resort to overt threats of violence. The threat was already implied. There was no need to state it outright and make matters worse. Plus, no one was going to hurt the girl. I had made that clear and Grady knew me well enough to know I'd hurt him and his boys before I let him hurt the girl.

When I saw Jess leave the girl's room and lock the door, I took the opportunity to catch her up on our prep for the call and how we meant to proceed. Her expression, however, caused me to abandon my train of thought.

"What's wrong?" I asked. "Having second thoughts about all this?"

"No, it's not that," she said, sliding down the exterior wall to sit. "It's the girl. There's something weird about her."

"She's in shock," I said. "She's been kidnapped, you know. No matter how sweet you are to her, she's still scared."

Jess shook her head.

"What?"

"She creeps me out," Jess said. "I had to get out of there for a minute. Felt like I was going to scream."

I laughed until she gave me a look that choked it out of me.

"What do you mean she creeps you out?"

"I-I'm not sure how to explain it," Jess said. "She looks at me like—"

I slid down the wall to sit next to her.

"Like what?"

"I don't know, Jazz. Like she knows more than I do. Or like she's in on some joke completely lost on me."

"That's ridiculous. You're just feeling creeped out that we've stooped this low."

"No. That isn't it. I don't like it, but I was onboard. Hell, I got *you* onboard. It's her. She's weird. And I don't mean for a kid, Jazz."

"Relax," I said, taking her hand and giving it a squeeze. "We make the call in a few hours. Her parents have to be climbing the walls by now. They'll move on this quickly. Once we get our merry bushels of cash, we'll leave the kid and this life in the rearview. Her parents will get a call about where they can pick her up and it's happy endings all around."

"I don't believe in happy endings," Jess grumped.

"That's because you date guys like Grady."

"Screw you, Jazz."

"That's my girl."

AFTER I POWERED UP THE EQUIPMENT THAT would ensure our signal couldn't be traced back to our location, I attached the voice scrambler to the burner phone and handed it to Grady. He had the script in front of him, including responses to things the parents might say. If the cops answered, we had a script for that, too. Luckily, it was the father who answered.

"Devereaux," he said.

"We have your daughter," Grady said through the scrambler. "She remains unharmed. Her continued health, however, will depend upon your compliance."

The line went dead, prompting Grady to look at me like I had shot him in the face.

"What the hell, Jazz?"

"I'm not sure," I said, checking my tech. "Everything here is solid and reading five by five. Maybe the dad hung up?"

"Sure," Grady snapped back, "We called the one father on the whole fucking globe who doesn't give a shit about his kid!"

"Clearly, you never met *my* old man," I fired back. "There's a lot of shitty ones out there. But it could also be the cops were on the line and are trying to unnerve us. So howsabout we don't go getting our feathers ruffled until we know what's what."

"What do you suggest?"

"Call back. Try again."

Grady redialed and stared a hole through me as it rang. And rang. And rang.

"Give it a minute," I said. "They may have feds feeding them instructions. They want to put us off-guard. Give it a few more rings."

Grady pointed his finger at me as if it was loaded. The threat didn't need to be verbalized.

"Devereaux," said the male voice on the line. Whether or not it was the real Devereaux or some cop stringing us along, who could say?

"Hang up on me again and the girl dies," Grady practically growled into the voice scrambler. The result was frightening. "You get one chance to—"

The sound of the line going dead again was deafening.

"What the hell, man?" Sonny asked, scratching at the grandmother whiskers on his chin.

"What is this?" Brick asked, grabbing me by the collar.

"Hands off, dipshit. I didn't do this. I need this score as much as anyone," I said. "Most likely more."

"He's right," Grady relented, though his eyes were still on me like I had propositioned his mother. "Jazz is in too deep to blow this."

"Says you," Brick said, yanking me a bit closer to his other fist, clenched and ready to have a brief meeting with my face.

"Let go of Jazz before he decides to make you," Grady said. "You got brawn but he's got brains and moves." He pulled his gun and pointed it in the brute's general direction. "Besides, between the two of you, you are far more expendable, ya dig? Play nice so we can figure this shit out, yeah?"

Brick turned my collar loose and paced back and forth like a caged lion.

"Why would a rich prick like Devereaux pull this shit?" Sonny asked. "Are we sure he ain't in some sort of financial trouble? Could it be we overestimated his bank and what he's able to part with?"

"What am I, a street rat fresh offa Grand and Reseda? I do my fucking homework, Sonny! I don't pull the trigger on a job until I've come at it from all angles. This cat is flush in cash, credit, and property," Grady argued. "Now, I haven't got the first damn clue what's going on with Devereaux, but we'll sort it out. We're too deep into this thing to get squirrely now. So, we chalk this up to the feds and their tricks and we try him back tonight. Let them sweat a few more hours."

"Nah, man," Brick said, kicking the table holding all my equipment. It wasn't enough to knock everything over, but it was enough that I felt a strong urge to take out a couple of his teeth the hard way. "This is bullshit," he continued. "They're onto us or something, man. They've got to be. I say we do the kid and split up. This job is burned."

"Nobody touches the kid," I said as calmly as I could muster. "That was the deal."

"He's right," Grady said.

"Man, fuck the deal," Brick said, stepping up into my face: his breath a mélange of cheap beer and hot wings. "I ain't doing no kidnapping time."

"M-maybe Brick has a point," Sonny said. "Everything seems to be going sideways on this and the kid—"

"The kid hasn't seen any of our faces," Grady said.

"Doesn't know our names, either. She ain't no danger to us. But I'm beginning to think you idiots might be."

He waved his gun at Brick, who stepped back and turned his attention to the gun.

"Right now," Grady said, "this whole thing is on pause. Maybe that's the feds. Maybe Devereaux is playing games. Whatever the hell is going on, we wait. And anybody who touches that girl had better be good at dodging lead, you hear?"

Brick reluctantly nodded. Sonny mumbled something apologetic.

"You two go walk the perimeter," Grady told them. "When you're done, take the car and get food for everybody…including the kid. Cash is in the glove box."

I watched them leave and turned my attention back toward the tech, knowing Grady wasn't done with me.

"I'll keep 'em in check, Jazz, but I can only do it for so long," he said, stuffing his Sig P226 into the back of his waistband. "Whatever is going on here, it's got them on edge. Same with me, I just know how to keep my head cooler. Ain't nothing good ever came from throwing the plan out the window."

"It's not the tech," I reiterated. "Even after Brick took a boot to the table, it's all reading fine. We're untraceable and the line was not lost from this end."

"So, what are you thinkin'? Devereaux, the technology guru, uses a crappy cell with bad reception? I ain't buying it."

"No. It has to be something else."

"Like?"

I shook my head.

"Well, we need an answer, Jazz, or it's gonna get a damn sight harder to keep Brick and Sonny corralled in the notion of doing no harm," Grady said.

"We could put eyes on the house," I said. "If the feds are running the show, it'll be clear and we'll wait out their game. They won't play us for long. The girl's parents wouldn't stand for it. If it's the parents trying to flex on us, knowing that detail will help us strategize a fix."

"Well, if I send one of those lunkheads, they're bound to miss something or get their asses caught in a federal net," he replied. "And I don't dare go lest they decide to start thinking for themselves and screw us over something fierce. Maybe Jess could—"

"No," I said. "Jess needs to stay with the girl. I can do it."

"I need you here for the call."

"No, you don't. It's all set up. You can leave it powered up and call once I have eyes on the house."

Grady needed a way out of our unprecedented situation. He clearly didn't like *my* idea, but it was the only play we had left.

"Wait until the boys are back with the food," he said, "and take the car. Be sure and keep your distance. Could be blue crawling all over the joint."

"There's a spot in the hills to the east of there," I said. "It should give me a good view of their property so long as I have powerful enough binoculars. I'll call you when I'm set up."

Grady tossed me his keys.

"Stop by my place first," he said. "I've got what you need. I'm talking military-grade shit. They've even got a built-in thermal scope so you can keep track of anything that isn't in your line of sight."

'Thanks. And Grady?"

"Yeah?"

"Be careful with that Brick character. He strikes me as someone who doesn't take to the leash, if you know what I mean."

"Just find out what's going on with Devereaux so we can put this shit behind us. And don't worry about Jess. You know I'd take a bullet for that girl."

"Better if you don't have to," I said. "I'll let her know the food's coming."

AFTER A COLD BURGER, LIMP FRIES AND A warm beer, I said my goodbyes to Jess. I didn't realize then that it would be the last time I would see the *real* her.

"I don't like it," she said.

"I'll be fine," I said. "I'm not engaging, only scoping the place out."

"I don't mean you," Jess said. We were sitting in rusted metal deck chairs outside the motel room where we were stashing the girl.

"Then what?"

"That girl is…well, there's something wrong with her. The way she looks at me—hell, the way she *talks* to me— it's like I'm a pet or something."

"She's scared and lonely," I offered.

"She's not scared," Jess said. "That's the trouble. She

seems to think we're dolls in her dollhouse. And she says some truly creepy shit. She told me I was going to be her big sister and we could find ourselves a brand-new mommy and daddy once the boys were dead."

"What boys?"

"That's what I asked her. She said, 'Grady, Brick, and Sonny. They all have to die…but not Jazz. I know you love Jazz, so we won't hurt him, Jess.' Then she stares at me with this weird smile like she's reading my mind or something."

There was a pit in my stomach threatening to come out through my esophagus.

"Who said our names, Jess? How does she know our names?"

"How the hell should I know? I wear a mask in there like you told me to, and not a one of you has been around her since we got to this rat trap."

"We didn't use names on the drive here," I reminded her. "She had to have heard them from someone, Jess. You can't chalk it up to her being a good guesser and I don't believe in mind readers."

"You haven't been around her like I have," she said. "There's something wrong with her, Jazz. She says shit like that and I…I believe her."

"She's getting into your head," I argued. "You just need some distance. I can have Sonny spell you in there while I'm gone."

"No," she said. "I don't want anyone to get hurt. No matter how creeptacular she is, she at least likes me. After what she said about the others, I don't want them going in there."

"She's a little girl," I reminded her. "She can't do anything to Sonny."

"I know. At least, I think I do."

"Do you want me to stay?" I asked. "Maybe Grady can send Brick or—"

"No. You should go." She touched my cheek and looked at me. "You're the only family I have that I can stand, ya know? I'd have given up on life long ago if you hadn't been with me."

"Same here," I said. And I meant it. Jess was my angel.

"I'll be fine," she said, and I believed her...because I needed to.

"I'll get back as quickly as I can," I promised. I was true to my word, but it didn't make any difference.

THE DEVEREAUX HOUSE SAT A GOOD MILE back from the front gate and was surrounded on three sides by hills which, for the most part, remained undeveloped. To the east of their estate, was the smallest of the three hills. I was perched there with Grady's thermal binoculars, spying on the people I hoped would prove to be my salvation.

The weaknesses of my plan were numerous. For one, I could only see the east side of the estate and, with a place so large, I would only be able to see them when they occupied that side of the house near a window. The thermal scope helped, but it didn't solve my other problem: no audio. With nearly blind eyes and deaf ears, it hardly counted as surveillance. My hope rested in the notion that observing what I could of their behavior— along with the presence or lack thereof of the police— would give Grady and me a clue as to how to proceed.

The binoculars were military grade and a prototype at that, far beyond anything available on the open market. The thermal imaging worked like a dream. In spite of my limited view, I could adjust the depth of field and get thermal readings on the whole joint. It was like having x-ray vision.

After observing for several hours, I called Grady.

"Give me some good news, Jazz," he said.

"I wish I could," I said, "but I'd be lying. I've been watching the Devereaux place for several hours. There's no one in there but the two of them and what I assume is a servant."

"You assume?"

"She was setting the table for them, so I don't think she's a fed."

"No cops at the entrance?"

"Not of whiff of them anywhere," I said. "I don't think they even called them."

"Why the hell would…? What do we do here, Jazz? I've got no frame of reference for this shit," Grady admitted. "I checked the girl's history. She's never run away or done the kind of shit that would make them feel like it's some play for attention."

"No trouble at school?"

"Couldn't find a line into the school," Grady said. "It's some private thing in the city. Scoped it out myself but the windows were all blacked out, so I couldn't see for shit.

Not even a website for the place. But every day, they ship the kid there during school hours and every afternoon, she comes back."

"Weird."

"Yeah. So, what are we going to do, Jazz?"

"Well, I have an idea…but it isn't a good one. In fact, it's downright foolhardy in the sense of risking my neck to make it happen," I said. "But it's the only thing I can think of that might still salvage this job."

"Maybe we let the kid go and call it a day," Grady said. "You do something stupid that lands you in jail and that's one thing. Bad enough, yeah? But Dust has people everywhere, Jazz. Even jail ain't safe from his reach. And Jess would still be on the hook, too."

"Not exactly a different outcome than bailing on this now," I argued. "The only way we live long enough to get clear of Dust is to finish the job."

"But, Jazz…it's all going foul, brother. It's—there's something wrong with this girl."

I took a deep breath and tried my best to strain all the panic and accusation from my voice before I spoke.

"What were you doing around the girl, Grady?"

"Look, don't panic or nothin' but Jess is coming unglued. She came out of the kid's room screaming bloody murder about something, but none of us could make sense of it. We finally got her calmed down, but I didn't want to send her back in the with the kid if she was a couple of fuses short, ya know? So, I stepped in and let her get some air."

"You think she's using again?" I asked.

"No, she's clean," Grady said. "I know what that sort of

sick looks like, Jazz, and this ain't it. This is something else. And when I went into that room, I finally understood."

"Understood what exactly?"

"That this kid ain't no kid," Grady said. "She's something else. A devil, maybe. A demon. Not—not human."

"That's crazy talk, Grady," I said. "You're letting Jess's freakout get you all worked up. Keep your head in the game and we'll get through this."

"Yeah, sure. You're right, Jazz. All this is damned upside-down, I—"

"I know, man. Keep it together. Keep those other two away from the kid. Let me figure out something on this end. Don't even make the ransom call. I'll be back by morning with a plan. Swear to God."

There was silence on the other end of the line, but I could hear Grady breathing, the ragged breathing you hear from someone on the verge of tears.

"Grady?"

"Did you hear it, Jazz?"

"Hear what?"

"The whisper?"

"No, man. I didn't. Sorry. Look, are you solid?"

"I-I think I—"

"Grady, just keep it together, man. I'll be back as soon as I can."

I disconnected the call and ran toward the Devereaux house like a man with hell at his heels. I didn't know yet how accurate that feeling would prove to be.

THE DEVEREAUX ESTATE, LIKE ANY HOME, had its security weaknesses. For all the money invested in alarm systems and motion sensors, a smart criminal such as yours truly can find and exploit a weakness to find a way in. For the Devereaux family, the weak spot was a small rectangular casement window at the back of the house, near the ground—leading into a workroom in their finished basement. Although wired for security, it had been left open. The smell of fresh spray paint lingered in the air and a half-dozen works in progress—sculptures I will graciously call "abstract"—were scattered across several work tables. Seemed Mrs. Devereaux was an aspiring artist.

Inside the house, I drew my weapon—a Glock 19 Grady had demanded I take "just in case"—and boldly went to look for the home owners and resident pains in my ass. First, I found the garage and the breaker box. I cut power to the alarm system, fired up my cell phone jammer, and cut the land lines. I didn't need the cops arriving before I got what I needed. I put on my angry face and stormed through the house until I found the Devereauxs warming themselves near a fireplace in the study. They were seated in posh, overstuffed chairs, each nursing a brandy as if they were about to welcome everyone to Masterpiece Theater.

"Put the gun away," Mr. Devereaux said, showing no fear of the gun I had aimed at his face. "We'll answer your questions. There's no need for violence."

"I think I'll be the one to decide if there's a need for violence, chief," I spat, turning my weapon toward the wife. "Either one of you makes a move and you'll find out I'm desperate enough to turn my conscience off for the evening."

"You're one of the kidnappers," the woman said. "You want to know about Lucinda."

"I want to know why you haven't fucking paid!" I screamed. "I want to know what the hell you think you're playing at!"

"Lucinda is a...special girl," Angela Devereaux said. Her words and tone did not match. Her words insinuated affection. Her tone suggested fear.

"She is willful," Peter said, "and very much her own. We serve her as best we are able, of course, but her existence is still quite limited. Sometimes she needs to...let go...and have some fun."

"What the hell is going on here?" I asked, moving the gun back and forth between the two of them. I wasn't looking to shoot anyone, but there was a chill crawling up my spine I couldn't explain and a growing suspicion that I was nothing but a cockroach already under the shadow of someone else's boot.

"Lucinda has a standing rule," Devereaux said. "We aren't to interfere. Not ever. She will take care of herself and when she requires our servitude, she will inform us of her needs."

"We made that mistake once," Angela Devereaux said, her voice breaking at the memory. "We thought we were helping her. Thought she would appreciate that—"

Mrs. Devereaux began to weep and rock gently in the elegantly upholstered chair which cost more than I had managed to scrape together in my entire, miserable life.

"She killed our Sophie," her husband said, no doubt

sensing she would be unable to finish. "She said she wanted a big sister…someone like her. And Sophie was too
kind for that. Not *broken* enough, she told us. Apparently,
the broken ones work best."

"I don't know what you're saying," I said through
clenched teeth. "She's a kid. She's just a kid."

"She's a monster," Devereaux said. "You and your as-
sociates were an unexpected delight, no doubt. But soon-
er or later, Lucinda will return to us. After she's had her
fun. After she's grown bored by her little holiday. She'll
come home. And, as we always have, we will serve her in
fear."

The weight of the gun took it back to my side. Whatever the hell was going on—and, thanks to all the cryp-
tic nonsense from the Devereauxs, I felt three steps behind—it was clear I had nothing to fear from Momma or
Poppa Devereaux.

"You're saying your daughter is a killer," I repeated, to
make sure I was hearing this insanity properly.

"She isn't our daughter," Angela Devereaux said. "We
only had Sophie."

"Lucinda simply showed up on our doorstep one
night," Peter said. "We invited her in, offered to get her
some help. But, once inside, she showed us the truth…
and we've been her captives ever since."

"The truth?" I asked.

"That she's not human," Peter said. "I know she looks
like any other little girl, but she's something else. Something evil. Something ancient. Because she looks as she
does, she needed a family to act as her cover. She chose
us to be her emissaries out in the waking world."

"And you're saying what? We kidnapped her and held her for ransom and that's little Lucinda having fun?"

"Did she seem scared to you?" Peter asked. "Did you and your friends intimidate her? Or was her calm resolve a bit unnatural—perhaps a tad unnerving?"

That chill in my spine had spread to my intestines. I felt like I was turning to ice from the inside out. My legs shook, and everything inside me wanted to retreat. I wanted to run back to the motel, grab Jess, and get as far away from Lucinda Devereaux as I could. But I had one final question.

"You said that my friends and I were an unexpected delight. Why would Lucinda let us kidnap her? How is that fun for her?"

Peter Devereaux turned to look me in the eye. I've never seen more sorrow and horror in one man. He was broken beyond the telling of it.

"Lucinda no longer finds joy in most of what this world has to offer," he told me, "but she *does* enjoy playing with her food before she feeds."

IF YOU WERE TO ASK ME WHY I BELIEVED PETER and Angela Devereaux's bizarre and impossible story of being held prisoner by some sort of horror posing as a small child—enough to leave them sitting there next to a blazing hearth and go ripping asphalt back to the abandoned motel, no less—I would tell you I didn't. Or, at least, I didn't push Grady's stolen beater to the limit just because of those two wingnuts. It was Jess. Her instincts. The ones I had ignored. No, not ignored. Mocked. Gaslighted.

I had Grady's rusted out Monte Carlo topped out at 90 mph most of the way back and the engine—hell, even calling it an engine is damn generous—sounded as if someone dropped a handful of bolts into a meat grinder. The fact that it didn't explode into a fiery ball of twisted metal and crispy Jazz was nothing short of a miracle.

I practically slid into the crumbling parking lot on two wheels and jumped out of the car with the engine still running. Gun drawn, I decided discretion wasn't called for. We were past all that.

"Jess?" I screamed. "Jess, come out!"

The wind was still and fetid. My gut screamed to get the hell out of there. My heart answered, "Not without Jess."

"Grady? Brick? Sonny? Somebody fuckin' answer me!" I screamed. "Jess? Grady?"

I ran to the room Grady and Brick had been bunking in and entered gun-first, only to find it empty. Burger wrappers and empty beer bottles still covered the little table where weary travelers once choked down their dry complimentary continental breakfasts. The off-brand flat screen on the wall was still on, trying to sell me one pharmaceutical or another. A pack of Grady's cheap cigarettes sat unopened on the bedside table.

"Jess?"

I pushed the door open to the next room—the double Sonny and I had shared. It, too, was empty save for the Pelican cases that had housed my comm gear before I had set it up in the adjacent room. The gear was still standing next door, and still powered on as if Grady had still hoped to make a play for the ransom. The voice-scrambled cell was on the table next to it, but no one would be making the call.

The acrid scent which had been trying to upend my stomach was growing stronger the closer I got to the girl's room. The coward in me was clawing to get out and take control of my legs. My love for Jess was stronger than that bastard, though, so it won the fight and I walked slowly toward the last room.

As I traversed those last few steps, I mentally prepared myself for what I might see. I let my imagination go to the darkest places because, once you've prepared for the absolute worst, anything less will seem survivable by contrast. I pictured wall to wall blood. I pictured Jess hanging by her own intestines while Grady and his crew lay naked and headless at her feet as if worshipping some foul goddess. I pictured the girl, Lucinda, smiling at me with her teeth full of my friends. Nothing I had imagined, however, prepared me for what awaited me beyond the door.

The room looked cleaner than when we had first stashed the girl there. The bed was made. The pictures had all been straightened. The small table and its accompanying chairs were free of dust. The door to the bathroom was closed, but there was a note carefully taped to its center.

> Big Sis and I have gone to play. She has a lot to learn before we find our new Mommy and Daddy. Don't come looking for us, Jazz. My kindness has limits.
>
> Lucinda
>
> P.S. The boys are in the bathroom. Best not to look.

I *did* look, of course. There was nothing left of them but their heads which Lucinda had hung from the shower curtain rings by tiny braids she had no doubt lovingly braided herself.

IT TOOK YEARS FOR THE HORROR OF THAT night to stop rushing back to me every time I tried to sleep. My only hope for sanity was to drive all thought and memory of Jess far from my mind. I couldn't mourn someone I had never known. I couldn't miss someone who had never existed. I spent years convincing myself I had always been alone. I grew old bouncing from identity to identity, trying to stay one step ahead of Dust and his long memory for transgression. Eventually, Dust was killed by an up-and-comer and I was free to be me once again.

I met a woman, fell in love, and got married. It didn't last. I tried again a few years later. Different girl, same me...same baggage. Once again, it didn't take. Stayed on the straight and narrow and got myself a solid gig with a telecom giant. It was blue collar shit, but it paid enough and kept me out of trouble. By the time I retired at 68, I had saved enough to see Europe for the first time. Booked myself a senior tour. Got to see Abbey Road, the Eiffel Tower, the Parthenon, and a whole slew of other sights that made me wish I had someone I loved enough to share them with.

It was on my second night in Rome when I saw Jess one last time. I woke in the middle of the night to find her sitting at the foot of my bed, looking as young and full of life as she had when I left her to go shake down Peter Devereaux. Lucinda sat out on the balcony, her attention drawn to the plaza below.

"You're *old*, Jazz," Jess said, her voice just as I remembered, yet different...as if there was another, softer voice speaking behind it. Something older. Something harder.

"Jess?"

"It won't be long now," she said. "That ticker of yours is already beating a tad out of kilter. Sorry. I know waking up to find me here likely doesn't help."

"Jess?"

"Yeah, Jazz. It's me. Decided I might like to see you again while you've still got some life in those old bones."

She put her hand on my knee and, even through the covers, it felt impossibly heavy.

"Where have you been?" I asked weakly, my eyes fighting to adjust to the darkness of the room.

"Everywhere," she said, a slight smile curling her lips. "While you were embracing the straight life, I was…not."

"Are you okay? You look so—"

"I do look so, don't I?" she repeated with a strange smile. "I've missed you, Jazz. Even so, I'm glad you didn't come looking for us all those years ago."

"I wanted to," I said.

"Better you didn't," she repeated. "Lucinda would've gutted you, Jazz. And, as much as I love ya, I wouldn't have stopped her. We can't really live by the same rules humans do."

"Humans?"

"I don't really have the time to educate you, Jazz. The only thing you needed to learn was left for you in that motel bathroom."

"I'm so sorry," I said, tears burning hot in the corners of my eyes. "I should've listened to you, Jess. I should've never left you there."

"Nonsense, my decrepit old cousin," she said, leaning into my face to smile at me. There was an unnatural shine in her eyes that chilled me. "I'm better than I've ever been. I've seen things you wouldn't believe. Done things you'd never have approved of. I am a goddess surveying all that is beneath her."

"Like me," I whispered.

"It doesn't have to be this way, Jazz. That's why I came. As I said, you don't have long with that plodding pumper of yours, but I can change that. I can make you like me."

I cast a glance out to Lucinda. She was staring at me. Though she still looked ten years old, her smile made my stomach turn.

"Don't worry about *her*," Jess said. "She's fine with it."

"And if I decline your offer?" I asked, quite afraid of her answer.

"You'll die," she said. "Not by my hand, or Lucinda's. We love you. You're the closest thing we have to a brother, Jazz. But the gift is a one-time offer. If you decline, your ticker will eventually go and that'll be that."

"I've made some pretty sketchy deals in my day," I said, "but I'm not sure immortality is worth a deal with the devil."

"Flatterer," Jess said with a laugh. "Final answer?"

"I'm afraid so. I love you. Always have, Jess. But I let you go a long, long time ago. And I don't ever want to be the sort of…thing…that does what she did to Grady and the others.

She grinned at me for a little too long. I began to wonder if she had changed her mind and put me on the menu.

"Suit yourself," she finally said. She rose from the bed and we both watched as Lucinda jumped off my 13th floor balcony. "I won't be seeing you again, Jazz. I don't like watching you people get sickly. It's pathetic and beneath us."

"I loved you," I said, as she stepped out onto the balcony.

"You loved her," she corrected, not bothering to look back at me. "And she loved you. Soon, you'll *both* be dead. Bye, Jazz."

And suddenly she was gone. And I was all alone. That night was over two years ago. I'm pleased to report my heart is still pumping—albeit irregularly—the trouble is, it feels damn empty.

MARK YOUR CALENDARS

"SIMMONS."

I wrote the name on the steno pad even though I thought Trent was a vindictive dick for throwing that particular name into the ring. There were three other names already on the list, but we still had half the council to go.

"Why Simmons?" I asked, not so much because I didn't know—we all knew—but to force Trent to justify it. "What are his qualifications?"

"Simmons is a retired minister," Trent said, "who spent more than a decade as a missionary to Honduras. He was married to his wife, Tammy, for 47 years before she passed away after a long bout with pancreatic cancer. He stayed by her side through the entire ordeal. It's why he retired from ministry. He needed to devote all his time to her care."

"That's swell," I said. "Not *convincing*, but swell."

Trent gave me a toothy smile. "He's made an impact in this community, Paul. His influence hasn't diminished since his retirement."

"Who's your choice, Paul?"

The woman asking was Pamela Branch, the wife of our mayor and head of the Women's Auxiliary League. She flirted with me incessantly before the others arrived. She wasn't my type, but she hated Trent as much as I did, and it never hurts to have allies when you want the vote to go your way.

"Karla Boyd." I looked around the table, daring any of my compatriots to argue. "She's a single mom raising four boys on her own. Her husband, Vic, was a firefighter who lost his life saving those disabled kids last spring. The whole school was turned to ash. I'm sure you all saw it on the news. Well, it turns out Vic wasn't the only hero in the family. Karla, who got a hefty insurance check when Vic died, donated half of it to rebuild the school. They were privately funded, see, and though they had fire insurance, their backers had already begun falling away. They could rebuild, but they wouldn't last long without donations. Karla Boyd saved the day. She could have been sitting pretty with that insurance money, but now she's got to have a day job just to support her kids."

"Pretty weak," Trent said. "I'm not sure—"

"She's been a Sunday School teacher for the last 6 years and visits her aunt in the nursing home every Thursday evening, often bringing baked goods for the other residents," I added.

Trent rolled his eyes. I jotted down the name Boyd as all eyes turned to Caesura Flint, the eldest member of the council. He wore his years well and bore a charm unmatched by any of his peers. I'm guessing it was the suave Spanish accent that sealed the deal.

"Friends," he said, "you know how difficult it is for me to choose. There are so many worthy candidates."

I nodded. "Still, we each bring a name to the table. You're the one who created that particular rule, if I recall."

"Forgive me," Flint said. "I'm a rule-breaker at heart. I suppose I break even my own rules. Let us hear from Mrs. Branch first, hmm?"

"That's fine. Pamela?"

"I'd like to submit my husband, Richard Branch."

Some members of the council groaned. Others shook their heads. She had nominated her husband three times in the past year. It was understandable, of course, but had grown as wearisome as Trent nominating Rev. Simmons.

"I know you think he isn't as deserving as the others," she said, "but Richard's got this new proposal he's working on. It could put an end to the homelessness problem if it passes. He's always working with the local charities to—"

"It isn't enough," Larry Nowlin said. Nowlin was the principal at Emit Posh Jr. High. He was as gay as The English Patient and a bigger tool than John Mayer, but he had a say in the matter just like the rest of us. "We all know he bought the last election, Pamela."

"Not to mention his philandering," Trent said. "He doesn't cover his tracks very well. For a politician, I mean."

"I'm sorry," I said. "I have to agree. I know you want this for him in the worst way, but Richard isn't the sort we're looking for."

Pamela looked like she wanted to argue, but she looked to Mr. Flint instead. When he shook his head, she let it go.

"Go ahead and put it on the list," Flint said. "We won't vote for him, but I don't think Pamela has anyone else in mind."

"I will next time," she said. "I'm sorry if I—"

"Please, my dear," Flint said, placing his hand over hers. "Don't apologize. Who's left, Paul?"

"Reverend Chatham is next," I said. "Who's it going to be, Reverend?"

Phillip Chatham was young for a minister, but well-respected by his Presbyterian flock. He had been a controversial choice, at first, not because of his age but because his ideology was more liberal than that of other ministers in town.

"Morris Baum," he said, drawing no reaction from my compatriots. "He's a member of my congregation. I suppose, story-wise, there isn't much to tell. Morris isn't a war hero. He isn't very active in the community or in the church. He's not a widower raising a house full of kids on his own."

"So, you're selling us on why he's a bad choice?" Trent said. "I'm not sure I get it. Why him?"

"He's got this way about him," Chatham said, "like the cruelty of this world can't touch him. He wears this contagious smile and has a peace about him like I've never seen in anyone else."

"But what does he do?" Pamela asked.

Chatham shook his head. "Little things. It's difficult to explain. He touches people in small ways, doing what he can when he can. He loves and gives and—" He stopped and shook his head again.

Flint leaned forward, gripping the table's edge. "And what, Reverend?"

"He may be the most *Christ*-like man I've ever encountered."

We all looked at each other, uncertain of what to say. Flint, at last, broke the uncomfortable silence by addressing Calvin Olsen.

"That brings us to you, Calvin. Then myself."

"Pete Stratton," he said. Calvin had been quiet the entire meeting, but he threw his choice out there loud and clear. "I think most of you know him."

I knew Stratton as did several others at the table. Calvin was the Worshipful Master of our town's Masonic Lodge. Calvin's candidates were usually out of left field, but Pete Stratton made perfect sense.

"Pete moved here from Cleveland, so he's new to the community, but he's already made an impact. He started art classes at the rec center for the under-privileged kids and volunteers at the VA center on the weekends. Turns out his dad was a vet and Pete took care of him near the end. When his dad passed, he moved here to make a fresh go of it."

He took a sip of his water and said, "He's got people talking, you know? I mean, if a stranger can come in here and have such an impact, why aren't the older families in town taking more of an interest?"

I wrote Pete's name below Baum's. "Can't stall any longer, Mr. Flint," I said. "It's down to you."

Flint grinned and pulled a Cuban from the holder he always kept in the inner pocket of his suit coat. While we waited for him to submit a name, he took the time to guillotine the tip of his corona and proceed through, what appeared to the uninitiated, to be a lighting ritual. Only after he had taken a few puffs did he grace us with his attention.

"When I had you pass me earlier, it was not because I hadn't made a selection as I led you to believe," he said. "I merely wanted to know if any of you had the insight to make the same selection as I have." He exhaled smoke through his nostrils, the Spanish dragon so full of his own praise. "I'm pleased to say one among you had the wisdom to see beyond the common qualifications to find a *truly* worthy submission."

I tapped my pen on the steno pad. "So, let's have it, Flint. Name your flavor."

"The good Reverend made, in my mind, the proper choice. Oh, of course, Baum is not as flashy as the other candidates, but he possesses the most important attribute of all—his Christ-likeness. When we boil down the qualities we look for in our nominees, I believe you will find the result is this Christ-likeness the Reverend spoke of. If anyone disagrees though, I would be happy to entertain the argument."

"It's not likely anyone wants to argue with *you*," Trent said.

"Or could win an argument with you even if they tried," I added. "I think we can put it to a vote and get on with our evening." I looked at my list. "Since two of you suggested Mr. Baum, we'll begin there. All those in favor?"

I watched as, one after one, the other members of the council showed their approval. I was the last to raise my hand.

"That makes it unanimous," I said. "First time we've managed that in quite a while."

"Whose turn is it to notify our winner?" Pamela asked.

I searched through my notes. "It looks like Trent's turn."

"I'll get you the chloroform," Doc Walker told Trent. "Just swing by my office tomorrow."

"I'll get the altar down to the clearing," Sherriff Long said. "Who's up for the big job?"

"According to my notes," I said, "it's Mr. Flint." Flint grinned at the thought. "I'll make sure to bring everything else we need for the sacrifice. Any other new business? If not, I make a motion we adjourn."

"I second," Doc Walker said.

"Then we stand adjourned. Our meeting next month will be on the 23rd. Please mark your calendars."

BOB AND JULIA

JULIA TAPPED HER TEASPOON ON THE AVOCADO green countertop, oblivious to the dirty looks coming her way from several other diner patrons. There had been a song in her head—no, in her *heart*—all morning, and even the looming thunderheads scraping the top of the Sears tower couldn't dampen her spirits. Though it was far from a common occurrence, she loved it when her morning started off on the right foot. Julia was so lost in the tune that she was wholly unaware of her utensil percussion until the bulky waitress cleared her throat.

"I'm sorry," Julia said. Her smile was wide and warm, yet seemingly powerless to melt the menopausal menu matron. "Did you say something?"

"Yeah." The waitress chewed her gum with the decorum of a syphilitic porn star. "I said, unless your name happens to be Tito Puente, you need to can the drum solo and order something."

"Ah, well, just a refill of iced tea, then."

"And?" Julia glanced at the waitress's name tag expecting to find a name like Greta, Claudette, or perhaps even Trixie. It read Bob.

"Pie, I guess?"

"Pizza or Pecan?" Bob asked.

Julia's smile remained, though she could feel it growing phony around the edges. "Surprise me."

She left the spoon on her napkin, but the tune was relentless. It morphed into a hum that played about her lips.

"All I have is Peach," Bob said, sliding the plate in front of her alongside a full glass of cloudy iced tea. On top of the pie was a slice of cheddar cheese, sweaty to the point of translucence. "Bon appétit."

Julia sipped her iced tea as she studied the wreck of a dessert and its chipped vessel, slowly turning the plate until it had rotated back to its original position. "I'm gonna go out on a limb and guess this wasn't baked fresh this morning."

"Pie is pie, lady," Bob said, as she rang up a breakfast patron on a register so old Julia imagined it was powered by hamsters in a wheel. "No one forced you to order it."

"That's not how *I* see it." Julia tilted the plate with the tip of her index finger. "Is it possible to get this carbon-dated? I don't want to pay for stale pie, but if it's the remnant of some ancient civilization or something—"

Bob ignored her and refilled the coffee cup of the Marine at the end of the counter. The soldier was lost in his newspaper, mumbling "Nank'oo" from the business section.

"You have anything in the way of a cake baked post-World War II?" Julia pushed the pie out of her line of sight, clinking it against the salt shaker. "Something from the cheesecake strain, perhaps?"

"Cheesecake? Are you hitting on me, lady?"

"No, but if this level of service stays on track—"

Bob leaned on the counter, her fat knuckles turning white with strain. "You got a real mouth on you, don't ya, girlie?"

Julia smiled a toothy smile. "It's where I'd like to put the cheesecake."

Bob was clearly not amused—nor was the Y-shaped vein in her temple which appeared (at least to Julia) to be dancing the Hippy-Hippy-Shake. As her sparring partner rallied her thoughts for the next verbal assault, Julia took note of Bob's plaque-edged canines and John Waters mustache. She wondered if Bob had been born with both, prompting the parents of the verbose diner despot to saddle her with a man's name.

"Listen, chickadee, you want pie? Eat pie. You want lip? Take it somewhere else." Bob was breathing heavily. Julia imagined her as a bull in one of those *Looney Tunes* shorts, her head growing bigger and redder until steam blew out her ears, all the while pawing at the ground. "I haven't got cheesecake, and I haven't got time to trade jabs like Ali and Frazier. Eat or don't, that's fine. If you *don't*, though, you need to free the seat."

"So that was a no on the cheesecake?" Julia's smile had become genuine again. "I do so love it."

"Tell ya what, lady," Bob said, her throat suddenly full of gravel, "You take your cheesecake-hole on out of here and your iced tea is on me."

"Can I ask you a question, Bob? It is alright if I call you Bob, isn't it?"

"No. It is not okay if you—"

"I've been wondering, Bob, what exactly is the function of your dysfunction?" Bob said nothing. She stood there slack-jawed and fuming. "I mean, I came in here with a song in my heart, Bob. I was having a good morning—a great morning, in fact. I'm curious why my cheery disposition gives you cancer of the smile gland. How did I become *persona au gratin*?"

The gentleman sitting to Julia's left had been listening to the exchange for some time, content to remain focused on his corned beef hash, until that moment. "No offense, ma'am, but I'm fairly certain the term is *persona non grata.*"

"No offense taken," Julia said. She gave him a wink that made him blush. "I know the correct phrase, I'm feeling extra cheesy today, is all."

"You wanna know why?" Bob said. If she had been a pot of the diner's infamous chili, she would have already boiled over. As it was, the waitress was, to the patrons who witnessed the moment, clearly simmering with lid-rattling impatience. "I'll tell you why."

"I'd like to know."

"Okay, I'll tell you."

"Now you're repeating yourself," Julia said, taking a large drought of her tea. "Repeating yourself."

"Lady, I work ten-hour shifts in this Taj Mahal of ptomaine, serving college kids and hobos some of the worst food in the city—aside from that Chinese place next door to the animal shelter. I come here day after day and work my tail off to pay my rent and electric bill. I get tipped a nickel here and a dime there by the lint of humanity's navel, and you want me to do it with a smile on my face?"

Julia nodded. "Here's the thing, Bob—"

"Bobette."

"Bobette?"

"Yeah."

"Right." She took a deep breath. "Bobette, I'm not claiming your life isn't hard, or even miserable." She took a quick look around the diner. "In fact, I don't think anyone here is trying to say that. Life sucks. Truly. Most mornings, I wake to a husband who is suffering from a terminal illness. I wake up in his arms praying I'll feel his chest rising and falling with one breath and then another. I go to work, not because I have a passion for the job but because my husband and I are nearly forty thousand dollars in debt and his ability to hold a job varies with his health."

Bobette's expression had gone from belligerent bulldog to bewildered in less than a second. There was still a sternness to her eyes, but they had softened enough for Julia to note they were a cashmere gray and not the icy blue she had previously thought.

"Last night, Bobette, I told my husband that he and I are expecting our first child. He was so excited that he called everyone he's ever met and told them he was going to keep fighting and living because he was going be here to see this baby of his born—hold it in his arms—sing it to sleep in the rocking chair his mom used to rock in with him."

Julia hadn't realized she was crying until that moment. She paused to wipe the saline on the back of her sleeve.

"We decided to drive to St. Louis today and tell his

folks in person, so I called in sick. Jon—that's my husband—is across the street at the Hertz rental place right now. He's renting us a car for the trip. I'm a sucker for diners, Bobette. My husband saw my eyes light up at the sight of this place, so he poked a little fun at me for my strange little passion and told me to come have a snack while he gets the car.'"

Bobette stumbled out of her silence. "Listen, lady, I don't know what—"

"The thing is, Bob, I was happy this morning. Happier than I've been in years. Something good—some kind of mad, astonishing hope came crashing into my life, past all the fear and pain and crap life keeps throwing around like a monkey in the zoo, and it feels *wonderful* to feel so wonderful."

Bobette still felt like interrupting. "And I suppose—"

"Let her finish," the marine said. His newspaper was folded neatly next to his oatmeal. The stern look in his eyes made the situation clear; he wasn't asking. He was telling. "She's got the floor, Bobette."

"And if you want a tip," Mr. Corned Beef Hash said, "I suggest you stop interrupting."

Julia tipped an imaginary hat to both men before continuing. "Like I said, Bobette. I know life sucks better than some, but I've made a determined effort every day not to let it corrupt me. Do you know why? Because grace still happens. There are always good, grace-filled moments that slip in just when you think you're never going to see one again. The way I figure it, there's enough pain and sorrow and disappointment in this world without me spreading it around. But—and this is the real trick—if I can see past all the fear, pain, and worry to attempt to put a smile on somebody's face or make them laugh a little, I figure I'm giving a bit better than I get, and maybe—just maybe—when I pray each night for my husband to still be breathing next to me in the morning – well, maybe God will keep my Jonathan with me for a while longer."

Bobette took a step back, resting her bulbous backside against the ice cream freezer.

"I came in here with a song," Julia said. "Even when you were rude to me, I tried to play with you. I enjoy sarcasm. I really do. But you weren't playing with me, Bobette. Maybe you forgot how to play."

Julia stood and dropped a ten-dollar bill on the counter. She got halfway to the door before she turned toward Bobette again. The waitress hadn't moved an inch. Every eye in the place was still on Julia.

"I'm sorry if your life is hard, Bobette. Sorrier still I couldn't put a smile on your face this morning. But you'll have to forgive me if I don't let your frustration cloud my sunny day. You see, God did me a solid, and I plan to celebrate. With cheesecake. Elsewhere. But I'll be praying that some of this mad hope manages to find you, too. It seems like you could use some."

Julia slipped outside into the fresh rain and began whistling. The tune was still hers to enjoy.

ON THE NAPE OF HER NECK

DANA FELT A COOL, WET BREATH ON THE tender isthmus of her neck, though her washroom mirror showed no source for that impression. Like the hum of dread reverberating beneath her sternum, the sensation had grown more noticeable over the preceding two weeks until, at present, it had become undeniable.

"Maybe you should see a doctor," her mother had suggested. "Just to make sure you don't have a brain tumor or something."

"Have I ever told you how comforting you aren't?" she had replied, but the recommendation had stuck with her, no doubt adding a bit of resonance to the infernal hum.

As she examined herself in the mirror and took a deep breath, she thought of Collin. Though three years her junior, Dana had found Collin to be everything she desired in a man. He was a contemplative listener. His thoughts were complex and seldom spoken aloud until fully formed and practically unassailable. His personal style was classic if a bit on the retro side, and his playlists could always find a way past your brain and dig deep into the root of your soul. He was charming and kind, gracious and carefree. He was as perfect as he was unavailable.

Three years earlier, on a calm, gray October day, Collin had married Dana's friend, Ashlyn, in a ceremony so sickeningly perfect it had brought a tear to Dana's eye and a pit to her stomach. He had never been hers, of course, outside of daydreams and too many sexual fantasies to count, but the loss of even the potential of Collin violating her secret places as he proclaimed how much better she was than his pitiful fiancée had nearly driven her mad.

"Nearly?" she wondered aloud, but her reflection was still smiling weakly back at her, so she hadn't lost it yet.

The ringing of her cell phone sent her back into the bedroom and scrambling through the contents of her oversized Kate Spade. When she found the phone and noted the name of the caller, however, she debated whether or not to answer.

It read: The Beast.

"Hello?" she asked timidly, ready to hang up if a telemarketer launched into some prerecorded pitch for life insurance.

"Hello, Dana."

"Who is this?" she asked.

"Why are you so worried, Dana? What is it that makes you so afraid?"

"Do…um, do I know you?"

"Yes. Now, answer me."

Instead, she hung up and walked to the kitchen to make herself some breakfast. She felt hungry for the first time in quite a while. Eggs and bacon were on the agenda. Toast, too—slathered with salty butter. And she wanted coffee to wash away the sleepiness in her soul.

The phone rang again. The name on the caller ID brought a frown.

"Please stop calling here," she said. "I don't know you and I don't know why you keep calling."

"Because you always answer when I call. You always have, Dana."

"I've sorry," she said, "but I have to go. Please don't call here again. I don't—"

"What were you hungry for, Dana? Hmm? Surely nothing from your refrigerator."

"Leave me alone!"

"You haven't opened the refrigerator since…well, you know. Or is that another little detail you've banished from your mind?"

Dana disconnected the call, tossed her phone onto the counter of the kitchen island, and turned to make her breakfast. The coffee carafe still held the cold remains of the last brew. She poured it down the sink and removed the filter and grounds. She was surprised to find white mold spreading out over the dry grounds and took extra care to scrub the filter basket with soap and the hottest water she could bear.

Once the coffee was brewing, Dana pulled a plate from the cupboard and decided to make toast only to find her loaf of whole grain bread speckled with green growth.

The phone rang, but Dana ignored it.

She grasped the stainless-steel handle of the fridge but hesitated. What was it the man on the phone had said?

Something about the refrigerator, she thought. A cool breath fell on her neck, and the tiny hairs there stood at attention like grateful athletes during the national anthem.

The phone rang again. It was The Beast. Again. Dana answered.

"Poor Dana," The Beast said. "What's become of you?"

"Why won't you leave me alone?"

"If I did," he asked with a sneer, "who would you talk to, my dear?"

"I have friends," she insisted.

"Did have, dear. 'Had' would be the more accurate term."

"You don't know me!" Her shout was so loud her neighbors surely heard, but Dana didn't care.

"Oh, but I *do* know you," The Beast insisted. "Do know. Have known. Will know. Always. Forever. Unending."

"Please! Please leave me alone!"

"Very well," he said, and the line went dead.

"Hello?"

Dana checked her phone and noticed that the battery icon was blinking. She placed the phone back on the island and returned to the refrigerator.

"What is that sound, Dana?" The Beast asked.

"Which sound?"

"There's a buzzing," he said. "I know you can hear it."

And she did hear it. A droning buzz as if somewhere nearby a contractor was busy playing a symphony on a table saw.

"They keep getting louder," The Beast said, his voice filled with no small amount of delight. "You keep tuning them out, but you can't hide forever, Dana."

"I'm not-I mean, I don't hide. I'm not—"

"From yourself, Dana. From the truth," The Beast said. "Even from reality itself."

"You always lie," she replied.

"I do? I thought you didn't know me?"

"I don't! You-you're trying to confuse me!"

"Oh, you don't need me for that, Dana. You're miles beyond confusion, my dear, and deep in the dark country of your own broken psyche."

"Don't! Don't ever call here again!" Dana screamed, wholly unconcerned with her neighbors or the nosy landlord. It felt good to unleash.

"Call you?" The Beast whispered in her ear. "I didn't call you, Dana. Your phone is still dead and sitting on the kitchen island where you left it."

She looked back at the phone. It lay exactly where she left it. Dana trembled as the cool breath washed over her neck like a lover's kisses, the dread in her soul replaced with an almost sexual thrill. She returned to her bathroom to inspect the woman in the mirror.

Pale and gaunt, Dana barely resembled the woman she used to know. Her once bright eyes had become bloodshot and old, her teeth discolored from neglect. For a moment, she thought she spotted a mole molesting her formerly lovely complexion, but it quickly flew away. Another fly soon took its place, but Dana paid it no mind. She had become distracted by how loose her teeth felt—as though a strong enough wind might send them tumbling out of her mouth.

She opened the medicine cabinet and reached for her

toothbrush, ignoring the phalanges placed neatly next to it.

"Is it easy, Dana?" The Beast asked.

"Is what easy?" she replied, closing the medicine cabinet and inspecting herself in the mirror. She looked as beautiful as she ever had. Her eyes were bright and filled with hope. Her skin was flawless and well-tanned. As she smiled at the woman in the mirror, she thought it might be a good day to visit Collin. Ashlyn would be there, of course—she was always in the way—but contrasted with Dana's beauty, Collin would surely see the error of his choice. An illicit affair might even be better than a marriage—especially if it made Ashlyn feel as betrayed and small as Dana had been made to feel.

"Is it easy to lie to yourself, Dana? To give yourself over to a reality which only exists in your mind?"

"I don't know what you mean," she said, brushing through what was left of her hair, ignorant of the strands falling in clumps into the grimy bathroom sink.

"How long have you been shut inside your apartment, Dana? Three weeks? Six? Do you even know? When was the last time you ate something? Or showered? When was the last time you spoke with anyone but me?"

"You always lie," Dana mumbled, shooing flies away from her stained mouth.

"Sure, I do," The Beast replied. "Go on, then. Have some breakfast, Dana. I'll leave you to eat it in peace."

Though Dana didn't believe The Beast, she still felt a slight thrill of satisfaction at the notion of asserting herself. Being heard was important even if she wasn't truly respected—and she had been heard, even if The

Beast was a liar.

As she returned to the kitchen, a sea of flies parted for her like she was some grim Moses crossing out of bondage. Dana, of course, could not see them. Or *would* not. She refused to acknowledge their presence in her reality, even as they landed near the corners of her mouth, sucking at the morbid nectar pooled there through their straw-like proboscides.

The rich smell of freshly brewed coffee could not mask the scent of putrefaction permeating the air, but Dana imagined it was all she could smell as she poured herself a wide-mouthed mug of the steaming brew. A good dose of dark roast—a "slug of the mug" as her late father would have said—would be just the thing to put a spring back in her step.

The cold sigh on her neck went mostly unnoticed as Dana focused on her growing hunger.

There was a knock at the door, but she chose to ignore it. She wasn't expecting company, nor did she want any. Not her busybody mother. Not her meddling neighbors. Not the annoyingly persistent building superintendent. They were always coming to her door under the pretense of being "worried" or "concerned" for her safety. It was nothing but bothersome, and Dana had taken to ignoring them all.

"What if it's Collin?" The Beast asked, sarcasm dripping from his voice. "What if he's realized how much he's *missed* you?"

She ran to the apartment entrance and placed her ear to the solid-core door.

"Collin?" she asked, her voice coming out rawer and

weaker than she had expected. "Collin, is that you?"

"Dana Caufield?" said a man from the other side of the door. "This is Officer Mike Kowalski of the SPPD. We've received several calls concerning your well-being, Ms. Caufield. Would you be willing to open the door and speak with me for a few minutes?"

"N-no," Dana said. "I'm about to have my breakfast. I'm quite fine. Dandy, in fact. Tell everyone I'm just—"

"We've been trying to call, Ms. Caufield. Your neighbors were concerned because you've stopped responding and haven't left your apartment in quite some time. And, ma'am, there's been several complaints of…well, an odor…emanating from your apartment. The super said he tried to talk to you about it, but you wouldn't answer your door."

Dana ignored the man at the door and walked back into the kitchen where she sipped on her warm coffee and imagined she could no longer hear the thumping at the door.

She opened the refrigerator and was overtaken by a fit of coughing.

"Maybe you should see a doctor," her mother had suggested. "Just to make sure you don't have a brain tumor or something."

"Ms. Caufield, the building super is here with me," the policeman shouted from the hallway, "and I have all the cause I need to come in, but I'd prefer for you to open the door for me. Will you do that, Ms. Caufield, or will I need to have the super let me in?"

Dana took the carving knife from the block on the countertop and leaned into the refrigerator, brushing dead flies and squirming maggots from the ham she imagined there. She cut a thin slice from butt to shank, ignoring the diamond anklet still attached to the shank.

The meat looked too raw to enjoy, but Dana's hunger drove everything else from her mind—the flies, the pounding at the door, the laughter of The Beast (which seemed so close now), and even the cool breath on the nape of her neck. Everything and everyone was driven from her mind…except Collin.

If only he had chosen wisely. If only he had understood what Dana had to offer him: how willing she would have been to debase herself in every vile way just to feel him and know him. If he had only chosen Dana, Ashlyn might still be alive. The Beast might never have broken free. The hunger might never have come.

"It's all over now," The Beast whispered. "They're coming in. They'll see what you've done, Dana—who you've become."

"Collin loves Ashlyn," Dana said, picking a bit of raw meat from between her teeth. "And, now, Ashlyn is inside of me. I'll be his everything. I'll be his goddess."

"Of course you will, Dana," The Beast said, chuckling in some corner of her mind. "Of course you will."

CAN YOU SEE ME?

EVERYTHING I'M ABOUT TO TELL YOU WILL sound crazy. I'm telling you that straight up. You don't know me from the man on the moon and, even if you did know me and knew I'm as honest a fella that ever worked the griddle, you'd still think I cracked something important in my brain pan. I can't help that. If I was you, I'd write me off as some pothead with a wild imagination. So, I get it. You should also know I ain't exactly Willy Shakespeare, if you catch my meaning. I'm gonna do my best to convey the story that was told to me in the hope you'll be better prepared than I was.

My name is Ricky Beventi, and I'm what you'd call a short order cook. I used to spend my days slinging hash and scrambling eggs. I worked down on 12th at a joint called The Hash Tag, a name the little hipster puke who bought out the joint thought would sell to the college puddin's. The new owner, Tad, spruced the joint up, but it's still pretty much a shithole—if you'll pardon the French.

Anyways, I normally worked the night shift, and last Halloween it weren't no different. In a dozen years workin' the griddle, we ain't never had any trouble on Halloween—just the usual traffic and a few bookworms from the local U coming in all dolled up in their costumes. No eggings. No flaming bags of dog sh—I mean, poop—at the front door. Nothing. So, last year come Halloween, I ain't expecting nothin' out of the ordinary 'cept maybe a few more college broads than usual dressed as hookers. And I truly didn't get nothin' out of the ordinary until after 2 a.m.

I remember the time specifically 'cause Joey Vitaglia was giving me grief about the Giants and I had glanced at the clock and was trying to convince him he should get on home to that pregnant wife of his and not leave her alone all hours. As Joey lobbed a few more insults at my team and paid his tab, a guy walks into the joint wearing a trench coat over some torn and bloody pajamas. As Halloween costumes go, I had seen more disturbing characters but something about the fella's expression made me think he might be more damaged than his getup made him appear.

Now, a fry cook ain't the same as a bartender, so let's get clear of that notion right off. I don't spend my time as some grease-splattered priest who's gotta listen to all the troubles and sorrows of every creep who walks into the place. That said, I usually know my customers—as long as they're from the neighborhood—and, like Joey and me, we might talk trash about the Giants or Jets, or some of the old timers might tell me what their grandkids are up to and the like. The point being, I don't go outta my way to get into the business of everyone who cops a squat at my counter, but it ain't outside the realm of possibility neither. This guy, though, I didn't know from Adam.

As he took a seat at the counter, the guy didn't take his eyes offa me. I was finishing a stack of flapjacks for an Elvira wannabe over in the corner booth, so I spoke to him over my shoulder.

"What can I get for ya, pal?"

"Can you...see me?" he asked—a question which might've drawn an insult from me had he not seemed so...I don't know...sincere, I guess.

Before I answered, I glanced over at Dave Krasinsky, a regular that time of night due to his trucking business being a 24-hour operation. Dave seemed uninterested in the weirdo at the counter. I say that on account of Dave asking me for another slice of pie instead of aiming his razor-sharp tongue at the guy clearly trying like hell to be spooky.

I turned back to the guy and shrugged. "What do you need, mister? Because I can whip you up the greasiest damn burger that ever gave you a coronary, but I can't stop everything I'm doing to play your little Halloween games."

"You can see me," was his only reply.

"Look, mister, my waitress called in sick so I'm running this botulism farm on my own. If you're gonna order something, order something. If you came in here to yank my chain, drag your ass back outside. You got me?"

He nodded.

"Good," I said. "So, what'll it be?"

"Do you have pie?"

I glanced over at the revolving pie case over near the

register. "I got peach, I got apple, and I got chocolate cream."

"Peach, please," he said, "and a cup of coffee."

"You got it."

Dave Krasinsky snorted back a laugh down at his end of the counter. "Say, Ricky, before you serve your ghost pal over there, howzabout you get me a slice of the apple?"

"Is that what he's supposed to be?"

"You tell me," Dave said.

"How about it, mister?" I asked. "You some sort of ghost or a walking pop culture reference I'm just not dork enough to get?"

I handed Dave his pie and put the last slice of the peach in front of the stranger. Then I grabbed a mug and poured him a steaming cup of joe before warming Dave's with a refill. The stranger said nothing.

"Cat's got his tongue, I guess," I whispered to Dave.

"Must be," Dave said, shaking his head.

I served Elvira her pancakes and, with no other orders waiting for my attention, I poured myself a cup of coffee and let my curiosity get the best of me.

"So, the costume…who are you supposed to be exactly?" I asked him. He stared at his pie. It wasn't the freshest peach pie in the world, but I was beginning to think I'd have to remind him it was supposed to be taken orally and not through sheer contemplation.

"Stop playing around," Dave said. "It ain't as creepy as you think it is."

"Yeah, pal, the silent act ain't gonna send *us* quaking," I said. "So why don't you tell me who you're supposed to be."

"I was asleep in my bed," the man said. "I'd had a long day at work and Millie, my secretary, had said that the next day would be even busier. So, I remember going home, eating dinner with my wife, kissing my toddler on the head, and crawling into bed. Sometime during the middle of the night, though, I woke to hear my daughter's cries coming from the baby monitor. She sometimes has bad dreams. I tried to nudge my wife, but she was out like a light. So, I put my slippers on and went downstairs to check on Dani—Danielle is my daughter's name, after my wife's grandmother. I thought maybe I could catch up on the snuggles I had missed by turning in early.

As I passed by the kitchen, I heard a strange noise. It was a tapping sound coming from the large window that looks out from our breakfast nook to the side yard on the east side of the house. From time to time, I see a cat perched outside on the window's tiny ledge. I guess, perhaps, the window was warm from the heat of the house and made a good place to sleep on a cold night. Anyway, thinking it was likely the cat again, I went and banged on the window a time or two, hoping to scare it away. I figured the tapping noise had frightened Dani so, cold night or not, the cat needed to go."

"Lemme guess, pal," I mocked. "The cat came back for revenge and clawed the hell out of you."

Dave apparently didn't think that was funny. I thought maybe he didn't want me to encourage the loon, but I figured it was Halloween. What the hell, right?

"I went to Dani's room and found her asleep," he continued. "Whatever had upset her clearly wasn't enough

117

to keep her awake. I went back to the kitchen and poured myself a glass of water. After I put the empty glass in the sink, I turned to head back upstairs to Anna, but I heard the noise again. The more I listened, the less it sounded like a cat and more like the branches of a tree moving in the wind… first tapping and then squeaking against the glass. The problem with that explanation, however, was we had no trees in the side yard. I tried to move the blinds enough to peer outside and find the source of the sound, but the light from the kitchen prevented me from seeing past my own reflection.

I rubbed my eyes and glanced at the clock on the microwave. It was a little after 4 in the morning and I had to be up in under three hours. I realized, though, it was a trash night. Normally, I'd take the garbage out to the curb right after dinner but, since I had gone to bed early, I had forgotten. I grabbed my trench coat from the entryway closet and walked it out to the curb."

"And that's when a mutant creature made outta all the garbage in Jersey rose up to avenge its children who you so callously bagged up and threw on the curb," I said. "Or did a drunk garbage man run you over—oh, or maybe he tossed you in the compactor?"

"Cut it out, Rickey," Dave warned.

"No, no," I said. "I want to hear how this story ends. Go ahead, Stephen King. Scare me."

"I put the bags of trash on the curb and suddenly had the strange feeling someone was behind me."

"The Middlesex Mangler!" I shouted, causing all my patrons to look at me as if I had taken a leak in their water glasses.

118

"There was no one there," the man said. "I whirled around prepared to defend myself but there was nothing to see but my lawn and the neighbor's fence. "

"For a second, I thought I had you figured out," I told him. "I thought maybe you were telling me about the Middlesex Mangler, which—no offense—would've been a bit of a letdown. That guy's been on the news so much it would've seemed too obvious."

The man stared into his pie like he was expecting Jesus Christ to come galloping out of it on a unicorn. Now, normally, if I felt a guy was messing with me—and I mean really trying to play me for the fool, you know?—well, hell, I'd give him the boot and go on with my shift. But this guy, in spite of being a walking question mark of a character, came off as utterly sincere...like he believed every word coming out of his mouth. And, at that point, he hadn't said anything *too* weird, right? I mean, if that was his idea of scary, he needed to save it for a Boy Scout campfire.

He mumbled something I didn't quite make out, so I asked him to repeat himself. When he declined, I made the rounds with a fresh pot of coffee and bussed a table or three. A young couple came in looking for a malt, so I whipped up something sweet for them and, after dropping their order at their booth, returned to the stranger. He still hadn't touched his pie...or the coffee, for that matter.

"Not hungry?" I asked him.

"I need to tell you," he said. "But you won't listen."

"Do you believe this guy?" I asked Dave.

"I thought you were over that," Dave replied. "Why keep this gag going, Ricky?"

"I want to hear what he has to say," I said. "Especially now that he lays in on me I'm not listening. Let's hear the man out." I pushed the guy's peach pie and coffee out of the way and leaned in close. "Shoot, mister. You got my full attention. But I can't promise you I won't call you on your BS once you're done. You've gotta be one of the strangest cats that ever wandered in here. So, either you're trying to get a reaction from me or you're off your nut. Whatever the case, I'm willing to humor you a bit longer, so get on with it already."

"Ricky—" Dave started.

I gave him the look. You know the one: the look your parents get when you're saying something so incredibly stupid it's about to get you some one-on-one time with the switch. Ol' Dave swallowed hard and went back to what remained of his apple pie.

The stranger sighed, rubbed his eyes with the palms of his hands, and continued.

"There was no one there. No monster hiding behind me waiting to devour my soft organs. No demon of fire sent to drag my soul down to the flames and torment. Yet, I still felt—and I know this sounds crazy—but I felt like I was in real danger. I felt as if, just by standing there alone in the cold early morning, I was dying a little inside.

I went back inside and locked the door behind me. I've never been a brave man, you see, but I was suddenly frightened beyond all reason. I had seen nothing unusual outside, but I had the tremendous sense that there was something or someone out there wanting to do me harm. That perhaps beyond my vision, there was a great and terrible evil waiting for me. Logically, I knew that I was back inside safe and sound, but I could still feel the chill of the morning air, and the whistle of the northern wind was still in my ears.

Once again, I heard the tap-tap-tap screeeech at the kitchen window and, once again, I went to see what was making that noise. This time, though, I left the lights out in the kitchen and felt my way through the dark to the window. I wanted to make sure I could see more than my own reflection. I was afraid to raise the blinds, which seemed silly. I knew there was nothing out there. I knew there was every possibility I would open those blinds and see nothing but an old tabby cat cleaning herself on the ledge, or maybe a raccoon trying to figure out how to jimmy the window so he could raid the pantry like a real bandit would. I tried to convince myself that nothing dangerous or frightening could be found on the other side of the glass, but my heart was pounding incessantly, and I could feel every muscle in my body yearning to break into a run—as though some primitive fight-or-flight response was keenly aware of some danger I was not.

So, I took a deep breath or two and grabbed onto the pull cord which raised the blinds. I gave myself a silent three count, yanked the chord, and peered outside into the frigid morning."

If I had been seated, I woulda been on the edge of my seat, you know? So, I looked over at Dave to see if he was as interested in what the fella was about to say as I was, but he was just sipping his coffee and reading a newspaper.

"What'd you see out there?" I asked the stranger. "What was waitin' on the other side of the window?"

"Me," he said just above a whisper. "I saw *me*."

"You mean you saw your reflection again," I corrected.

"No. I saw me—er, myself. But—"

"But what?"

"I was dead. Dead and decaying as though I had sprouted up out of the ground like some ragged robin and come to give myself a good scare. But, as soon as I realized it was me out there, all dead and pointless and far beyond the usefulness of fear, I remembered *everything*."

"What everything?" I asked, suddenly too caught up in his spooky tale to remember it was bullshit. "What did you remember?"

"I had died one morning taking the trash out in my trench coat and pajamas. I had felt someone behind me and had turned to find a man in a mask… with a knife that pierced my flesh as if it offered no more resistance to his blade than tissue paper. I had died there in the cold, not twenty feet from the warmth of my own house where, as I drew my last breath, my wife and daughter slept like angels."

I laughed with a sudden realization and took a step back from the counter to look the clown over.

"That's pretty good, mister. You sort of had me going a bit. I can admit it. You're supposed to be George Nichols, right? I mean, that's who you're dressed as."

"George Nichols," the man said, as though rolling it around on his tongue had a familiar flavor. "Yes. I was George Nichols. That was my name. It was my name in life."

"You don't think your costume's in bad taste?" I asked. "I only figured it out because I read the papers every day.

The way you sold that story, man, you truly were going for broke. But, as soon as you got to the murder, I had it all figured out. I was half right when I guessed the Middlesex Mangler. I just didn't catch on that you were dressed as the first victim."

"First?" he asked.

"Yeah. It's been in all the papers. The Middlesex Mangler has been killing folks all over the county. First, as you must've learned researching your costume, there was George Nichols, a businessman with a wife and kid. He was found like you said: wearing a trench coat and PJs and slumped over the garbage he had taken out. Some woman bought it too, at one of those walk-up ATMs. That's how the cops first got a look at the guy. Again, just like you said. He was wearing a mask and had some sort of knife the cops seem to think he made himself. Two more since then, so the papers and TV news had to give him a name and, since all the murders have taken place right here in Middlesex county, the Middlesex Mangler has become quite the morbid sensation. But I shouldn't have to tell you that."

"He's still out there," the guy said, though less like he was asking a question and more like I had confirmed his worst fear. "That's why I'm here."

"What's that mean?" I asked him.

"Even though I had just realized I was dead, I felt the need to wake my wife. I guess I thought maybe she could wake me from the nightmare I found myself in. But as I walked back upstairs, I noticed what, previously, my mind had not allowed. The house was empty. Boxes full of our possessions lined the hallway, and no one remained in the house but me. Time had passed since my death although, until you told me about this Middlesex Mangler, I had no idea how much.

I walked here tonight like a dog on a leash goes where he is led. I was being pulled along, dragged here by some force greater than death. Along the way, I tried to ask people on the street if they could help me figure out where Anna and Dani had gone, but no one could see me…not until I came in here. When you spoke to me, I knew I had to tell you my story. I think—I'm not entirely sure—but I think I was sent here to warn you. I think, perhaps, you can only see me because you're the killer's next victim. You can see me because you must. You can see me because there is still hope for *you* to escape my cruel fate."

Now, I felt like I'd been pretty patient with ol' George or whatever his name really was, but the way he laid out those last few statements convinced me that maybe I really was in danger…of looking like a damn fool for listening to some loon tell his nutty story without showing him the door. For the first time since he had walked into The Hash Tag, I felt like the stranger was truly bent in the head. He looked at me with some sort of sadness, like I was a puppy dog that had just been run over, and he wanted to help me—only he couldn't quite figure out how. But he also seemed more detached than he had been when he was telling his story. It was almost like his concern for me was some half-remembered notion. He could give it voice, but he couldn't bring himself to feel any real concern. To say it gave me the creeps would be a helluva understatement.

I ain't never been the type to pick a fight, but I've finished quite a few in my time, and I suddenly had the urge to smack the guy. Still, I didn't quite know whether I should be angry at him for trying to threaten me or at myself for giving him the opportunity. At a loss for words, I turned back to Dave Krasinsky.

"You believe this guy? I play along real nice to let him tell his Halloween stories, and he has the gall to threaten me? Dave, you got my back, right, if this creep tries to say I attacked him or something? I just want to throw him out on his ass and get back to my night."

Dave, typically a calm and cool type, slammed his coffee mug on the counter and stood. He leaned in so close that his nose was practically touching mine.

"Listen, Ricky," Dave said. "I get it's Halloween, and I get you're pissed for getting stuck runnin' this joint on your own for the night, but my patience with you has just about run out."

"Your patience with me?" I said. "What about ol' George Nichols over there? I'm not the guy trying to convince everyone he's the first victim of the Middlesex Mangler!"

"No, you're the guy who's spent the past 20 minutes giving pie, coffee, and conversation to an empty seat! I don't know if you're cracking up, if you've been drinking on the job, or you're trying to annoy the shit out of me. Either way, I've had enough. Give me my check and let me get the hell out of here."

"It's not me, Dave," I said. "It's this idiot that—"

When I turned back to George, I saw what Dave and all the other diner patrons had seen all along: an empty seat at the counter that had been served a slice of peach pie and a mug of joe. They hadn't been witness to a man dressed like a homicide victim telling his crazy-ass horror story. They had watched the cook at their favorite greasy spoon carrying out his half of a conversation with an empty stool.

Some instinct screamed out for me to look around for the man who had called himself George Nichols, but some deeper instinct made me certain I'd never find him. Part of me wanted to ask each customer if they had seen the man walk in and order his pie, but another part of me knew I would only be more frightened when they told me they saw nothing but a lunatic fry cook putting on a little Halloween theater.

"I'm sorry, Dave," I managed, though my throat had gone as dry as a Mormon wedding. "I was just, you know, trying to liven things up a bit. I didn't mean nothin' by it."

Dave dropped back onto his stool and shook his head.

"You're alright, Ricky. You were starting to creep me out is all. I was seriously beginning to think something had happened to you...like maybe your brain was stroking out."

"I'm fine," I lied. "And don't sweat the bill. It's on me since you were such a good sport and all."

Now, I don't have to tell you how confused I was. I wasn't sure if I should feel relieved that I was no longer seeing things or—and I know how this sounds—if maybe I truly had been sent some sort of warning. After all, the Middlesex Mangler was still on the loose, and ol' George Nichols had seemed as real to me as Dave, Joey, and the rest of the diners had. Could the real George

Nichols have been sent to save me from the violence that had come to call upon him one cold, dark morning? No matter how I put the question to myself, I couldn't feel confident in any answer.

I FINISHED MY SHIFT AND WAS RELIEVED BY Carl Loomis, the morning griddle man and manager, and Doreen Clark, a waitress that the owner, Tad, was banging every time his wife went out of town. I counted my tips—which was a rarity since I usually didn't have to wait on tables—and said my goodbyes. It was just after 7 a.m. and the sun was already out. Home was only a few blocks away, so I hoofed it back to my place.

As you can imagine, I was a bit on edge. Every sound—whether it was an argument among sedge wrens or an empty soda can clattering down the street—seemed to be the sound of menace. I ain't what you'd call paranoid, but damned if I didn't look over my shoulder a dozen or more times on my walk home, half-expecting to see the Mangler ready to greet me with his steel. Each time I glanced back, though, I found nothing worthy of my fear.

Away from the bodegas and bakeries, the streets were quiet, and I began to feel more foolish than fearful. I wondered if reading all them news stories about the Mangler had poisoned me with such an intense understanding of how looney tunes the world had grown that it had me hallucinating phantom pie contemplators and filling in the gaps with details from the papers. I had read, after all, that Nichols had been found in his trench coat and pajamas with multiple stab wounds. So maybe the whole experience had been my mind's way of saying, "Yo, Ricky, this world has gone topsy-turvy and you gotta be more careful."

Anyway, I took the steps of my stoop two at a time and fished in my pocket for the keys. Somewhere off in the distance, I heard a train whistle and the honking of cars. And in my right side, I felt something like a needle. Before I could even utter a curse, I sensed something wet running down my leg. It was warm and, for a split second, I thought maybe I had pissed myself. I looked down thinking a dog may have mistaken me for a hydrant, only to find a flow of crimson spilling out onto my right shoe. Suddenly, those needles were everywhere, stinging my left shoulder…my lower back…just behind my left knee. Over and over, like a hornet with a thousand stingers, something bit deep into my flesh. I felt dizzy and had to grip the doorknob to stay standing.

I managed to turn, but my assailant was already cleaning his knife—a hawksbill blade nearly a foot in length—and walking back toward the street as calmly as if he had delivered my mail. He glanced back at me, and I got a good look at his mask. It looked like one of them ceremonial masks you sometimes see in those National Geographics. I'd say it looked Egyptian, but I don't know Egyptian from Greek or Martian so why the hell should anyone believe me? I remember sliding down the door until I was sitting in a pool of my own blood. I could feel it seeping into the seat of my pants, but there wasn't a damn thing I could do about it. I have the vague recollection of my neighbor, Janie Freeman, finding me there and calling for an ambulance, but I don't know how long I'd been bleeding out when that happened. "Too long" is about all I can say.

I know you probably can't bring yourself to believe my story, but I'm telling you—no, I'm *swearing* to you on all I hold holy and sacred—that every word of it is true. I met whatever part of George Nichols still lingered in Middlesex county on Halloween night and, on November the 1st, I became the fifth victim of the man the newspapers call the Middlesex Mangler.

Now, I don't remember how I got here today. I only remember feeling pulled along street after street until I walked in here and found you reading your book. I didn't know what I was supposed to do until you said hello to me but then it finally hit me. See, I was sent here to warn you. I was sent here to tell you that you're next—the Mangler is coming for you. I know this because of what you did.

You saw me.

THE CINDER MAN

I TOOK MY FIRST ROAD TRIP WHEN I WAS SEVEN years old. My father, the late, great Howard Kinneman, loaded the entire family into our rust bait Suburban and drove us from deep within the bowels of western Arkansas to the splendor of Florida's stunning monument to capitalism, Disney World. Along the way, down highway mile after highway mile, I watched a country I barely knew fly past my window. Even before we left our little 3-bedroom tract house in Mountainburg, I was less excited about the famous, bustling amusement park and its equally famous rodent mascot than I was getting out of my armpit of a hometown.

Our blue and gray Suburban C20 was packed to the gills with the assorted nonsense my mother, Helen, deemed necessary for a lengthy excursion into gator country. Roughly three changes of clothing per day "just in case" was her rule of thumb. By the time you factored in swimsuits, a duffle bag filled with toiletries—including but not limited to four different brands of mosquito repellent and a first aid kit that would make a paramedic jealous—along with an assortment of jackets and scarves in the off chance we ran into a freak summer snow storm while passing through Yawn-n-Scratch, Alabama or Bumblefart, Georgia, the old Suburban, which Dad affectionately referred to as "Betsy", was so overweight with the fruit of my mother's packing anxiety that her shocks had all the bounce of an octogenarian stripper.

I couldn't exactly remember going to Disney World or even the long drive back home, but I remembered how good it felt to be on the road to adventure, speeding away from my tiny dead-end town. Truth told, I hadn't thought of that trip in years until my wife, Megan, and I were making the eight-hour return trip to Indianapolis from her parents' place on Mackinac Island, Michigan. I was brooding, which—to be fair—isn't exactly an uncommon occurrence, and Megan picked up on it after we stopped for gas and snacks in Munro.

"Got you a Zero bar, Gloomy Gus," Megan said, plopping into the passenger seat, "and a giant bottle of water good for hydration and, if we get into a real bind, urination."

"Gross," I said, grasping for the Zero bar only to have her snatch it away. The sunlight stretching through the Impreza's windshield warmed the tiny array of freckles which mapped her face from just under her left eye and over the gentle slope of her nose only to stop beneath her right eye. She hates those freckles. I've always thought they add to her charm.

"You can eat the Zero bar after you tell me what's eating *you*," she said. "You've been glum ever since we hit the road."

"It's nothing to worry your pretty little head about," I joked.

"My head may, in fact, be pretty, Mr. Kinneman," Meg said, handing me the oversized bottle of water she had purchased while I topped off the tank with gas, "but it isn't just for looks, you know. It houses a brain, and that brain houses an intellect quite equal to yours."

"Oh, no! Not my equal," I said sincerely, "I bow to my intellectual *superior*. That brain of yours is one of the sexiest things about you."

"Remind me to ask you what the others are the next time we're alone with a modicum of privacy."

"See? You said 'modicum.' Even your vocabulary is sexy."

"You're changing the subject," she said, kicking her sandals off in the floorboard and tucking her legs under her. "My dad said something, didn't he?"

"It doesn't matter," I lied. "He's your dad. Dads worry about their kids. Comes with the gig. If he wasn't concerned, he'd be one of the bad ones who flat doesn't care."

"Are you going to tell me or not?" The look she gave me was one I had seen before. Continuing the avoidance game was only going to upset her and that was something I vowed never to do willingly.

"Ed may have mentioned a friend of his with a startup in Indy. Said it was a 'once-in-a-lifetime opportunity for anyone smart enough to latch onto it' and reminded me that guys who never finished college should be grateful to have an easy in."

Meg studied my eyes for a minute. I'm not sure what she found there, but I saw hurt and not a little bit of anger in hers as her eyelids narrowed and she took a deep breath.

"He's trying to help," I offered. "He doesn't understand me—"

"Because he's never given it a moment's effort," she grumbled.

"—and he might not *ever* understand me. That's okay. He means well."

"I don't care what he means," she argued, leaning in to touch her forehead to mine. "No one talks to my man that way. Not even my Dad. And he knows better, which is why he waited until I wasn't around to pull that crap."

"To be fair, very few men from his generation understand guys like me."

"Well, it's dumb," Meg said just before pressing her lips to mine. The kiss was soft and sweet and, as always, I felt it ended too soon. "I love you," she said, "and Dad may not understand art, but your being at home working on it allows me to do what I do. So, if he's going to praise me for my accomplishments, he'd damn well better lay off pressuring you on the 9 to 5 horsesh—er, crap."

I smiled at her like a Grade A dope. After eight years as the Mister to her Missus, I was still hopelessly in love with Meg.

"That swear jar is losing money on the daily," I said.

"I'm working on it. While we're on the subject of parental units and secret conversations, you weren't the only one who had an awkward encounter dumped in your lap," she said. "Mom sang all the greatest hits from her

Wannabe Grandmother's Blues album."

"She hummed a few bars for me, too," I admitted. "Reminded me that you're not getting any younger."

"Thanks, Ma!" Meg chimed with her cheesiest grin. "Geez, when did our family planning become everyone else's business?"

"I think when we hit our 5th anniversary and hadn't produced any progeny, the filter fell off. It's just one more thing they can blame me for. I'm pretty sure there's a master list with subcategories, illustrations, and the like."

"I never lay it at your feet when they ask," Meg said. "And I won't. Not ever."

"I know," I said. "But it kind of belongs there. I've kept *you* waiting, too."

"We'll have kids when we're both ready," she said, handing me the Zero bar. "And I'm not ready until *you're* ready. Until such a day comes, it's not anyone's business."

As we drove out of Munro, I questioned my unyielding hesitation to bring children into the world. My own childhood had been relatively happy. On the cosmic scales where joy and sorrow are forever weighed against each other, the former tipped the scales with little competition. Yet some dark worry haunted me whenever Megan brought up the notion of parenthood—a fear whose grip I could never quite shake. It was suffocating.

Meg was asleep before we even made it 20 miles out of Munro. Mist had settled on my windshield and the sky had turned as gray as my mood. The rhythm of the windshield wipers was grating on my nerves, but I didn't want to wake Meg with the radio, so I retreated into the past. Hoping to recall at least something of my trip to

Kissimmee, I rummaged through the steamer trunk of tangled memory fragments and tried to piece together something of substance. My struggle, however, was in vain.

As we drove into Gaylord, my eyes were getting heavy, so I turned the radio on as low as it could go. WMJZ "The Eagle" greeted me with some Creedence Clearwater Revival which mingled with a yawn from the passenger seat.

"Where are we?" Meg asked, searching through her purse for some gum.

"About two miles outside of Gaylord," I said. "Sorry about the radio. I was getting sleepy."

"Not surprising, Mr. Insomniac. I think you got a total of 6 hours the whole weekend."

"I don't travel well," I admitted.

"Crab salad doesn't travel well, David," she said, poking my belly with her finger. "You're a disaster. You get moody and quiet. It's a good thing I love you."

"Yes, it is."

"Pull over, Droopy, and I'll take the wheel," she said. "I'll even drive the speed limit this time."

"I'd pretend I believe you, but I'm too tired for that."

I took us off the highway into Gaylord and pulled into the parking lot at Timothy's Pub, where I entered and ordered a bourbon neat and a black coffee for Megan. I don't know what it is about bourbon, but it has always calmed my nerves. Just a sip or two, mind you, but it's my go-to nightcap.

Back in the car, I adjusted the passenger seat for sleep and secured myself with the seatbelt as Meg repositioned the side mirrors.

"No drag racing," I half-yawned.

"But I won $75 last time," Meg teased.

"Don't let me nap more than 45 miles or so, Leadfoot," I said, drifting further away from consciousness.

"Sure thing, Killjoy."

I ADMIT THAT, MUCH LIKE MY MOTHER BEFORE me, I'm a tad obsessive when it comes to road trips. But, instead of it driving me to overpack, my hyperactive brain conjures every scenario for potential catastrophe and I actively plan for the worst. I replaced the pitiful factory jack and tool combo with something more reliable the day after we bought the car. There's a go bag permanently stored in the back jam-packed with ponchos, emergency blankets, flashlights with extra batteries, an extra power supply for charging our phones, along with a fire starter and other survival tools. It's a sickness. I blame my mother.

Before we left Indy to set out for Mackinac Island, I had taken the car to have the brakes checked, the oil changed, and the tires rotated. None of my preparation, however, prevented my head from impacting with the dashboard when Megan slammed on the Impreza's brakes and left a trail of rubber down the interstate. I was woozy and dazed. Darkness crept into the edges of my vision as unconsciousness threatened to overwhelm me, but I shook it off to tend to more important things.

"Are you okay?" I asked, trying to get my eyes to focus

on Meg.

"Scared shitless," she said, breathing heavy. "You?"

"A bit of a love tap from the dash, but I'll live. And you owe the swear jar, lady."

"Fuck the swear jar."

"Fair enough. What happened?"

When she didn't answer, I turned to find Meg had exited the car and was cautiously making her way toward whatever lay in the road beyond the hood.

"Babe?"

I opened the passenger door and tried to follow. Standing, however, proved to be a problem. I was suddenly the axis of the world and I felt sick as I watched it revolve around me. The Zero bar made an unexpected return appearance along with the remnants of my breakfast. I gripped the door tightly, desperate not to drop to my knees in the mess I had made on the pavement. Megan was speaking, but only bits and pieces broke through the haze of overwhelming nausea.

"...thought...animal...nearly hit...won't talk to me... try, David..."

Perhaps it was my concern for Megan which cleared my head and calmed my stomach but, as soon as she said my name, the world stopped spinning and I could stand.

"What happened?" I asked, walking around to see what she was kneeling over in the street. There was a young boy at her feet, curled up like a cat in the sunlight and trembling.

"He ran in front of us," Meg said, stroking his head. "Thank God I stopped in time. But something's wrong with him, David. I can't get him to speak to me."

"Where are we?" I asked, not recognizing the wooded area on either side of the highway.

"I'm not sure," Meg replied. "It's all a blur when I'm highway driving. Haven't seen a sign for a bit."

I knelt next to her and looked at the boy. He was filthy. His clothes, out of fashion and ripped in numerous places, were stained by grass and mud. And there was a smell about him...like bad liquor.

"Are you okay, kid?" I asked. "Do we need to call an ambulance?"

He shook his head. Hooray for communication.

"I'm sorry I almost hit you," Meg offered. "What are you doing out here by yourself?"

The boy said nothing.

"Do your parents live around here?" I asked. He shook his head. "Did you run away?"

"David..." Meg started.

"It's a fair question. Did you run away, kid?"

He shook his head again.

"Can you walk?"

This time, he nodded.

"Okay. Let's get you on our feet and in the car. It's way too cold out here for little boys in Swiss cheese clothes." I helped him stand but, when I took his hand, the staggering dizziness returned. "I think you'll have to steer the boat, babe. I hit my head a lot harder than I thought. My vertical hold seems to be on the fritz."

"You're going to the hospital," Meg said. Her tone was one I knew well. It assured me that no amount of arguing would keep her from having her way.

"That's gonna be tough if you don't know where we

are, Magellan," I said, watching her strap the boy into the back seat. "We'd be better off calling the police and letting them do the driving."

As Megan pulled out her phone, my attention drifted to the back seat where the boy shivered and sniffed back tears. I turned the heat up before pulling the visor down and inspecting my head in the small makeup mirror. Thankfully, I found no blood or wound, but I had a big enough goose egg to make me look like I'd soon be sprouting an alien. And, given that I had trouble getting my eyes to focus on the injury, I assumed a concussion was in play, as well.

"Damn it. Nothing," Meg said, turning on the flashlight feature of her smartphone. "There's no 911 service out here in…wherever the hell we are. And when I try to search for the closest police station, my phone just processes. The service out here must be screwy."

"Then we drive," I said. "Or *you* do. Once we hit the next town, we'll either find the police or have the service to call them."

"Let me see your head," she said, grabbing my chin and turning my injury toward her light. "Oh, babe, you look like an aspiring unicorn."

She shined her light in my eyes and it took all my willpower not to shrink away from it. The brightness made my head feel like an echo chamber in which a hundred or more giants with sledgehammers were playing The Anvil Chorus on rusty oil barrels.

"You're concussed, babe, so I need you to stay awake and keep talking to me while I drive. Deal?"

"Deal," I said. I moved my visor so the mirror would

give me a view of the boy in the back seat. "You got a name, kid?"

The boy nodded but didn't move or make any attempt to look at us.

"You feel like sharing it, you let us know. As for us, I'm David. The nice lady who almost hit you with our car is Megan."

"Thanks, babe," Meg said, putting the car in drive but keeping her foot on the break.

"I know you're scared," she told the kid, "but David and I will get you some help. Try to relax."

In the mirror, I saw the boy sit up and peer out the nearest window. There was fear in his eyes and his trembling became more pronounced. Meg saw it, too.

"What is it?" she asked. "What's—David, look!"

I turned to my own window to follow her gaze out into the darkness surrounding us. There was nothing but wild brush out there and... and something else. My eyes were too unfocused to make it out, but there was something brighter off in the distance. A campfire? A torch?

The boy said something. It was little more than a whisper, but Meg and I both heard it.

"The Cinder Man," the boy had said, and despite having no idea what those words could mean, something inside me froze over. It must have had the same effect on Megan, because she disengaged the brake and used her infamous lead foot to get us out of there.

Putting distance between us and whatever had frightened the kid didn't seem to calm him. He continued to whimper and shake like a wounded animal. He didn't seem to understand he was safe with us, which made me consider what sort of torment he had endured before running in front of our car.

As we drove on, I grew more and more concerned. Nothing about the highway—a route we had taken more times than the Beatles went to the toppermost of the poppermost—seemed familiar. Interstate 75 was littered with places to stop even before you made it to Saginaw, but there were no signs along that stretch of macadam announcing rest stops, gas stations, or greasy spoons. And no matter how many times I checked for a signal on my own smartphone, I ended up with a bigger goose egg than I was wearing on my forehead.

"Where are we?" Meg asked, as if she'd been strolling through my thoughts. "We should be close to West Branch, but—"

"Yeah," was all I could muster. "Did you take 127 by mistake? It would've been a few miles past Grayling. It's easy to do."

"No, David, I took 75. I was very careful."

"Okay."

"You don't believe me," she grumped. "I took 75."

"I believe you, babe, I just don't know what to make of it. Let's give it a few more miles."

"He's coming," the boy said. It wasn't merely a statement of fact. It had the tone of a warning.

"Who's coming?" I asked.

"The Cinder Man," he replied. "He's coming for me."

"Whoever you think is coming for you, you don't have to worry," Meg said. "David and I will protect you. I can swing a mean tire iron and David will puke on them. Right, David?"

"You're safe with us, kiddo," I said, trying my best to sound reassuring. "Next town we see, we'll stop for help."

"No one can help," the kid said. "He's coming. And he won't stop."

"Who's the Cinder Man?" I asked. "Is that, like, a nickname or something? Is it someone you know? Like a relative or something?"

The boy gave no answer. Instead, he retreated into staring out the side window.

"How's your head?" Meg asked.

"Still attached," I replied. "I know this because it hurts like unholy hell."

"I'd offer to kiss it, but...*eww*."

"Thanks, love."

"Is that a gas station?" she asked, squinting to see something in the distance. "Over there. On the right. Is it a—it is!"

"Pull over," I said. I'm not usually so demanding, but my nausea was returning like gangbusters and I didn't feel like decorating the car interior with a frat house splatter painting.

Have you ever had a moment of clarity? A moment in which everything around you seemed to stop and you suddenly knew something so bone deep, so clearly that no one would ever be able to convince you otherwise? That's how I felt as soon as Megan brought the car to a stop under the fading lights of that apparently abandoned gas station. I knew, even as the compulsion to vomit faded, that there was something out there in the darkness coming for the boy and Megan and I were powerless to stop it from happening. Before I could share my epiphany with my wife, however, she exited the car.

"It seems deserted," she yelled back to me. "Stay with the boy. I'm going to see if there's anything resembling a phone in there."

"She shouldn't go in there," the boy in the back seat whispered.

"The Cinder Man is coming," I replied with certainty.

The door to the small convenience store portion of the old gas station was little more than a metal frame and door pull. Whatever glass had made up its greater portion was nothing but a memory…its former presence proven only by the few shards still clinging to the corners of the frame like art deco spider webs. Before I could cry out for her to stop, Megan disappeared into the station.

"She's gonna find a phone, kid," I lied, bile rising in my throat. "Everything will be okay."

"There's no phone," the kid said. "There was never a phone. It wasn't safe in there."

From my perspective, an eternity passed from the moment I lost sight of Meg until the moment I willed myself to open the passenger door and step outside. I've never been a fearful man, but something was gripping me that I couldn't shake. It weakened my knees, bent my spine, and made me think I might lose control of my bladder.

"Stay in the car," I managed to say to the kid. "I'm going to go get her."

"He's almost here," he said.

"I know."

I had lost my line of sight with Megan as soon as she crossed the threshold of the station. As I drew nearer to that same spot, I gave a quick glance back to the kid to make sure he wasn't following me. The back door of the Impreza was open and the boy was nowhere in sight.

"Damn it," I mumbled, hoping I'd make it back to the safety of my home where I would add a dollar to my wife's swear jar.

I stepped over the broken glass which littered the pavement near the doorway and through the metal frame Megan had traversed a moment or two ahead of me.

"Meg?"

She appeared from a narrow door in the back which must have been—when the place was still in operation—a storage room for the air fresheners, candy bars, and cigarettes typically sold in such a place.

"David? Why are you out of the car? Your head—"

"We have to go," I insisted, feeling every bit the lunatic. "There's something…well, I can't explain it, but—"

"I couldn't find a phone," she said. "I found a little desk back there in the storage room, but no phone. There was, however, a frighteningly sexist wall calendar suggesting this place hasn't been in operation since the Carter administration. Either way, no phone means we're going to have to keep driving until we find something else, so let's get you back to the car, Dizzy Miss Lizzy."

"The boy is gone. We need to find him," I said as the whole dusty and ruined station tilted on me. "Something's…coming."

Before I could drop to my knees, Meg steadied me and moved me slowly toward the car.

"This is exactly why I told you to stay with the kid, babe. You're in no condition to wander around playing tough guy. Let's get you back to the car and I'll look for the boy."

"No, we...we need to go," I said, fighting to stay upright and conscious. "Can't you feel it, Meg?"

"Feel what?"

"The danger. It's covering everything around us like the dust on these shelves. Everything seems still now, but if the right gust of wind should come along—"

"As soon as I find the boy, we'll ghost," she promised. "Now, see if you can mobilize those legs and help me out. You weigh more than you look."

"He's here," the boy said. How or when he had entered the dilapidated station, I couldn't tell you, but he was there alright, cringing behind a display that had once been filled with magazines and comic books.

"Who's here?" Megan asked. I knew the answer to her question, but the boy beat me to the punch.

"The Cinder Man," he replied, followed by a whisper I alone heard like a shout. "He's always here. I never get away."

Megan propped me up near where the register had once rung up tins of Skoal, packets of Chiclets gum, and soft drinks for weary travelers. The boy cautiously made his way to my side and gripped the bottom hem of my gray Oxford shirt as if holding onto the leash of a dog prone to bolt at the first sign of a squirrel or grackle.

Megan, however, approached the remnant of the glass door we had entered through to investigate what had the boy so scared. Had I not been crippled by fear and nausea, I would've pleaded with her to stay away from the door. The Cinder Man was coming...and we never get away.

Before she even made it to the door, he entered—a trail of fire marking every step. Megan rightly screamed at the sight of him, but I could not hear the depth of its terror. The only sound that registered in my ears was the whispered words of the boy cowering behind me.

"He'll never let us get away."

I'd love to tell you that seeing my wife standing so near that thing brought out the beast in me—some heroic alter ego who impulsively leapt between them and rattled off a clever one-liner before sending that awful creature back to whatever hellish pit it came from, but the truth is I'm more likely to be mistaken for Barney Fife than John Rambo.

"David, run!"

That much I heard and, as Megan bolted back toward the storage room/office combo she had explored earlier in search of a phone, I chased after her with the boy hot on my heels. Once we were all inside, she turned the deadbolt behind us and propped the desk chair under the doorknob.

"He was on fire," I mumbled. "He was on fire and alive. All together. Both at once."

"Yeah, I got that part, but we can process and panic later," Megan said. "That deadbolt's not meant to hold long. Follow me."

The room was deeper than it was wide. The front third, where the Cinder Man would soon burn through deadbolt, door, and chair alike, housed a filing cabinet and small desk where undoubtedly the owner of the mom and pop establishment once rifled through invoices while smoking a cigar so cheap it would make Groucho jealous.

The other two-thirds, though, was storage consisting of shelving units lined up like dominos. On the right side of each unit was an aisle barely wide enough for an adult to shimmy through sideways. How the owner ever moved product back and forth without bringing the whole precarious arrangement down on his own head, I couldn't fathom.

"There's a door in the back," Megan said, slipping past the first shelving unit. "Get the kid and let's go."

I looked back at the boy and there was a deadness in his eyes—a weariness which belied his youthful exterior.

"Can you help me, kid?" I asked. "I seem to be a bit clumsy since greeting the dashboard with my melon, and we need to get out of here."

He obliged by taking my right hand. I used my left to hold onto the shelving which, by that point, held nothing more than half-empty boxes of toilet paper and a few gallon jugs of wiper fluid. We followed Megan to the back where we found the delivery door closed and padlocked. Megan kicked it as hard as she could and bounced backward, her ever-so-cute butt landing on the dusty concrete floor.

"Damn," she said, standing and dusting off her backside. "That always looks so easy on television."

"Most things do," I said. "We need a hammer. Or maybe a crowbar or something."

"He's coming," the boy said.

"A fact not lost on us, kiddo," Megan said. "I think I saw a hammer on top of the filing cabinet."

As she made her way back to the front of the room, I gave the back door another kick, only to feel an awkward but not-quite-painful pop in my knee.

"Stupid, lying police procedurals," I grumped. "Meg?"

"Got it," she said, rounding the corner of the nearest shelving unit and handing me a hammer that looked like it could've been brand new...in 1876.

"Yikes," was all I could muster before launching my attack on the padlock.

"What the fu—I mean, what the heck is that thing, kid?" Meg asked the boy. "Is that the Cinder Man?"

The boy nodded but said nothing.

"Why is it after us? Better still, why you?"

Silence.

Meg looked back toward the office door.

"That door turned to ash, David," she said. "It didn't burn, it just—"

"Doesn't matter," I said, as my seventh strike with the tool broke the lock. "Go!"

As Megan and the boy ran through the back door into what had once been a quarter car wash, I threw my body into the closest shelving unit and watched intently as it crashed into the next unit. Down they went like dominoes, speed and weight being added to each subsequent collapse until, at last, the rack closest to the Cinder Man toppled toward him. He hit the ground hard but, even as I rejoiced for a moment in my haphazard victory, I knew it wasn't enough to stop him. The Cinder Man was coming, as the boy said, and I could feel his relentlessness like a hand on my throat.

My wife, the boy, and I raced through the abandoned car wash and back toward the front of the station where our car was idling right where we left it. Megan threw

148

open the passenger door and climbed across to get behind the wheel. The boy scrambled after her as I followed and closed the door behind us. As soon as the final seatbelt clicked into place, Megan broke what had to have been the previous land speed record for a foreign-made compact sedan.

"Okay, let's get back to my previous question. What the hell was that thing?" Meg asked, white-knuckling the steering wheel as she maxed out the Impreza's capacity for speed.

"The Cinder Man," was all I could think to say.

"Not helpful, David! That thing was on fire and moving around as if it hadn't even noticed. That's not possible. It's the stuff of nightmares and cheesy B-movies."

I had nothing to say. At that moment, I didn't understand what was happening or why. Even if I had, I doubt that I would have been able to explain it.

"Why is this thing after you, kid? If we're in danger, we need to understand what we're up against," Megan said. "This whole nonverbal thing you've got going isn't doing us any favors."

"It's trauma," I said. "He's not trying to be difficult, babe."

"Understood," she replied. "And I'm not upset with you, kiddo. Not at all. I just need all the info if I'm going to get us out of this."

"He won't stop coming," the boy said. "He'll never let me go."

"We're going to drive far, far away from him," Meg said. "No more stopping until we find a town."

"No one ever helps," the boy replied. "No one comes

for us."

"I know it must feel that way," Meg offered, "and I'm scared as all get out, too. But we'll figure this out together. You can trust me."

"She's right," I said. "I've never known someone truer to her word than my missus. You can take her word to the bank."

"How's your head? You still wibbly?" Meg asked me.

"Better than before," I said. "I wouldn't trust my math, though."

"I never did."

"Nice."

"Why aren't we finding a town, David? I know I didn't get off the highway, but none of this looks familiar."

"None of this makes any sense," I said. "Let's try to find some other people. Or a phone. Or some other people with a phone."

"I'd feel better if the person with a phone was a priest," Meg said. "That thing was on fire, David. Literal fire."

"We saw, babe."

"I mean 'Cinder Man' my ass. That guy was like the Human Torch without the lackluster box office."

"We saw him, Meg."

"I know. I know," she said. "I'm all panicky. It happens when I panic. It's the panic that makes me panicky."

"Megan?"

"Yeah?"

"Shut up, huh? I need to think."

"Yep."

The next 30 miles or so rolled by with no sight of the Cinder Man. Unfortunately, it also lacked anything resembling sanctuary. No towns. No rest stops. No greasy spoons advertising "Breakfast Menu Available 24 Hrs a Day!" No cheap motels, strip malls, or warehouse stores. For all we could tell, we were alone in the world—and the further down the highway we got, the more that feeling began to weigh on us.

"It's the Twilight Zone," Meg said, breaking a solid 20 minutes of silence.

I said nothing. I had the distinct feeling Megan wasn't actually trying to convince me of anything. She just needed to hear herself talk. Proof of life, I suppose.

"It's like someone turned our channel and suddenly life is all a Serling-inspired frightfest and we can't find the remote to get us back on *I Love Lucy*."

"Life doesn't work that way," I offered, only half sure I believed it. "People don't blink out of reality and into something altogether different. There's an explanation. I'm sure of it. As sure as I've ever been of anything. We simply can't sort it out quite yet."

"That isn't comforting," Meg said flatly.

"I wasn't exactly shooting for comfort," I replied. "I was aiming more for honesty."

"And?"

"Bullseye."

"Okay, then."

"It'll all make sense," I said, desperately hoping my spiritual CB radio was on the right frequency and God had His ears on.

Miles rolled by in rapid succession but, no matter how much distance we put between ourselves and the abandoned gas station, we couldn't escape the fear bubbling away in our guts like week-old chili. Our smartphones were still useless and the car stereo, equipped with factory-installed satellite radio, produced nothing but static. The highway had narrowed, and the sky had grown preternaturally dark, so much so that it prompted me to look at my watch—a lovely Invicta Diver Meg had given me on our first anniversary.

"What time did we leave Munro with our snacks?" I asked. "Around ten?"

"Thereabouts," Meg replied. "Why?"

"And we stopped in Gaylord maybe half an hour later so you could spell me. How long would you say you were driving before we nearly hit our young passenger back there?"

"What does it matter?"

"It couldn't have been more than 45 minutes or so, right?" I surmised.

"And?"

"It was almost dusk when we put him in the car. Later still when we had our run-in with the walking fire sale… and, now, it's night. Like night night. We haven't been driving long enough for that to make sense."

"We saw a man on fire, David," Megan reminded me, though it had hardly slipped my mind. "Nothing about this day makes any sense. *The Twilight Zone*'s got nothing on us, remember?"

"Yeah, but…how? Why?"

"You're looking for sense where there doesn't seem to be any, babe," she replied, leaning over to stroke my leg. "There's no meaning to be found in this insanity."

"Everything has meaning," I said. "Our stories are all

interwoven—a tapestry of tales written by the unseen hand. We can't always see how they connect because our scope is so small, but they all have meaning forged within them."

"That's weirdly deep, David. And doesn't sound like *you* at all."

"Well, I'm not the one who said it. I was quoting the Mysterious Dr. Meridian."

She looked over at me with concern. I didn't bother to ask, but I assumed Megan thought I was losing my mind.

"Don't look at me that way," I snickered. "I'm not making things up. The Mysterious Dr. Meridian was the pay-by-the-hour magician my parents hired for my 9th birthday party. He was quite the character, too. He told me all about how he had once been a proper wizard but had to settle for minor tricks because he had been banished from his own story. I don't know why I was so mesmerized by his silly stories, but he told me that nothing was accidental—that he had been hired for my birthday party because our stories were meant to cross over and only he could give me—"

"What?" Meg asked.

"I, uh, I don't remember. I remember *him*, of course, right down to the weird writing on his long coat which seemed to morph and move around on its own. He had some amazingly real illusions, so I'm guessing my folks had paid him a pretty penny to be there. I remember him suddenly growing serious and telling me that he had a gift for me from my parents but, even as I think back on it in detail, I can't remember if he gave me an actual gift."

"What does any of this have to do with the Cinder Man and our sudden lack of daylight?"

"I'm not sure," I admitted. "I'm still piecing it together. But my gut says that this train of thought is going somewhere."

"Well, let me off at the depot," Meg replied. "I don't hear any sense in it. I think you hit your head harder than either of us realized."

"Probably."

She pulled the Impreza to the shoulder of the highway and turned in her seat to look back at the kid. "This is a pee stop, kiddo. I've been holding it for miles. You need to go?"

The boy shook his head and shrunk back into a near fetal position.

"Suit yourself," Meg said, before glancing over at me. "David?"

"I'm good," I lied. "I don't—I mean, I'm not sure that stopping here is the greatest plan. Maybe we can find a restroom up ahead."

"I can't wait, babe," she replied. "I may have a cast iron stomach, but my bladder is—I don't know—balsa wood or something."

I raised an eyebrow.

"I know, I know. But I have to go. So, you and the kid keep an eye out for…you know who…and I'll be back in the car before you can say, 'Where's a porta-potty when you need one?' Okay?"

She was out of the car before my overtaxed brain could formulate a better argument. I watched as she walked around to the passenger side and stepped into a crop of trees for some privacy.

Aside from the waxing crescent moon, the car's headlights provided our only source of light. The road ahead was empty and seemed to go in a straight line for miles. Behind us, at least as far back as I could see, was more of the same. On the driver's side, past the shoulder and guardrail, was a gentle slope into a valley where a field of feed corn was gently shifting in the breeze. I focused my eyes—which was still a chore, thanks to the painful lump on my noggin—but saw no sign of the Cinder Man.

"We shouldn't be here," the boy said, his voice quivering and frail. "This place isn't safe. It's his place. It's where he puts them when they've been bad."

"Give her a minute," I answered. "When you've got to go, you've got to go. That's kindergarten 101, pal."

"Not here," he whispered. "He was waiting."

"I know you're scared, kid. I am, too. But we have to—"

I stopped when I caught a glimpse of something in the corner of my eye. A pinprick of light in the dark expanse not there a mere moment before. I leaned over toward the driver's side window and, once again, fought to focus my eyes on the corn field. He was there in the distance. Nothing but a flicker of flame at first, but it was him. There was determination in his movement as the flames of his rage set the corn ablaze.

I rolled down my window and screamed for Megan. Seconds later, she stumbled into sight and ran for the car. I glanced back toward the valley and could no longer make out the Cinder Man's shape amid the flames. But he was coming, and destruction was at his heels.

"He's moving fast," I said, as Megan dropped into the driver's seat. "Get us out of here."

She put the car in gear and lit out of there like a bat out of Ozzy Osbourne's house. I looked back as we sped away and saw the Cinder Man standing there in the middle of the highway, flames whipping about him like lashes from his belt. He did nothing but watch as we drove away. And I knew, as surely as the boy did, it was because he had no need to chase us. There was no distance that could thwart his coming. No place upon the earth that could shelter us from his wrath. He was coming. He would not stop. Not until we were all dead.

AFTER ANOTHER 20 MILES OR SO, THE HIGHWAY became a one-lane stretch of asphalt. Five miles further and it became a dirt road.

"I'm turning the car around, David," Meg whispered, as if saying it too loud was the surest way to make the Cinder Man reappear.

"Don't," I replied. "Keep driving. See where this road leads."

"I don't want to. I want to turn around."

"Me, too," I said. "That's why we shouldn't."

"You can't know that, babe," she reminded.

"No. But I feel it. Our way out of—whatever this is—lies in front of us, not behind us."

"You feel it?"

"I do," I said. And I did. I just wasn't sure why.

"Then we go forward," she said, gripping my left hand with her right. "Together. Always."

"You should stop here," the boy said from the back seat. "There's a cabin back there in the trees. It's where the Cinder Man comes from."

"And he's in there?" Meg asked. "He's in this cabin, what, waiting for us?"

"No," the boy said. "He's not there. Gone away for a little while. But he came back. He always comes back."

"We need to know what we're fighting," I said. "Or, if not fighting, trying to survive."

"Knowledge is power," my wife mumbled. "We have to go in there."

"We don't," I said. "I can go alone."

"Yes, you can. You can also go as limp as a boneless trout the next time that injury of yours sends you reeling. No way, hon. We're a team. Better together than apart. It's always been true, so I'm not changing things now."

"You didn't say that when you went into the creepy gas station alone," I reminded.

"Lesson learned," she replied, pulling the car over into a small patch of grass. "I won't make the same mistake twice."

"She's not supposed to be there," the boy said.

"The hell I'm not," Meg said, giving the boy an angry glance. "Where David goes, I go. Period."

"And vice versa," I offered.

"Damn straight."

"Jar, babe. Twice."

"Crap."

If, at this point, you are questioning why we would be so foolish as to do the sort of thing that gets stupid people killed in horror movies every year, I can only say that I was moving on instinct. From the moment I laid eyes on the boy, I had felt the pull of something bigger than myself. Call it destiny. Call it instinct. Call it divine intervention. However you choose to look at it, I was being led deeper into something beyond my understanding. And, because my wife is built entirely of awesome, she followed me.

The boy knew what he was talking about. Less than a quarter of a mile off the dirt road, hidden from sight by a dense population of yellow pines and turkey oaks, sat a hunting cabin which, from the condition of its exterior, I would guess was roughly 3 trillion years old. I exaggerate, of course. The fact is that the cabin was so overtaken by Pandora vines that most everything but the front door was hidden in natural camouflage.

There was no path or drive leading to the cabin. No mailbox for bills or birthday cards. No porch swing for lazy Sunday afternoons. No welcome mat to greet visitors. There were no telephone or electrical lines. No pink plastic flamingos perched precariously on one foot or a bubbling fountain with a nude little cupid to suggest any streak of frivolity might exist within the owner of the cabin. It was a hideout, plain and simple. A camouflaged horror house where undoubtedly bad things had happened to good people. No amount of hope or faith would change that.

We approached silently, though we both believed the boy when he said that the Cinder Man was gone. We were in a mouse trap sniffing at the cheese and stepping lightly around the catch, our tender necks tense with fear of the hammer. The boy had stayed in the car, but it was nothing more than a formality. If we died, he would die, too. But he *didn't* die. Not then. And part of me understood that, even though I didn't fully know it yet.

Megan was the first to try the door. It wasn't recklessness or a lack of fear that made her so brave. I had lived with fear long enough to know the difference. My wife's courage came from seeing past her fear to what she hoped waited on the other side of it—a home shared by two frail humans in love with the notion of spending their lives together and committed to that end, Cinder Man be damned. So, with little hesitation, she turned the knob. The door opened, and we stepped inside.

The "cabin" was little more than a wooden box with a small fireplace built into the north wall to warm it. In one corner was a military-style cot (most likely purchased at an Army Surplus store) and a wooden stool employed as a night stand. On it sat an old-fashioned windup alarm clock. Above the cot, bolted to the wall, was a rusty iron hitch ring. In the center of the room sat a small table and two wooden chairs. A bare bulb, dangling from its own wiring, was the sole source of light in the place. My eyes traced the wires across the ceiling and down the west wall to find it attached to a car battery which, in turn, was wired to a small generator parked on the right of the door by which we had entered. A rusty 5-gallon gas can bearing the painted-on words "Wizard Gasoline & Utility Container" sat beside it just as I remembered—though I could not recall how I remembered.

The smoldering embers in the fireplace could not cover up the scent of human waste coming from the tin pail stowed beneath the cot. We couldn't see it from the door, of course, but I knew it was there. Somehow, I knew. Just as I knew what was in the corked porcelain jug on the table. Something was happening to me that I couldn't explain and, once more, dizziness and nausea fought to overwhelm me.

"What is this place, David?" Meg asked me as she slowly made her way around the Spartan room. "This isn't some hellish cave or alien spawning ground. It's a shabby little cabin—not exactly the kind of place a monster would live."

"There are no windows," I said, so softly I thought she couldn't hear me. "They let the hope in. The daylight causes it to spring up in your heart."

"What?"

"There are no photos of people he cares for," I said, swooning so that I barely knew I was speaking. "No magazines or books. No televisions or phones. It's his own world and he thinks he's a god here."

"The Cinder Man?" she asked.

I nodded, and the motion made me fall to my knees. My stomach was blessedly empty, but the dry heaving continued for several minutes.

"What do you know about this, David?" Meg asked, crouching to hold me. "What's happening?"

"I don't know," I confessed. "I'm remembering things…things I shouldn't know."

"How is that possible?"

"How is any of this possible?" I answered.

"You're trembling," she said, pulling me into her arms.

"I'm afraid. Fear is…it's like a drill boring into the core

of me. It's been gnawing at my insides ever since we found the boy."

"He's scared, too," she said. "You can feel it coming off him in waves. I think he's afraid that, if he talks about it too much, it will bring the monster back."

"It doesn't matter what you do," I replied. "Whether you talk about the Cinder Man or not, he's out there, and he's coming for us. He'll never let us go. Never let us rest."

"You're scaring me, David. We should get out of here before that thing comes back."

"It's too late."

We turned to see the boy sitting on the bed. His right wrist was bound by a 3-foot length of nylon rope to the hitch ring above the bed. The knot around his wrist had been wrapped around and around with duct tape to prevent tampering.

"He's coming back," the boy said. "After what I did, he's gonna kill me. I think he only left to tell the others."

"What others?" Megan asked, whereas my head was full of the question 'How did you get in here without us seeing you and who tied you to the hitch ring?'

"There are others," the boy said. "He only keeps us until they come and pay."

"Who keeps you? The Cinder Man?" she asked.

"That isn't his name," I whispered. "Not his *real* name."

"How do you know this, David?" There were tears perched on her lower eyelids. Megan's mind hadn't caught up yet…but her heart knew the truth.

"You got away," I told the boy. "You finished this."

"No," the kid said. "I only thought I did. I tried to

put him away, but he was always still there. Always in the distance but always coming. I never get away. He'll never let it happen."

"He's dead," I said. "You saw him die!"

"His body died. I burned him good. Left nothing but a cinder," the boy said, "but he's still with me. I feel the heat of him sometimes when I'm afraid."

"I don't understand," Megan admitted. "One of you, please, tell me what's happening!"

"He's coming for me," I said. "He's always coming. And it has to stop."

"You can't stop that thing, David. It isn't human."

"I know," I said. "The boy stopped it before but…I can finish it."

As if he was the most menacing dinner theater actor to ever enter on cue, the Cinder Man appeared behind us. The heat was overwhelming, and the scent of burning flesh and the black smoke rolling out of his flames overpowered my senses. I stumbled backward a few steps and tripped on the cot, falling butt first over the end rail into the canvas. The boy was gone. The nylon rope no longer bound him. It had found a new home on my wrist.

"David!" Megan screamed, looking for a way around the Cinder Man's flames.

"Stay there," I ordered. It was the only order I had ever given my wife, and I don't regret it in the least.

I looked up at the Cinder Man as he lumbered toward me. For the first time, I noticed that there was little purpose to his walk. It was all instinct. It was primal—the last attempt of a dying animal to run away. To survive.

"It's me you want," I said, staring past the flames to

the dark, ashen figure within. "But I learned something a moment ago that you won't like. No, you won't like it at all."

He drew closer, but I had found my courage again and refused to shrink away from him like a child on his rope.

"Those flames are not meant for me," I said. There was no need to shout. I knew he could hear me. "They are *your* torment to bear, not mine. You only live on to torture me because I let you. I locked you away in some room in my mind, but my fear of you continued to burn. I guess I could never evict you because I had forgotten you were in there."

The Cinder Man had stopped. He stood there, trapped and blazing in the moment of his death.

"I don't know how much of my life you've turned to ash and dust, Bryce, but it ends today." I don't know when the tears had come, but it was in that moment that I felt them making a trail through the soot on my face. "I won't be the victim anymore. I won't live in your cage of fear. I'm done with you. I proved it all those years ago and I'll prove it now. I won't let you hurt me anymore."

I knew Megan had stopped shouting, but when I looked over to make sure she was okay, I found that—like the boy before her—she had disappeared.

"You don't get to rest in peace," I told the Cinder Man, "but I'll have mine. And thanks to a brave boy, you have less than *nothing* to say about it."

The flaming creature before me took a lumbering step forward, but I did not cower.

"We're done, you and me," I said, feeling once more the overwhelming dizziness and nausea. "Even if I die in this place, I'll never be afraid of you again."

Just before I lost consciousness, I blinked and found myself alone in the room.

I AWOKE TO THE SOUND OF MEGAN HUMMING The Beatles tune, "Please Please Me" somewhere nearby. Everything was so bright, I was afraid to open my eyes, but I had to see Meg. I needed to know she was all right. I squinted until my eyes adjusted enough to see her sitting in the window of the small hospital room I found myself in. Beside me, a pudgy nurse who reminded me a bit of my aunt Fiona stood hanging a fresh bag of lactated Ringers solution. I watched as she traced the tubing with her fingertips before inserting the connector into the IV someone had placed in my right arm while I was unconscious.

"Mr. Kinneman," the nurse said, leaning in and checking my pupils with her pen light, "How are you feeling?"

"Like my head is three sizes too big," I said. My throat was dry—my voice raspy. "And filled with clay."

"I caught a look at your CT scans," she said, putting her light away. "I can promise there's no clay in there. A bit of a concussion, of course, but no clay."

I felt Megan's right hand slip over my left.

"There she is," I said, turning my head to get a good look at her. She was beautiful, even though I could tell she had been crying.

"You scared the shit out of me, babe," she said, giving

my hand a squeeze.

"Jar," I replied, which made her smile.

The nurse asked a few more questions and said Dr. Tarar—a kind, soft-spoken Pakistani man to hear Meg tell it—would stop by to assess me when he made his rounds. As soon as she left us alone, Meg leaned down and gently kissed my lips.

"Don't ever scare me like that again, David," she said. "I was freaked big time."

"How did I get here?" I asked.

"Ambulance. I called 911 and they had you here within 20 minutes."

"And the boy?"

"The boy?" A look of concern crawled across her lovely features. "What boy?"

I shook my head.

"David, what boy?"

"I thought we swerved to avoid hitting a boy who ran in front of the car," I said.

"It was a dog," she said. "When I swerved, we slid sideways and hit a tree. The airbag did its job, but you had been sleeping and positioned yourself in a weird way. When we impacted, your head cracked the passenger window. For about a second-and-a-half there, I thought I had lost you. Should've known you're too damn stubborn to die young."

"That's me," I said hoarsely.

"I've already talked to our insurance company. Dad is meeting them at the site. He'll have it towed and take care of the details until they call me about the claim."

"That's fine."

"You were out for quite some time," she said. "For a while you seemed…agitated."

"I was healing," I said, because it was true. "My mind was working through some old trauma while the rest of my body was recovering, I guess."

"What kind of trauma?"

"When I was seven, my family took a road trip to Disney World," I said, "only I never got there."

"What do you mean?"

"Mom was driving the old man crazy with bathroom breaks. She always did, of course, but this trip was the worst. I had lost count of how many times we stopped. But, somewhere in Alabama along I-22, it was *my* bladder that became the issue. Not wanting any more delays, Dad pulled over and told me to walk out into a crop of trees, relieve myself, and come back. I was only able to follow the first two instructions. A man named Alton Bryce was in that particular patch of woods where he had just finished burying a 9-year-old boy named Scotty Haines. He had planned to sell Scotty to the highest bidder through a sex trafficking ring he had been supplying off and on for three years.

"Scotty, you see, had become a problem. No one was ever sure what he had done, but Bryce had decided whatever money he would get for the kid wasn't worth the trouble. They found pieces of that boy buried in several different unmarked graves spread throughout those woods once they began to search them for me."

"Why did you never tell me this?" Megan asked, tears from both eyes meeting at her chin.

"I didn't remember," I admitted. "Not until now. Bryce

had me for nearly three weeks, hidden away in a secluded cabin off a dirt road in the middle of nowhere. I was tied to the wall while he terrorized me. Apparently, there was a program in place to make boys and girls less troublesome for the buyers. I wasn't to be touched sexually, but I could be beaten and mentally worn down until all my resistance was broken.

"Bryce drank a lot—vodka, I think, which he kept in a jug on the table. I managed to untie myself one night after he got drunk enough to pass out. I made my way down the dirt road, desperate for help. I thought I'd found it around dawn when I saw a service station in the distance. It had been abandoned by its owner, one of the many victims of the 70s oil crisis. I broke in, though. I found an old hammer laying near the pumps and smashed the glass door in. I envisioned myself finding a phone, telling the operator to send the police, and watching as they threw Bryce into the deepest, darkest pit they could find. But that didn't happen."

"He found you?" Meg asked and I nodded.

"He beat me so badly I thought he was going to kill me. It was then that he told me all about what had happened to little Scotty Haines. He said that if I tried something like that again, my parents would *never* find all the pieces of me."

"Oh, my God," my wife whispered. There was a hesitation in her eyes. She wasn't sure she wanted to hear any more of my story, but I had to tell it. It was the final step to freedom.

"I remember praying. It's hard to explain. It was like I wasn't actively thinking the words of a prayer, but something inside me was praying all the same. And I realized with a clarity no kid that age should ever have to have that I was never going to be sold into whatever hell Bryce had in mind for me. God would either help me find my way free or…or I would die. And I knew deep in the soul of me that either of those options was better than whatever the buyers wanted from me.

"So, I waited and prayed. And one afternoon, nineteen days after Bryce snatched me out of those woods, I found my moment. Bryce left to buy cigarettes. There were no windows in the cabin and he always locked the door, but I knew what needed doing and that I would only get one shot at it. As soon as he was gone, I chewed through the duct tape Bryce had used to cover my knots and spent what felt like an eternity getting free of the rope. I wasn't sure how long I had before Bryce returned, so I got to work.

"He came back expecting to find a frightened kid tied to a wall. I robbed him of that notion when I smashed his own jug of liquor over his head. He stumbled backward with a gash in his scalp, and I ran at him hard. He was already so off-balance even a malnourished 7-year-old could push him over into the fire. I didn't know much about how alcohol burned and, truth is, it likely would've done the job on its own. But, as he rolled around trying to extinguish the flames, I added the contents of the gasoline can he kept near his generator, and I ran.

"I only looked back once to make sure he wasn't following. I saw him standing there in the flames, nothing but a dark shape screaming out in agony and rage. I ran. And I ran some more. Then, somewhere outside of

Mulga, Alabama, a middle-aged married couple found me wandering along the road and took me to the police. Less than 24 hours and several medical examinations later, I was back with my family. By that point, the cops had found the remains of the Haines boy and my poor parents had feared the worst. The state police found the burnt husk of Bryce's cabin with what was left of him still inside. Nothing but a cinder, I heard one cop tell my dad. I never made it to Disney World.

"I remember now that I had nightmares. I would see Bryce or, at least, what was left of him still walking around in the fire. He was dead but the terror of him and the hopelessness he made me feel was still haunting me. I buried him over and over and—eventually, I guess—I buried him so deeply that I put the whole thing out of my mind. It simply never happened. If you were to ask me just last week about my family's Florida vacation, I'd have told you I remembered the drive but couldn't remember much about Disney World or what rides I enjoyed. There was only static where those memories should have been."

"But you didn't make your parents forget, David. You couldn't have. So why would they let you block out such a huge event in your life?"

"Why wouldn't they? If forgetting got me past my fear and the effects of my terror, why force me to remember? My brain did what it needed to do for 7-year-old Davey Kinneman to survive. It erased the horror. It buried Bryce down so deep it was as if I had never been taken."

Meg sniffed and took a tissue from a box on the bedside table.

"I think those memories were still in there, though,

haunting me," I told her. "I'd wager they were the root of my hesitance to have children. I had felt so...powerless. I think some part of me has always been afraid that I wouldn't be able to protect a child from the evil lurking out there just beyond the trees."

"No one is untouchable," Meg said. "Whether you're an adult or a child, the world can sometimes be a dangerous place. I-I can't even imagine what you went through, babe, or how heavy this burden has been...even if you didn't remember it."

"I don't know how exactly, but I feel like, in remembering, that I've faced Bryce and the terror he caused me all over again. And now I'm free of him. I won't allow him to haunt me anymore."

A FEW MONTHS HAVE NOW PASSED SINCE that fateful drive back from Mackinac Island, and my therapist—a matronly Texas transplant with a small practice in Indy—suggested writing out my story. Acknowledging what happened to me all those years ago, and the life I was forced to take to escape it, is necessary for me to finally be free. And, if the plus sign on the pregnancy test Megan showed me yesterday is any indication, my freedom will be sweet indeed.

WEEDS

MAE WALKER WAS THE ONLY BLACK GIRL IN her 4th grade class. She had noticed, of course, that no one looked quite like her, but it had never bothered her. At least, not until Brian Fallon used the 'N' word as they were coming back in from recess. Brian had been reprimanded by Ms. McElhaney in front of the whole class and sent to the principal's office for good measure. There, Mr. Dalworth, the school principal, called Brian's mother and father and made them come to the school for a talk. Mae wasn't sure exactly what Mr. Dalworth said to the Fallons, but 9-year-old Brian had not returned to class for two days.

The 'N' word. Even abbreviating it in her mind made Mae cringe. It was a foul word with a foul meaning that her mother had hoped she would never have to hear.

"But that isn't the way of the world, Little Miss," she told Mae as they sat at the kitchen table shelling peas. "Every time we get comfortable and get to thinking the worst is over, some little ignorant man, woman, or child reminds us that it's still out there growing like weeds."

"What is, momma?" Mae asked.

"Evil. Hatred. Sinfulness." Mae's mother said each word as though they grieved her as much as the word which had prompted the conversation. "It tells white folks the black man's out to rob them or hurt them. It tells the black man that the Jew is going to swindle or cheat them. It tells men the lie that women aren't worthy of their respect or of equality. It convinces women that most men only want them for one thing and are always looking for ways to keep them down. Those weeds come in many varieties, and they just keep right on growing. They're always at work trying to make us think 'different' means 'less than.'"

"Is the 'N' word a weed?" Mae asked.

"No, Little Miss. That word is nothing but a nasty symptom. When you've got a fever, it's a symptom of whatever it is that's really making you sick. If I treat only the fever, I might get it down and have you feeling better for a moment or two but, so long as the sickness remains, your fever's gonna keep creeping back up."

"Like when my tonsils got angry," Mae said.

Momma laughed. "Yes, baby. Like those angry ol' tonsils. And how did Doctor Nguyen fix you up right as rain?"

"He took 'em out."

"That's right. Because the tonsils were the real problem, not the fever. So it is with *most* troubles. The word the little Fallon boy threw around was nothing more than the fever. It was a chill—a rattling of the teeth—telling us something's gone wrong. But stopping a boy from saying that word isn't apt to fix anything. We need to dig deeper. Did the word spring up out of hatred, or was it ignorance that moved him? If it was hatred, was it his *own* hate or was he just echoing someone he looks up to? And, if he *was* repeating what someone else believes, can he still learn to be someone better before he's so lost he can't see reason?"

"I used to think Brian was a nice boy," Mae told her mother, scratching absentmindedly at the kitchen table. "He was rude sometimes, but not mean."

"He may be a nice boy who simply doesn't know any better," her mother replied. "Or he might be a weed pretending to be a flower. Only time will tell the whole story, Little Miss. But, until he proves himself to be a flower, you should figure him for a weed."

"That seems mean, momma."

"Not mean, baby. Cautious. You know what that word means?"

"Careful," Mae replied.

"That's right," her momma said. "See, the weeds of evil and hatred—whether that hatred shouts out loud like racism or whispers softly like disregard—can grow in anyone's garden. And those weeds have thorns and sharp edges, you see? And it's a mother's job to protect her babies."

Mae hugged her mom tightly.

"I'll be okay, Momma," she said. "Tommy Evans said if Brian ever says the 'N' word again, he'll make him stop."

"Tommy Evans? Is he the little red-headed boy with the braces?"

"And the freckles that look like star drawings on his

face," Mae said.

"Constellations," Momma said. "He's your friend, this Tommy?"

"Yes, Momma. Sometimes people make fun of him for his red hair," she explained, "but we stick up for each other. Tommy said his daddy told him there was way too much same in the world so being different is a good thing."

"I agree with his daddy," Momma said, giving Mae a kiss on the forehead. "Do you remember when we drove over to Holland with your daddy and went to the farmer's market?"

"With the stinky cheeses?"

"Yes. And the purple potatoes," Momma said. "You were all excited about those purple potatoes until I went to cook them. You didn't want to eat them, remember?"

"I had never had them before," Mae said. "I liked the regular kind."

"But there is no regular kind, Little Miss," Momma said. "There's only the kind you know, and the kind you don't. So, momma made you both kinds and had you close your eyes."

"And I couldn't tell the difference," Mae admitted. "All I could taste was the butter and the salt."

"But there are so many kinds of potatoes...varieties even I don't know about," Momma said, "and they come in so many shapes, sizes, and colors. What a boring place the world would be if you ate only the kind you had grown used to."

"Me and Tommy are like purple potatoes?" Mae asked.

"Or red. Or blue. The point is that people like the

Fallon boy might like the same old potatoes instead of the purple ones. It's ignorant, for sure. But maybe he just needs to learn that variety is a good thing…and, come the end of the day, a potato is good no matter what color it is."

"As long as they have lots of butter and salt!"

Momma laughed. "That's right."

"But he might be a weed," Mae said, "on account of him saying that bad word."

"And it's best to be?"

"Cautious."

"Right."

"What if he learns his lesson?" Mae asked.

"How will you know, baby?

Mae thought for a moment. "He'd stop saying the word."

"But the word is only a symptom, remember?" Momma said. "When we first moved into this house, your daddy had to struggle with the back yard. It had been left unattended for so long that the weeds were choking out the good grass. That's what weeds do, Little Miss…choke out the good grass and take over the yard. So, Daddy went to work out there digging up stinkweed with a spade and yanking it out by the root. But digging weeds is hard, hot work. It makes your knees and back ache and you know your daddy's back gives him pain on the *best* day. So, after a week or two of battling those weeds, he surrendered the fight and finally took the mower to them. And he was so proud of his work, your daddy. The yard finally looked clean and trim. The trouble was that he treated the weeds the same as he treated the grass. It hid the problem, alright, and made the yard look pretty as a picture for a little while…but the weeds were still there amid the grass, and barely a day or two later they were peeking out again.

"Lots of folks know how to cover up the weeds, Little Miss. That bit of work isn't so hard. In fact, it's a great deal easier than digging up those roots. But it only hides the troubles and cleans things up for a bit. But, hidden by all the good green grass, those weeds are still growing. They're still choking out the good grass and will eventually make a mess of the whole yard. That's how it is with prejudice or any other evil. You can call it out and punish it, but until we get to the roots, it isn't ever going to be gone for good."

"So how will I know if Brian learned his lesson about saying the mean word?"

"He'll *own* it," Momma said. "Everybody in the world makes mistakes—some big and some small—but, we all make them. Good people own what they do. They apologize for what they've done and not just by saying they are sorry…but by doing the hard, *hard* work of pulling up those weeds by the root. We all got our issues, and we all need the Lord's help to overcome them, but a man can't get help if he never admits he needs it. Like Pastor Jenkins always says, "First comes confession, then comes grace. And grace changes everything."

"Can grace change Brian Fallon?" Mae asked.

"God can do anything," Momma said. "But folks who can't confess their wrongdoing can't change. If the Fallon boy realizes how badly that word can hurt, he might truly be sorry for what he did. God might choose to use such a moment to grow some proper grass. If not—"

"The weeds will keep growing?"

"Exactly, Little Miss."

"Can I, um... Can I help Brian grow some good grass?" Mae asked. Her question prompted Momma to kiss her forehead again. And brush back a tear.

"I'm awful proud you *want* to," Momma said. "And I suppose you could try, so long as you're...tell me the word again."

"Cautious?"

"Yes, baby."

"How can I help?"

"You can start by telling him exactly how that word made you feel," Momma said. "Truth is, if he was just repeating someone else, he might not have known how it could hurt. Maybe hearing it from you will help him see the weed he needs to uproot. If so, he might truly be sorry and want to make it right. Then, you can help by forgiving him. Extend him some of the grace you hope for when you're the one who's done someone wrong. But, if he can't see that he did anything wrong, well...I suspect all you could do is leave him to God. No one should have to accept hatefulness, Little Miss, so you don't sleep on his nonsense if he keeps at it. You hear? It might be that you aren't the only student at your school affected by his hate, if that's what it is. You stand up for yourself and your friends when you spot those weeds. You are fearfully and *wonderfully* made, and being gracious doesn't mean letting yourself be abused."

Mae thought about her mother's words for a moment.

"I think I did wrong, Momma."

"How so, Little Miss?"

"Sometimes I hear kids at school teasing Tommy about his red hair and I don't say nothing."

"Anything," Momma corrected. "You don't say anything. And why is that so wrong?"

"Because I saw the weeds and didn't do nothing."

"Anything," Momma said. "Why not?"

"I guess I didn't think about how Tommy felt about it," Mae said. "I figured the kids teasing him were goofing around and didn't mean nothing by it."

"Anything," Momma replied. "And you're right. We should point out weeds when we see them. Good folks will dig them up and be better for it. It's a tough responsibility, though, Little Miss. Especially for little girls who shouldn't have to think about such things."

"I'm gonna tell Tommy I'll watch out for weeds same as he does for me," Mae said. "We'll be different together. It's *better* than same."

"It doesn't always feel that way," Momma said, "but it's true. And no weed gets to tell you otherwise."

"I love you, Momma," Mae said, pulling her homework from her backpack.

"I love you, too, Little Miss," her momma said. "You have math tonight?"

"Yes, ma'am."

"If you need any help, you'd best go get your father," Momma said with a laugh. "I'm already late finishing dinner."

"What are we having?"

"Pot roast and gravy with some fresh peas and potatoes."

"Purple potatoes?"

"Does it matter?" Momma asked.

"No, ma'am."

"Good," Momma replied. "Now, get your father to work some math with you and tell him we'll be ready to eat in half an hour or so."

"Yes, momma," Mae said, running out of the kitchen to seek out her father in the den.

As soon as the door swung closed, Mae's mother bowed her head, whispering a prayer that unleashed the tears she had been holding back far too long.

"Keep her safe," she whispered, "and help her little heart hang onto the spark of hope You put there. Don't let her grow callous and hard, but give her the strength to stand for what's right…no matter how wicked the days may seem. Give her good friends to watch her back and Your grace to be a light in the darkness. And may the sweet, green grass always outnumber the weeds."

Amen.

ROOT BEER FLOATS AND DAFFODILS

GEORGE ADDISON CAUGHT A GLIMPSE OF HIS reflection in the display window of the Bivens Appliance and Television Emporium and gave himself a wink. In his emerald green corduroy sport coat and gray gabardine slacks, he was certain he looked more distinguished than the young sweater jockeys vying for his girl's attention. True, his lemon-yellow shirt was open at the collar (after all, he wasn't exactly sniffing after an old maid or a librarian) and he had managed to lose his lucky handkerchief at the laundromat but, in comparison to the grease-stained coveralls typically draped across his beefy frame, he was looking as shiny as a newly-minted penny.

There was something else, though, in the appliance store window—something or someone lurking and watching from the corner of his eye—that sent a chill down George's spine. When he looked to see what it might be, however, he saw nothing but the black Pontiac Chieftain parked at the curb right where Old Man Bivens always left it. George checked his own reflection again, inspecting his teeth, and turned to take in the sights of Main Street.

On any other weekday night, the storefronts along the street would be closed by 6 p.m. and not reopen until 8 a.m. the following morning. This night, though, was something special. It was the first annual Welcome to Wimberley Festival. The city council had pitched the festival as a chance for the ever-growing population of Wimberley to venture out after work hours and meet neighbors, visit businesses, sample a few carnival foods (whose sales would benefit the township's library fund,) and get a little face time with the mayor and the rest of the local government. It was an easy sell to the fair citizens of Wimberley, and they turned out in droves on that cool autumn night, dressed in their finest clothes and warmest smiles.

Both lanes of Main Street had been blocked off to allow the festival crowd to fill the streets, so George had parked his cream colored (aside from the one black passenger door he had retrieved from the salvage yard) 1941 Chrysler Highlander convertible behind the First Methodist Church and beat feet into town. From a PA system set up on the steps of city hall, The Platters sang a siren song, "The Great Pretender," drawing the crowd deeper and deeper into the festivities.

The scents of popcorn and cotton candy filled the air, but George wouldn't be enticed by them. Not *yet*. His date was waiting for him at Winston's Soda Shoppe, and he didn't want to be late. Besides, knowing Helen, she would have her heart set on a root beer float and a slice of coconut cake.

At the edge of Larue Park, (the official name for what most locals thought of as the town square), George spied the town's only florist, Sal Montieth, peddling bouquets of flowers to any young couple who walked past. Most of them passed by without paying Sal much notice, drawn deeper into the festival by the scents of freshly popped popcorn and hot funnel cakes, but George made a beeline straight for him.

"Young Mr. Addison," Sal boomed, "looking sharp as a tack and twice as shiny! Must be a date night. Can I interest you in some flowers for the lucky lady?"

"You bet, Mr. Montieth," George replied, fishing in his back pocket for the worn leather wallet his father had given him on his fifteenth birthday. "I'd like a bouquet of your prettiest daffodils, please. They're Helen's favorite."

"I've got some lovely *narcissus elegans* I've been using to fill in the other bouquets. I'd be happy to group some together for you," Sal said, snatching some of the six-petal white daffodils from a few prearranged bouquets. "Would this Helen of yours be Helen Chamberlain by any chance?"

"Yessir," George said, "and, I'm sorry Mr. Montieth, but I can only afford two dollars' worth tonight. I already promised her something sweet over at Winston's."

"No worries, my boy," Sal said, tying a bit of yellow ribbon around the stems and offering it to George. "It's a five-dollar job, but the other three are on me. I owe you a debt after you helped get me back on the road last spring."

"That was nothing," George said, handing over two singles. "Just some loose wiring. A fella from Dardenville came to the shop with the same issue a couple of years back. I remembered how Dad fixed it. Easy-peasy."

A sensation washed over George as Sal Montieth turned toward him with the flowers. It was the same feeling as before—that he was being watched. He turned and scanned the crowd of festivalgoers but saw nothing out of the ordinary.

"Well, I'd have paid a fortune for a tow if you hadn't wandered by," Sal said, handing him the bouquet, "so you take those extra flowers on the house and have yourself a fine time with Miss Chamberlain. She's a sweet girl, that Helen. Tutored my Rose in algebra last year. Even got her onto the honor roll."

"She's the smartest girl I've ever known," George admitted. "Thanks for the flowers, Mr. Montieth. Have a good night."

"You too, son," Sal said, before turning his attention to an approaching couple. "Flowers for your lovely date, good sir?"

WINSTON'S SODA SHOPPE WAS A BEEHIVE OF activity, filled with teens and young adults abuzz with excitement for the festival and swooning in the throes of young love. The jukebox in the back corner was playing Nat King Cole's version of "Smile," but it could hardly be heard over the sounds of laughter and reverie. The mood of the place was quite intoxicating, but none of it compared to the sight of Helen Chamberlain.

A few weeks shy of her eighteenth birthday, Helen Chamberlain was everything a young man like George Addison found irresistible. She was smart but not full of herself. Beautiful but not vain. Elegant without being extravagant. And, most importantly, charming without being a flirt. Every red-blooded male in Wimberley under the age of twenty-five was at least mildly infatuated with her, which might have made her classmates a bit jealous were she not so sweet and nearly oblivious to that sort of attention. Had George seen her type in a movie, he'd have laughed her off as Hollywood make-believe...no more real than Lon Chaney's Wolf Man or Bela Lugosi's Dracula. But Helen was real alright and had, for reasons unknown to George and her other would-be Don Juans, agreed to go out with him. Two months later, he was her guy and she was his girl.

Seated at a table near the jukebox, Helen was engaged in conversation with Patti Wallace, one of the many girls Helen had tutored in math. Patti happened to be a waitress at Winston's on the weekend and had been called in to work the crowds drawn by the festival. Dressed in a simple floral print dress with a cummerbund waist accented by a single string of pearls—no doubt borrowed from her mother—Helen seemed, at least to George, to be the only technicolor character in a black and white world, vibrant and impossible to ignore.

"Speak of the devil," Helen said as he approached, flashing him a smile. "I was just telling Patti that I didn't want to order without you."

"You two think about your order," Patti said as she smoothed her apron. "I'll be back in a jiff...as soon as I

184

sling some sherbet for Mrs. Herbert's little monsters."

"Those for me, George?" Helen asked, noting the flowers in his right hand. "Or do you have some other girl on the side that I should know about?"

The grin on her face was unmistakable. She was pulling his chain.

"No others in Wimberley," he teased. "You gotta keep 'em spread out in different towns if you don't want to get caught."

"I see."

"But I'm thinking of giving up my wandering ways and making you my only gal."

He handed her the flowers and after giving them a long, slow sniff, she replied. "Oh, yeah?"

"Yeah. See, it's getting awful expensive to keep seeing these gals all over the state. I must've filled my tank three times last week alone."

Helen cocked her left eyebrow, which made him laugh.

"You know I've only got eyes for you," he said, reaching across the table and taking her hand. It was a decidedly bold move to hold her hand in public, but he had big plans for the evening.

She blushed.

"Would you care to share some french fries, or are you hungry enough for a hamburger?" she asked. "I wasn't sure if you'd had a chance to eat today, you staying so busy at work and all."

"Thought you'd want the coconut cake you love," he said, giving her hand a gentle squeeze. "That sweet tooth of yours is usually in charge of the ordering."

"Not tonight. Smelling the popcorn outside made me

crave something salty."

"Fries it is," George said. "And maybe a couple of root beer floats?"

"Hold the whipped cream and you have a deal," she laughed. "In fact, let me pop over and tell Patti now. I want to be able to finish here and walk the square with you before it gets too late."

Her seat had been vacant less than thirty seconds when Stew Conklin dropped into it with a thud. Dressed in dungarees and a cardigan, Stew blended in with all the teens in the place in spite of being a good ten years their senior.

"Whatcha say, gearhead?" There was liquor on his breath mixed with the scent of cheap cigarettes. "You give any more thought to the, uh, situation we discussed?"

George glanced to make sure Helen wasn't watching and leaned across the table.

"Not here," he said between clenched teeth. "Not in front of Helen. Not ever."

"Yeah, well, nobody put you in charge o' nothin'," Stew said, scratching at the whiskers on his chin. "I done right by you, gearhead, and I like having you in my crew, but I ain't about to take lip from a grease monkey."

"Yeah. Okay," George said, taking a deep breath. "I'm sorry, alright? I'm in, but...I can't have Helen involved in any of this. You understand? This is too new. I'm not about to lose her because *you* can't pick a more private spot to talk."

Stew stood and sneered.

"Your priorities are out of whack, boy," he said. "You find me tomorrow near the bus terminal. My boys and I will go over the plan then...with or without you."

George kept an eye on Stew as he made his way past a throng of teens and back out into the street where he quickly disappeared in the bustling town square. Every muscle in George's body tightened, and he had half a mind to go after Stew and let his fists remind the criminal he wasn't going to be intimidated by some little creep who hadn't possessed the brains to finish high school.

"What's with the scowl?" Helen asked, reclaiming her seat.

"What'd Patti say?"

"She said they were super-duper busy, but she'd do her best to rush our order along," Helen said. "Now stop dodging me, mister. What's bothering you?"

"Not sure," he lied. "I'm tired, I guess. Not used to so many people being around."

"We can go if you'd rather," she offered. "I can tell Patti to—"

"No, no. I want you to have your root beer float," he said. "I'm not going to let a momentary bout with grumpiness ruin a lovely evening."

That made her smile but, for the briefest of moments, George thought he saw someone standing behind her and to his right, barely visible in the corner of his eye. When he looked, as before, there was nothing there. No rubbernecking teen. No overzealous chaperone. No plainclothes cop.

"George?" she asked, the concern in her voice something he had not heard before.

"I'm sorry," he said. "I guess I'm a bit distracted."

"It is a tad noisy in here," she admitted, taking his

hand. "But I'm here. And I'm happy to see you."

"You look beautiful," he said without an ounce of flattery. "The dress, of course, and the pearls, but... mostly just you."

That made her blush, but she was saved from an awkward silence when Patti Wallace arrived with a basket of french fries and two filled-to-the-brim root beer floats.

LESS THAN TWENTY MINUTES AFTER THEIR treats arrived, Helen took her last sip of float and stared at her date. He had fallen silent halfway through her story about the senior bake sale and had been staring at the jukebox ever since. George's half of the french fries remained untouched and his face had taken on a disturbing pallor.

"Penny for 'em," she offered but, wherever George's attention was, it was far away from their two-top at Winston's.

It was then that she noticed his lips moving. At first, it seemed to be nothing but a twitch but, after watching for a moment, she realized he was mouthing words.

"George!"

Startled out of his stupor, the young man shook his head as if to clear away whatever cobwebs had been gathered in the corners of his mind.

"I'm sorry, Helen," he said. "I was distracted by whatever is wrong with the jukebox."

"You don't like Doris Day?" she asked, mildly amused

by his befuddlement.

"No, I mean…that *thing* it's doing," he said, noticing for the first time the cool sweat clinging to his brow.

Helen looked over at the jukebox, scrutinizing it. All the lights were aglow. Doris Day's "Secret Love" ended and was quickly and efficiently replaced by Perry Como singing "Wanted." She studied the face of her date. He looked pale. Disturbed.

"Are you feeling alright, George?" she asked. "You look ill."

"I'm fine. Really. But…I can't concentrate with the jukebox doing that."

"Doing what?"

"You don't hear it?" he asked. She shook her head. "It sounds like…like the record is playing at the wrong speed. Too slow one minute, even slower the next, and then back to normal…over and over and over again. And there's…there's a whisper or something. It's like a foreign language or gibberish, and it's making my stomach turn."

Helen leaned across the table and gripped George's wrist. She spoke softly so as not to draw unwanted attention.

"Let me walk you home, George. There's nothing wrong with the jukebox. It's been playing fine since we got here."

"That's impossible," he argued. "I heard it."

"Maybe you have a headache coming on," she said. "Or maybe you're running a fever. Sometimes a fever can make your head go all loopy."

"I don't have a fever!" he snapped, and the booth closest to their table turned their attention his way.

If Helen was wounded by his shouting at her, she didn't let it dampen her concern.

"Something is wrong," she said. "You said it. I believe you. But the jukebox isn't the problem, George. You know, I'd bet Doc Starlin is out there on the square somewhere. Let's go for a walk and maybe, when we see him, he can look you over."

Had it been anyone but Helen suggesting he was cracking up, George Addison would have met their suspicion with a shot to the jaw. Helen's kindness and concern, however, proved to be a balm, and the tension in his body melted away at the sight of her.

"Maybe I've blown a gasket up in the old noodle," he admitted. "It sounds alright now, but a minute ago…it was…like something out of a nightmare."

"Let's take that walk," Helen said. "The fresh air will make you feel better and, if we happen to bump into him, you can decide if you want to have the doc look you over."

He offered her a weak smile.

"Fresh air sounds good. Even better with you on my arm…so long as you aren't embarrassed to be seen with a mechanic."

"You're my guy, George Addison," she replied. "I've never been embarrassed to be your girl."

A LEISURELY WALK AROUND THE SQUARE calmed George's nerves. In fact, by the time he and Helen spotted Tom Haggerty standing in front of his furniture store, George was all smiles and laughter.

"You two seem to be enjoying yourselves," Tom said, shaking George's hand. "Hello, Helen. Hello, George."

"Mr. Haggerty," Helen replied with a slight curtsy. "Sold anything tonight?"

"Nah," the elderly man said. "Just a few look-sees. It's okay, though. Tonight isn't about selling. It's about getting to know the friendly faces of Wimberley's newcomers."

"It's a lovely night for it," Helen said. "Where's Mrs. Haggerty?"

"Mary stayed home tonight," Tom replied. "Her arthritis came on something fierce, and I told her that I could handle things here on my own."

"I'll pray for her," Helen offered. "I got so used to seeing her weekly for my piano lessons I've come to miss her. Please send her my love."

"Of course, dear," Tom said. "How's your Dad, George? Keeping you busy down at the shop?"

"Yessir," George said. "There's always something in need of fixing, and fixing's what Addisons do best. So, whether it's the mayor's Hornet or Widow Franklin's Studebaker sedan, we get 'em fixed and back on the road in a jiffy."

"Well, Norris Addison has kept my delivery truck running well past its prime," Tom praised, "and is still one of the humbler men I've had the good pleasure to meet. I know it couldn't have been easy raising you boys without—what I mean is, Carol was such a *kind* woman and…."

As the older gentleman fumbled for his next word,

Helen rescued him.

"I don't mean to interrupt, Mr. Haggerty," she fibbed, "but my mom will worry if George keeps me out too late, and there's still an awful lot of festival to take in."

"Of course, dear," he said. "You two have a nice time. I'll let Mary know you asked after her."

George was about to say goodbye when he felt a cool breath on the nape of his neck. The sensation startled him so that he spun around only to find no one there.

"Something the matter, George?" Haggerty asked.

"No, sir," George said. "I, uh…thought someone I knew passed by."

Haggerty laughed.

"That could be darned near anyone tonight, son," he said.

George faked a laugh. "Good point, sir."

Helen laughed, too. But her laughter did nothing to diminish the growing concern she felt for George Addison.

LLOYD JENSEN HAD GROWN WEARY OF SHAKING hands with his constituents a mere twenty minutes into the evening's festivities. By the time Helen Chamberlain approached his booth with her date, the Deputy Mayor wanted to run for the proverbial hills. Nevertheless, he plastered on his best politician smile and greeted them.

"Miss Chamberlain," he said, offering her his hand. After she shook it, he turned to her date. "Mr. Addison, correct?"

"That's what they tell me," George replied.

"Norris's boy, yes? The one who works with him at the garage?"

"Since I turned twelve," George confirmed, "and every summer thereafter, until I graduated last year. Been full-time ever since."

"George is an absolute *genius* with engines," Helen bragged. "His dad says, when it comes to anything powered by gasoline, George is a regular Harry Blackstone."

"Good for you, George," Jensen said. "If you're ever interested, I know a foreman over at the manufacturing plant in Sadley. I'd be happy to put in a good word for you, if you'd like. They've been looking for young men with mechanical knowhow. It wouldn't pay much to start, but lots of room for advancement, you know?"

George blushed, but seemed distracted again. Helen ignored it and continued her conversation.

"I see you were conned into the raffle booth," Helen said. "What are they raffling?"

"A freezer full of meat from the butcher," Jensen said, "a town holiday in honor of the winner, and four passes to Michener's Drive-In Cinema over in Martinville. Tickets are only a nickel and all the proceeds are going to the Christmas Toy Drive. You and George had best fill out a ticket. You have to play to win, after all."

"I don't think I even have a nickel," Helen said. "Would you mind, George?"

She turned to find George walking away from the raffle booth and his date without a word.

"Did I say something to offend?" Jensen asked.

"No, sir," Helen replied. "He's been distracted all evening. I think maybe he's coming down with something."

"Dr. Starlin has a booth near the library. Perhaps young Mr. Addison could stop by and make an appointment."

"Perhaps," she said, watching George disappear into the crowd. "It was nice seeing you, Mr. Jensen, but I think I need to catch up to George."

"Okay, then," he said. "Swing back by if you like. The raffle won't close until 9 p.m."

THE MAN GEORGE KEPT SEEING IN THE CORNER of his eye was unusual, not for his attire—as he was dressed in a crisp wool suit of ashen gray—but for his gait. The stranger walked with a bit of a limp which caused his left leg to drag a bit on the pavement. Having finally seen the stranger in the crowd, albeit from behind, George wasted no time giving chase. Unfortunately, he had lost the man in a horde of citizens gathered near the gazebo at the center of the square, which often acted as the bandstand for the Wimberley Chorale.

As he scanned the crowd for the man's gait, George heard a sound—a buzzing so deep it could never be mistaken for the sound of an insect. No, this sound was more akin to a growl and seemed to be coming from deep beneath the park. No one else, however, seemed to notice. Then, suddenly, there he was again. That blasted man was watching him from the corner of his eye. George broke into a sprint, nearly knocking over the elderly couple who owned Wright Drugs and Discount Store.

As the limping man approached the fire station, he ducked into the alley and disappeared into the night. George stared into the pitch black of the alleyway and considered continuing his pursuit. He was stopped by Stew Conklin.

"What do you think you're doing, George?" Stew asked, grabbing George by the arm. "You've been calling a lot of attention to yourself. Heard a couple o' small-chested sophomores talking all about you makin' a stink over at the soda joint after I left. Now the one and only Helen Chamberlain is roaming the square looking for her date while I catch you running around with a crazed look in your eyes. We're supposed to be playing things *cool*, George. You on something?"

"What? No," George said. "It was the man I was chasing. He was—"

"What man?" Stew asked. "Ain't nobody but you I seen running this direction."

"There was a man and he—"

"Look," Stew said, shoving George against the outer wall of the fire house, "I don't care what you're playing at, Georgie. You might be losing your marbles faster than you were runnin'. I don't give a damn. You've been dodgy all night, ya grease monkey. First about the job and now whatever *this* nonsense is. You'd better get your head on straight or I might have to straighten it out for you."

Stew Conklin had taken more than his share of punches. None had hurt worse than the ones thrown by his father, a career grifter serving a 7-year stint in a medium security prison on the other side of the state. The punch George

Addison delivered to his jaw, however, felt like all of his father's blows combined. He fell unconscious, his head impacting the pavement with a sick thud.

"Good God! What happened?"

George turned to see Dr. Marshall Starlin, Wimberley's only physician, staring down at Stew Conklin. He immediately knelt next to the young man and checked his pulse.

"Is he dead?" George asked, suddenly quite afraid of the answer.

"He's alive," Starlin replied, "no thanks to you. His shoulder likely hit first, or he would have cracked his skull open. Why'd you hit him?"

"I didn't—"

"Don't bother lying, son," Starlin said. "I saw the whole thing as I approached. He had shoved you against the wall and you punched him. Bad blood?"

"Something like that," George said. "It's a bit of a long story, Doc."

The doctor pulled a small penlight from his breast pocket and checked Conklin's eyes.

"He's got a concussion," Starlin said. "Help me get him onto the bench and then talk to Joe Mills inside the fire station. He runs the show in there. Tell him I said to bring his car around. I need him to drive this boy and me to the hospital."

"The hospital?"

"He'll be fine, but I want him looked after," Starlin said. "Head injuries can be tricky business."

George helped the doctor lift Stew off the pavement and set the still-unconscious criminal in the bench on the corner. Before he could turn to enter the station, he noticed that a small crowd had gathered, including police officer Bob Dowdy who rushed to the doctor's side.

"What happened here?" he asked. "Some sort of accident?"

"You'd have to ask these two," the doctor said, tilting his head in George's direction. "Seems some sort of argument took place which led directly to fisticuffs."

"I see," Dowdy said, giving George the once over. "What happened here, son?"

"Just a bit of a misunderstanding," George said. "But Stew was mad enough to start shoving me around and I…hit him. I shouldn't have, I know. It was all I could think to do in the moment."

"Any witnesses?" Dowdy asked.

"I saw the unconscious fellow shoving the boy around," Dr. Starlin offered. "He seemed rather intense."

"Sounds like self-defense to me," Dowdy offered. "Still, you can't go solving your problems with your fists, kid. This fella gonna be okay, Doc?"

"Provided we get him to Martinville General in a timely matter, I don't see why not. I told the boy to get Joe Mills to drive me."

"My squad car is down the block," Dowdy said. "I'll use the lights and get you there faster. Be right back."

He turned and addressed the crowd, ordering them to disperse. And they did, save one lovely blonde girl wearing a floral print dress accented with a string of her mother's pearls. The look on Helen's face spoke volumes. George couldn't bring himself to look her in the eye. She stayed on the other side of the street until Officer Dowdy and

Dr. Starlin carefully loaded Stew Conklin into the squad car and departed, sirens wailing, for the closest hospital.

"I haven't been a very good date tonight," he offered as she approached.

"You have a talent for understatement, George," she said. "Or was that meant to be a joke?"

"I can explain," he said, mentally concocting a lie that he hoped would turn the whole situation to his favor.

"Explain what exactly, George? Your odd, detached behavior this evening? Or the violence which erupted out of you and sent a man to the hospital?"

"Stew Conklin is a criminal," he tried to explain. "I know you don't *know* the guy, but he has a reputation around town. He's a thief and a crook and the kind of fella who does bad things to people who get in his way."

"I know," she said, noting the shock registered on George's face. "Just because I don't run in the same circles as a man like Conklin doesn't mean I'm oblivious to him and his kind. Wimberley is too small a town for me *not* to have heard things."

"Okay," George said. "So, you know it's not like I randomly punched a guy for looking at me funny. Conklin is a bad egg."

"A bad egg you had a conversation with while I was placing our order at Winston's," she said. "Or did you think I hadn't noticed?"

George didn't know what to say, so he remained silent.

"If a man like Stew Conklin dropped into a chair at *my* table, I'd have been shocked," she said. "I don't know the man. I don't *want* to know the man. But, aside from being a bit embarrassed, George, you didn't seem at all surprised he wanted to talk to you. In fact, one might be led to believe you two know each other pretty well."

"You didn't say anything," George said. "Why?"

"I didn't want to believe it," she said. "I made excuses. Maybe he was bullying you. Maybe your father had borrowed some money or something. I was worried about you for other reasons, so I let Conklin and whatever relationship you might have with him go and focused on you. Because I care about you, George."

He reached out to touch her arm, but she recoiled as if his touch wounded her.

"I'm not a girl who likes being lied to, George. Everyone's days are filled with choices. Mine are no different, and I'd be a hypocrite to pretend I haven't made more than my fair share of mistakes. I've needed as much of God's grace as any man or woman alive, and I've pledged myself to being all He could want of me. I choose my friends carefully. I conduct *myself* carefully. See, George, for all the good we can find in it, the world is a messy, messy place and I'm determined not to add to the mess. I can be gracious to the Stewart Conklins of the world and hope for their restoration. What I don't do, though, is let them into my life. That sort of compromise does me far more harm than it does them good."

"What are you saying?" George asked, ignoring the limping man approaching from the corner of his eye.

"I'm saying I want to know exactly what sort of man you mean to *become*, George Addison. I want you to tell me the truth about how you know a man like Stew Conklin. I want you to tell me because I believe I have the right to know who I'm entrusting my heart to. But you should know, before you say a word, that I won't compromise who I am or who I'm becoming for someone who doesn't respect me enough to tell the truth. If you lie to me, we're done."

"And if you don't like the truth?" he asked.

"I don't know yet," Helen replied. "I'd have to hear it first."

He took a slow, deep breath. Everything inside him wanted to turn and face the man with the limp, but George half expected he would turn to find no one there.

"I've done two jobs for Conklin," George admitted. "He came to my dad first and said he could promise a big payday for a little mechanical knowhow. Dad, of course, told him where he could go. And he wasn't nice about it."

"So, Conklin asked you," Helen said.

"No," George said. "I went to him. I didn't go away to school like my friends. The garage is all I have and, while we stay busy, it's never going to pay what I need it to. So, I asked Stew about the job and…it seemed easy enough. No one could get hurt. It was a hustle more than an outright crime. The pay was decent."

"I'm not sure I understand what a 19-year-old boy needs with more money than his job can provide," Helen replied. "Especially if earning it meant doing something dishonest."

"I was planning for the future, Helen. A future I hoped would have you in it. But you can't buy a home with what I was making. You can't keep gasoline in your tank or food on the table. After the first job, Stew came sniffing around again. He said he had a bigger score in mind and needed a driver and a tuned-up truck. It was a big score alright. He and his goons broke into a supply warehouse and stole tools he claimed he could fence easily out of state…only Stew failed to mention that there would be guards on duty at the warehouse. He beat those guards within an inch of their lives. When they weren't cheering him on, his buddies helped."

"And you didn't stop them?"

"How could I, Helen? Am I going to take on four guys on my own? Am I going to leave them there and call the cops? They'd just give me up and I'd go away, too."

"This happened over in Braydonville?" she asked. When George nodded, she sighed. "I read about it in the newspaper. Both men ended up in the hospital, George. One of them lost the use of his right eye. The article mentioned that he had been working there for seven years without a hitch until that night. He was a widower like your dad, raising three little girls on his own."

"You think I don't feel guilty?" he asked. "You think I don't think about that guard every day?"

"I don't know, George," Helen replied flatly. "Did you take the money?"

"What?"

"The money from the warehouse job," she said. "Did you take your share?"

"Yes," he said. "The job was done. I couldn't exactly undo what happened to those guards, Helen. So, I—"

"Enough, George," she said, rubbing her temples with her fingers. "I've heard more than enough."

"What does that mean?" he asked, though the bile in his throat said he already knew what she meant.

"It means I can't build a life with someone who would

stand by and watch a man beaten nearly to death just for doing his job. It means I have no hope for a future with a man who is more concerned with getting paid than doing what's right. It means every daydream I wandered into about how happy we might be together was built on a foundation of half-truths and lies. It means my heart is broken, George, and it was broken by the one person I trusted *not* to break it."

"That's a lot to put on me," George replied, looking down at his shoes. "I made a mistake, Helen. I'm not the devil."

"We're all the devil," Helen said, "if we let ourselves be. But I'd be more of one if I turned a blind eye to what you've done, George. I won't do that."

He looked into her eyes again and noted the anger behind the tears.

"So, this is goodbye?"

She touched his face gently with her fingertips.

"I don't understand why you've made the choices you've made," she said, "but no man is hopeless, George. People in this town have seen your talent. They've seen good in you. You don't have to drift farther and farther away from being the man I—from being a man I could build a life with. But who you are today? I can't be with him."

"That money was to build a life for *us*," he argued.

"I don't need money, George. You were enough for me."

"That's not how it works," he said, turning his back to her. "Love doesn't put bread on the table."

"And I won't eat bread your violence or thievery puts

on the table," Helen said. "Together, we could find a way without that money, George. You hid things from me—lied to me—because you knew exactly what I would think. You knew what you were becoming and still had enough conscience to be ashamed."

"You can't tell anyone what I did," he said, the words coming out with harsher edge than he had intended. "Stew won't talk. But if you…"

"I won't help put you away," Helen said, turning to leave. "But this road you're on only ends in jail or death, George. I happen to think you deserve better."

"I deserve you," he spat.

"You *had* me," she said, her voice breaking. "You wanted something else."

GEORGE WATCHED HELEN CHAMBERLAIN, THE sweetest, most beautiful girl he had ever known, walk out of his life and into the throng of citizens still milling about the park. There was a sick feeling in the pit of George's stomach. The limping man was still in the corner of his eye, leaning toward him incredibly close.

"Do you remember?" the man asked.

George dropped his head, a tear trembling near the edge of his left eye.

"Tell me," the limping man said. "Say it."

"I was angry," George said. "Hurt and angry and desperate to prove her wrong."

"Tell me," the man repeated, only George knew all too

well that it wasn't a man speaking, but some hellish beast wearing the form of a man.

"Stew was laid out for a week. I made things right between us by taking his boys and doing the job. Was going to give him my cut as a peace offering. But Stew got wind and wanted payback for his trip to the hospital. Had his boys ditch me in the middle of the job. Cops caught me and I got 3 years at a minimum security joint. By the time I was out, Helen had married and had a kid on the way."

"Tell me," the thing said, its voice ragged and hoarse.

"I had nothing else going for me. Dad wouldn't take me back, and the whole town knew what I'd done. I was talked about the way Stew Conklin always had been. So, I went crawling back to the crew. Told them I'd learned my lesson and they respected that I hadn't squealed on them. We had a good run of jobs for a few years until we tried to knock over an armored car. Conklin got himself shot by a guard."

"Yessss?"

"And I shot the guard. Did 15 years in maximum while my Dad was dying of cancer," George said. "Didn't even get to go to his funeral. Came back to town when I got out of the joint. Figured no one would remember me. First local paper I picked up had a big article on Helen's kid, a high school football talent destined for the AFC. The picture showed Helen and her husband with their arms around the boy…all three of them looking proud. *Happy*, even."

"How did that make you feeeeeel?" the thing whispered in his ear.

"Lost," George whispered back. "Alone. Hopeless."

"Yessss."

"I found an old .22 my father used to keep in his cashbox at the shop," George said, the memory of it as vivid as if he was standing there in his Dad's closet once again. "I didn't even check to make sure it was loaded. I just put it in my mouth and squeezed."

"And came to me," the thing said, a hint of laughter in his tone.

"Why this night?" George asked.

"So *close* to happiness," the thing said, delighted. "On the very cusp of all you wanted. But so far, *far* away all at once."

"How many times have I relived it?"

"Hard to sssssay," the thing said, it's breath cold and damp on George's cheek. "I lost count some time ago. The last time I recall counting wassss your 6,718th time. Yes, yessss. Long ago that was."

"I don't deserve this," George said, which caused the beast to cackle maniacally.

"Your thinking you don't deserve it," the creature said, "is one of the many reasons you most assuredly do."

"I couldn't even enjoy how close it felt," George said, his tears now falling freely. "It wasn't how things actually happened. I felt *you* there all night."

"Good," the limping thing said. "Now, let's begin again."

"Please," George begged. "Don't—"

GEORGE ADDISON CAUGHT A GLIMPSE OF HIS reflection in the display window of the Bivens Appliance and Television Emporium and gave himself a wink. In his emerald green corduroy sport coat and gray gabardine slacks, he was certain he looked more distinguished than the young sweater jockeys vying for his girl's attention. Yes, George felt as shiny as a new penny.

There was something else, though, in the appliance store window—something or someone lurking and watching from the corner of his eye—that sent a chill down George's spine.

AN IMPROMPTU CHAT

I WAS 24 YEARS OLD WHEN I FIRST ENCOUNTERED the embodiment of Death. She was seated on a park bench watching a small group of children on the playground. At first, I thought my eyes were playing a trick on me or, perhaps, I was experiencing the first symptom of some brain trauma or psychosis of which I was previously unaware. She was beautiful and frightening all at once. Everything within me wanted to look away—heck, to run away—yet I was drawn to her like a magnet. She felt it as soon as I sat next to her.

"How is it you can see me, Philip Hawkins?" she asked, not bothering to look my way. Her voice was a whisper that seemed to come from deep within me as much as from any audible source. It made my insides shake and my mouth go dry.

"I, uh, don't know what you mean," I offered limply.

"You cannot lie to one such as I, Philip Hawkins. Now, explain yourself."

"Wh-what exactly...I mean, who are you?"

"Who do you *believe* that I am?" she asked in return.

"Death," I said before I could stop myself. "I think you're…Death."

"So, how is it you can *see* me?"

"I don't know," I admitted. "I was on my way—"

"To the train station," she finished for me. "You ride it every day of the work week and sit in the same seat unless it is already occupied. Near the window at the rear of the second car."

"How do you—?"

"I am long-lived, Philip Hawkins. A story so old I am only told in whispers. You are a fruit fly on his 49th day."

I'll admit I didn't understand what she meant by that remark until much later when I researched the life span of the average fruit fly.

"If you know so much," I said, trying not to look at her, "why don't you know why I can see you?"

"I know a great deal more than you do, Philip Hawkins, but I am not omniscient. Only One knows all there is to know, and He has not graced me with this knowledge."

"Are you…um, I'm sorry if I'm out of line for asking, but…are you here for one of them?"

I pointed toward the playground, where half a dozen rugrats were working up a sweat on the monkey bars and merry-go-round.

"If I was," she said, "it would have nothing to do with you."

"I know, but—"

"I might not be here for them at all," she said, a sly smile playing at her pale lips. "I could be here for *you*."

"Well, yeah, I suppose it's a possibility," I said, "but I

don't think you are."

"And why is that?"

"Because you seem curious about why I can see you," I told her. "If I was your assignment, I don't imagine you'd waste time talking to me."

That hint of a smile returned.

"Perhaps I decided to postpone your fate long enough to satisfy my curiosity," she said.

"Or maybe you were lonely," I offered.

She turned to face me, and I was afraid. It was a warm 82 degrees outside, but a chill rattled through my bones as she looked me over. She looked every inch a beautiful woman. But I saw, then, as the object of her scrutiny, the fierce and unpredictable wildness of a lioness. No attempt to tame or understand her would lessen the danger in her gaze. No park bench conversation would make her my ally.

"I-I didn't mean to offend," I said weakly. "I just imagined, given the nature of your…profession, that you feel a certain weight of solitude."

"Is *that* what you imagine?" she said, her tone dripping with contempt. "And who are you, Philip Hawkins, to consider the nature of a being such as I?"

"A child, no doubt, to someone eternal," I said. "Perhaps even to some of the finite-minded folks in this city. But—"

Death raised an eyebrow.

"But?"

"You spoke of your boss before when you mentioned omniscience," I said.

"*Boss* is hardly the correct title," she said, turning her

gaze back to the children. "He is my king. My master. My lord."

"He's my father," I said, a swell of courage coming from somewhere deeper than my shoes. "Adoptive, but still."

Her attention snapped back to me so quickly I'll admit I scooted away from her.

"Your point?"

"That you and I may be built for far different purposes," I explained, "yet we serve the same kingdom and Lord. No doubt you do it more *successfully* than I, but…it bonds us, doesn't it?"

Something danced behind her eyes, but she remained silent.

"Maybe God opened my eyes so I could see you and acknowledge your loneliness?"

"To serve what purpose?" she asked.

"So you could know *He* sees it, too."

She was quiet for some time, turning back to watch the children as they ran and played with the sort of energy I only vaguely remember having. A cool breeze shuffled a herd of leaves past my sneakers and reminded me I was running late.

"You should go, Philip Hawkins. You will be late for work. Again."

"Promptness is overrated," I replied with a wink.

"Not where I come from," she said. "Then, again, time is not *my* enemy."

"I suppose that's true," I said, standing to go. "Before I leave, though, I should thank you."

She looked at me strangely, as if she had never heard

those words before. I suppose she hadn't. If I was the only human being to ever speak directly to her, I suppose anything I could say would be at least somewhat perplexing.

"Three times in my life," I told her, "I've held the hand of someone I love as they left this world behind."

She looked away.

"That is my purpose, Philip Hawkins. It is what I was made for."

"I know," I said. "All three of those times, I wept and mourned. It hurt. Perhaps in ways, from your perspective, you might struggle to understand. The first loss was my grandfather. He was a larger than life figure in my eyes…funny, loving, and generous. So, when cancer was eating him up, it hurt to see him wasting away into a frail caricature of himself. I knew I would miss him when he was gone, but…I also knew he was in pain and wanted to go home. You came and set him free."

She didn't look at me. She only nodded.

"By the time my father died, he had been through so much—in and out of the hospital more times than I could count—that every new struggle could've been the end. When it was finally his time, it was a grace to him. A grace you brought like a long-awaited gift. A ticket to a land where sorrow and pain, sickness and broken bodies are a thing of the past."

This time, she looked at me, her expression impossible to read.

"My mom passed suddenly 15 months later," I said. "I was convinced it wouldn't happen. She was too tough to die and I…well, I wasn't ready…though I suppose none of us are ever *ready* to lose someone we love. Her death hit me like a freight train and tunneled out the core of me. I was angry at everyone. Myself, of course, for all the times I hadn't appreciated her and the sacrifices she made for me. The doctors and nurses, too, for not being smart enough or fast enough to save her. But the main target of my anger and hurt was God."

My words pricked something inside her, but she was an angel and I am just a man. I didn't dare assume to know what she was thinking, so I kept talking. I'm good at running my mouth. Ask anyone.

"I prayed a lot," I continued, "but my prayers were often accusatory. How could God claim to love me and then take my parents away? How could He claim to love them both and then let them die before they even made it to 60? What sort of love is that?"

"It is not my place to question the One, Philip Hawkins. He is my Lord. I am His servant."

"Well, I'm His *son*," I said, "and I wanted answers. And I trusted His love enough to question it without the fear that…well, that He'd send someone like *you* after me just for being angry at Him. Instead, He spoke truth to me— burned it right into my soul."

"What did He say?" she asked, the sadness in her eyes so deep I didn't dare look into them for long.

"That He would bear all my pain and my anger. He would take it upon Himself much as the Son had taken my sin and shame upon His shoulders and borne them to Calvary. He also revealed where His grace could be found…namely in the nature of those relationships. So many children come from broken homes. So many don't know their fathers or get along with their mothers.

So many come from abuse or neglect. So many make it to adulthood without a single memory of laughter and joy. But my childhood was filled to the brim with those moments. My parents invested time and love and tears... again and again. I didn't *have* to have that. It wasn't owed me. It was given. It was grace.

"And when my dad left us, he also left the pain of a broken body for a homeland he had never seen but that called to him with deep murmurings which stirred his heart on toward home. He closed his eyes to our love and opened them to a love that eclipsed the very best we could offer. And mom said goodbye to a world without her husband and hello to a land they had only dreamed of. They were together again and home among countless saints. That, too, was grace.

"And I heard Him say to me, 'Your mourning is great because what you loved and lost was great. No man can lose something he never had. No man can mourn those he didn't love.' And I knew it was true. Even my heartache was a gift, for it meant I had been truly blessed."

Death sat perplexed, her front teeth gently scraping at her lower lip.

"So, thank you," I said. "For taking them home. For reuniting them with each other and the God they loved. And please know, when *my* time comes, I won't despair to see your lovely face again. I'll greet you like an old friend. Maybe that's why I can see you today. Maybe you needed to know that you, too, are an instrument of grace."

She smiled slightly, a gentle curve that briefly tamed the ferocity remaining in her features.

"Thank you, Philip Hawkins," the angel called Death

said to me. "May it be many years before we meet again."

I smiled at the thought and left her there on the park bench, pondering the children at play.

MONSTER/HUNTER

ED THE RAVEN HAD HIS BEAK BURIED IN A FRESH chicken egg—a gift from his young protégé, Dylan—when the door to the reading room burst open to reveal the master of the Great Library, the man most knew only as Darke. His sudden entrance startled the bird so that he dropped his dinner and flew from the reading table to perch on the bust of Antoninus Pius near the fireplace.

"For pity's sake, Master Darke, you nearly scared the life out of these old hollow bones!" he squawked, flicking his tail and stretching out his wings in anger. "I wasn't expecting you back until tomorrow."

"I know it's hard to keep track of time in this place," Darke said, dropping into one of the overstuffed leather chairs near the hearth with a thump, "but I'm right on schedule, old bird. *Punctual as lovers to the moment sworn.*"

"Didn't think you were a fan of Edward Young," the bird replied.

"I'm a fan of that line," Darke said. "I don't suppose there's any dinner to be had, hmm?"

"I was quite enjoying mine before *you* lumbered in," the raven said, gliding back down to the desk. "Master Dylan had furnished me with a fine, fresh egg. I had forgotten you were ever so thoughtful."

"Blame it on the devil in my brain," Darke replied, scratching the bird's head. "It's hard to be a saint with him always whispering in my ear."

"Who said, *A man can fail many times, but he isn't a failure until he begins to blame somebody else?*"

"Burroughs," Darke answered. "So, was that a 'no' to dinner?"

"All the cupboards have been replenished," Ed said. "There's wine, if you're staying put for a while. Root beer and cream soda if you're only passing through."

"Cream soda it is, then. And a ham sandwich or three. But, first, a change of clothes. I'll need more than jeans and a Led Zeppelin t-shirt for my next assignment."

"It's a shame, really," Ed replied. "I fancy those red sand shoes."

"They aren't sand shoes," Darke grumped. "At any rate, while I grab some gear and throw some fuel into the tank, I need you to fetch Dylan. He's got to venture into the field at some point, and part of this assignment is a perfect opportunity for getting his feet wet."

"Do you think it's wise to involve the boy? Having him study and work within the Great Library is *one* thing, but you risk a good deal—not to mention your very existence—by pushing him into the field too early."

"If what I suspect is true, Ed, namely that the library has *already* been breached by outside forces, I fear Dylan is no safer here than in someone else's tale," Darke said.

"Besides, I'll look after him. I understand the danger to the boy…and to myself. I trust the Author to guide us well."

"As do I," the raven squawked. "But I *am* prone to worry."

"I know, old bird," Darke replied, giving him another scratch on the head. "It's one of the many reasons I love you. By the way, with Dylan and me gone, you'd be the keeper of these old halls until we return. I assume you can handle the responsibility."

"I was soaring the mazes of these halls long before *you* blundered your way into this realm," Ed said. "I can surely keep an eye on it in your absence."

"And should you find someone in the stacks who doesn't belong?"

"I'll hide, of course. I'm a bird, not a barbarian," Ed harrumphed.

"Good man," Darke said. "Now fetch the boy and have him meet me in the kitchen."

"Yes, yes," the raven said, taking flight and winging his way toward a hall beyond one of several open doors. "I trust you'll find me a fresh egg to replace the one you cost me, eh, Master Darke?"

"If I come across one in the kitchen, old bird, it's yours to pillage."

DYLAN DRAKE HAD BEEN WAITING IN THE saloon for more than half an hour when the hunter walked in. Covered in mud, blood, and gore, the sight of him was enough to clear the room of everyone who wasn't too drunk to notice or already passed out.

"I'm owed another 20 gold," the man told the barkeep. "I was told there were six of those creatures hiding in the mines, but there was a seventh among them. A newly-turned girl. Couldn'ta been more than a breath before the coming of her blood."

"We agreed to 120," the keep said, leaning across the bar to look the man squarely in the eyes. "You agreed."

"Yes, I did," the hunter agreed. "Twenty gold for each head. You said there were six, so 120 was the price agreed upon. But 'twas *seven* critters preying on your town, so an extra 20 gold is called for. It ain't a point you'd do well to argue."

"Well, you'll get 120 and not a nickel more!" The bartender slammed his fist on the bar as if to punctuate his sentence. He produced a pouch and tossed it to the hunter. "Now you have our thanks *and* our gold. You'd best be on your way."

The hunter tucked the pouch into a larger leather pouch attached to his belt.

"I thought you'd say as much," he told the keep. "It's why I left the girl alive. Come nightfall, she'll be hungry and find there's none of her brothers left to bring the food to her. I reckon she'll make herself known before morning."

"Damn you," the barkeep said. "That girl was the one what drug us into this hell. Lucinda, she calls herself. Nobody knew where she came from, but she was the devil who killed Ty Greyson and his kin and started us down this piss-soaked path to ruin. And you mean to doom us all over 20 gold pieces?"

"Not at all," the hunter said. "But a man shouldn't be expected to work for an employer who refuses his wage. You see, the way I figure it, you and your townsfolk sent me into that nest without all the facts. You reckoned, while I was busy killing vampires, one or two more wouldn't count for much trouble. But a job is a job and my price is 20 gold per head. Had I known the girl was the one who turned the lot, I'd have killed her first and you would've gotten yourself quite a bargain. But you kept me in the dark and now, short of you coming up with another 20 in coin, your omission might be the death of you."

"I'll cover their 20, Mr. Cooke" Dylan offered, stepping up to the bar. "You take care of *their* little problem as an audition and, then, I'll give you a new problem… along with 500 gold to hear me out."

Charles Jamison Cooke laughed. In two decades of monster hunting, he had never had a payday like the one being offered by a boy barely old enough to shave.

"500 gold? From you, son?" The hunter looked the young man over. Though clad in appropriate attire for a lad his age, he seemed uncomfortable. As if he was wearing someone else's skin. "May as well sell me a unicorn like that Barnum fella tried to," he said. "Whatever it is you are, boy, you *ain't* what you appear to be."

Dylan removed his bowler and produced from it an envelope, which he handed to the hunter.

"There's enough gold certificates in there to cover finishing this job and bring you back here to discuss mine," he told the hunter. "And there's more where it came from."

Cooke counted the bills and stared at the boy a moment before saying, "What's your story, kid? Who do you work for?"

"All of mankind, actually," Dylan offered. "It's a long game, though, Mr. Cooke. So the 500 gold offer is only the first payment to bring you onboard. There's much more to be had. If you come with me and, after hearing my pitch, decide to decline the job, you can keep the first payment for your time and we'll part ways."

"You'll find I'm not the sort to be trifled with, son," Cooke told him, examining the gold notes more carefully. "If you come out of this deal looking anything short of honest, you're gonna meet your maker for wasting my time."

"I'm as honest as a child's prayer," Dylan said. "The job on offer is one only *you* can accomplish and, as such, will keep you in coin as long as you remain at work. Now, go take care of this unfinished business in the mine so we can be on our way. Time grows short and we have some traveling ahead of us."

"You're pushy for a beardless little snot," Cooke grumped. "But the notes are real and I've nothing *else* to do, so I'll entertain the notion of your sincerity...for now."

"It's all I ask," Dylan said.

Cooke stuffed the envelope filled with gold notes into the pouch on his belt and turned to go. He looked back at the kid and noted, "Your clothes don't fit ya, son. Whatever you are, it ain't what you're trying to sell me. I'm not sure I like that."

"I'm not the job," Dylan replied. "I dress to blend into my surroundings as a chameleon might."

"I prefer the truth," Cooke said.

"The truth of me is…complicated, I'm afraid."

"All the same," Cooke replied, "I'll expect some honesty to go with my coin."

"I'll do what I can," Dylan promised, "and I've no doubt you'll do the same."

LONDON WAS COLD AND EXCESSIVELY DAMP, and Darke felt ill at ease with what lay ahead. He had lost count long ago of how many stories he had journeyed into by the ineffable power of the Great Library. Each assignment was a new experience. Some were simple and straightforward, others more complex or downright dangerous. None, however, had proven to be completed without cost and, with young Dylan half a world away completing his half of the mission, Darke worried that the raven, Ed, might have been right about the boy. Perhaps he wasn't ready to take on a more active role. Perhaps he was simply too young to face the cost.

For his own part, Darke was required to remain out of sight until the proper moment which, in 1873 Knightsbridge, proved fairly simple. By staying on the rooftops, hidden within the frost-heavy fog, he would seem little more than a specter to anyone who spotted him from the streets below. A bit of borrowed future tech—procured from another assignment—allowed him to see everything below quite clearly across multiple spectrums. He would not lose sight of his target, nor would he be caught unaware by the monsters which hunted by night.

A few blocks away, on Brompton Road, workmen were busy adding a two-story expansion to Harrods, and much of the talk on the street revolved around the addition and what it would mean in the community. Only a few dared discuss the string of killings taking place in every borough of London. Lloyd's Weekly had called the murders "monstrous" and "barbaric," but Darke alone knew the truth of what stalked the streets and alleyways of London that autumn, and he had come to set in motion the means of their salvation.

Dusk was coming soon and with it, danger. Staying on mission meant Darke couldn't possibly protect everyone. He would, however, play his part and revisit the tale from time to time to nudge it toward a better ending. That was his job, after all, and the Great Library allowed him to come and go as he pleased.

A vibration in the brace on his left forearm alerted him to Dylan's success in hiring the hunter, Cooke. Poe, an artificial intelligence who guided Darke through more complex missions, had recently been damaged and no longer spoke to him audibly. Her screen, however, told him all he needed to know. The first task had been completed. The second was up to him.

"I miss your voice, you know," he told Poe. "Whatever is going on with you, I fear it has something to do with the mysterious figure who has managed to breach the Great Library's defenses. If you knew more about it, you'd tell me, yes?"

He gazed at the response on the screen for a moment before replying.

"You mean this incursion is part of *my* story and you aren't allowed to interfere?"

Poe's response was as brief as it was negative.

"Is the intruder responsible for your current state?"

Poe's reply was three words.

"Well, if *you* don't know, I suppose no one does but the Author…and the intruder himself."

Poe warbled a reminder.

"Or *her*self, yes."

CHARLES JAMISON COOKE HAD HEARD HIS FAIR share of tall tales over the years, from creatures that fell from the sky to ancient curses and spirits who haunt the living. Some, like vampires and werewolves, had proven to be true. A great many more, however, were bunk…as unlikely as an honest politician or a flying horse. After 4 days aboard a steamship bound for Liverpool, Cooke still wasn't sure he believed the story young Dylan had told him in fits and starts since leaving New York. But the gold notes were real enough and his gut said the job was good, even if the kid doing the hiring didn't have both oars in the water.

"You don't believe me," Dylan said. "I don't blame you, sir. It's a hard truth to swallow."

"It doesn't matter if I believe you about your magical library and whatnot," Cooke said, striking a match to light his cigar. "You have gold and I have time."

"But we need you for the duration," the boy replied. "So, perhaps I need to prove myself. If you bail a year or two in, you could blow the whole mission, which would cost a great many people their lives."

"If you say so, kid."

They were standing on the deck of the SS *Indiana*, passengers on the iron ship's maiden voyage to Queensland and on to Liverpool where Darke would be waiting for them. It was a cold autumn, and the salted winds whipping up from the water chilled young Dylan despite his many layers of the warmest clothes his coin could buy. The hunter, however, seemed not to notice the cold as he puffed on his cigar. He had already turned his mind toward other things—namely the missing vampire girl, Lucinda, who had escaped his clutches out west—when the boy said a name…a name the hunter had not heard in many years.

"Esmerelda Lucia Villalobos," Dylan said softly, knowing he must take great care in what he was about to do.

Cooke turned so fast he had the boy by the collar before he could twist out of his grasp. With a ferocity he typically reserved for monsters, Cooke threw the boy to the deck and drew his pistol.

"Explain yourself," he spat, "or I will end you right here, boy! How do you know her name?"

"Th-the Great Library," Dylan said, struggling to catch his breath. "Told you…already. I r-read all…about you."

"Liar," Cooke said, pulling the hammer back on his Smith and Wesson Model 3 pistol. "No one knows about her. No one ever knew."

"Your life, Mr. Cooke, is a story. So is mine. And in the Great Library, *all* stories are known. I haven't read them all. I doubt I ever could. But I read all about you because I needed to come for you and convince you to help me. So, you go ahead and ask me about anything you think I shouldn't know, and I'll do my best to convince you I'm in earnest."

Cooke kept his gun aimed squarely at the boy but moved his finger from the trigger to the guard.

"Tell me who she was, boy! You know the name. What else is it you think you know, eh?"

"You loved her," Dylan offered. "No one could know, of course. Her family would never approve of a white man taking their daughter north of the border. You meant to stay. You were tired of fighting other men's wars. You saw in her a chance to wash the blood from your hands and start a new life—a *simple* life. She loved you enough to leave, but you stayed. You wanted to do it the right way. You wanted to prove to her father that you were worthy of her hand. But a monster came in the night and took it all away from you."

Cooke's gun hand shook as his finger moved back to the trigger.

"Who? *Who* took her from me?"

"A man you knew," Dylan said, unable to gaze into the pain filling the hunter's eyes. "A man you thought you had killed in El Paso many months before you met Esmerelda. A man you couldn't possibly have known was more than a mere man. His name was Aldus Bennett. It was your first encounter with a vampire."

"You can't know this," Cooke said. "It's impossible."

"Bennett didn't kill you," the boy said. "He did so much worse."

"He tied me to a post," Cooke said, lowering his gun to his side. "He did the same to Esmerelda."

"I read all about what Bennett did to her family...and to her," Dylan said. He stood slowly, praying silently that he wouldn't be shot. "He made you watch it all, hoping to drive you mad."

"Some days I think he did," Cooke said, holstering his weapon. "I think all the good I ever had in me was left tied to that damned post."

"That isn't true," Dylan argued. "You may have become a hunter out of a desire for revenge, but you've saved countless lives and what I'm asking of you will save countless more. But I doubt you'll be up for the task if you cannot bring yourself to believe there is more at work here than the will of men and monsters."

"Like what, boy? Fate? God, perhaps? I've read the Good Book and I—"

"If your life is a story, Mr. Cooke, perhaps it's being written with a purpose and toward a greater end. Esmerelda's story may have been a shorter tale, but yours is still being told. And, if her love was a grace to you, perhaps it may *still* be employed toward that end."

"Is that what you've been taught by the mentor you've told me about?"

"It's what I *believe*," Dylan replied. "And I know where your story went from there. You nearly died from exposure. But you lived, and you traveled the world looking for knowledge in order to find and kill the creature who took her from you."

"I tracked him to Marrakesh," Cooke said, "and put an end to him. Slowly."

"And did it help?" Dylan asked. "Did it douse the flames of sorrow blazing in your soul?"

The hunter exhaled a steady stream of smoke, his gaze somewhere out at sea and his thoughts far beyond even that.

"What else do you know, boy?"

"That you were tired of killing long before you decided to hunt them. It's a millstone about your neck. You could free yourself of the burden, cast it aside for the sake of your own comfort and peace of mind, but you won't."

"They are out there…hunting and plotting while the world is asleep," the hunter said, flicking the remains of his cigar into the sea below. "We have been doomed since the moment those things were forged in the fires of hell. At most, I forestall the end…put off their victory for another day…another breath. It's less than nothing, but I will *not* stop."

"What I'm offering you is the chance to train someone to do what you cannot, Mr. Cooke. To prepare an individual to wage war on your behalf long after you pass on to better lands. To give a protégé the education and skills he needs to—one day, many years from now—end this nightmare once and for all time."

"This library of yours," Cooke said, "wherein you've read about my life, may I visit it? That would go a long way toward helping me to believe all this."

"You mentioned the Good Book earlier, Mr. Cooke. There is a passage within that book I am reminded of by your question: Faith is the assurance of things hoped for, the evidence of things unseen."

"The book of Hebrews," Cooke said. "Seems a bit of a dodge to me, at least where you're concerned, boy."

"Will it do?"

"For now," Cooke said, casting his gaze back out to the open sea. "It will have to do for now."

DARKE LEFT HIS PERCH ON THE ROOFTOPS AND dropped into the alley. Without the tech at work in his goggles, he would have had to depend on the moon as his only source of light. That would have left plenty of dark corners for danger to occupy. The warehouse that was his destination would be shut down for the night, its imported wares safely locked behind chained doors of iron and wood. By the time Darke arrived at those doors, however, the chains had been unlocked and removed, which could only mean his target was already inside.

Darke entered silently and sought the high ground among the rafters. He was fast and quiet. He could see the heat signatures of the six men circled about the boy. He positioned himself above them and listened.

"This boy is all you could manage?" one of them—a bald brute in a burlap shirt—asked.

"Saw the posh clothes and the clean skin and figured him for a dandy," one of the others said. He was a frail sort, his skin pock-marked and pallid. "Someone should be willing to pay to get 'im back, I'd wager. We'll be in for butter upon bacon, don't you go worryin' your fly rink about it. No need for the worries."

"Perhaps," the brute said. "What say you, lad? Who should the boys talk to about your ransom, eh? Got yerself any blood what gives a good damn?"

The boy was on the ground, his hands and feet bound. He made no attempt to answer the brutish man. He simply stared back at him, his thoughts a mystery to the cutthroats who had kidnapped him.

"You do not want to do this," Darke said. To the criminals, his voice seemed to come from the night itself, their torches far too weak to reveal his placement in the rafters. "Leave this place and come with me. There is hope for you still and great good in your future."

"Come out of the shadows," the brute cried. "Get within an arm's reach and see how bricky ya feel, ya lurker."

"Blood will not appease you," Darke said. "Death will not slake the thirst of your soul. You have been infected—corrupted by forces beyond you. Spilling more blood only drives you further from your salvation. If things turn violent, you'll leave me no choice but to stop you."

"Oh, violence we'll give ya fer certain, man o' the shadows," the pallid man said, grabbing an iron crow from the top of a nearby crate. "My lot thinks little of billy blinds and bluecaps, so best you shut your sauce box and back slang it out o' here, 'fore me lads remind ya who yer talking to with a right ol' batty-fang."

"But I'm not talking to you and your men," Darke said. "I was speaking to young Timothy there. This boy is not your meal ticket, gentlemen. In fact, he's not what you think he is at all."

The kidnapped boy looked into the rafters, his sight piercing the darkness to spot the traveler crouching in the rafters. He looked back toward the men who had taken him from the street and smiled.

"Don't sell us a dog, ya devil," the bald brute called back. "You seen us snatch the boy and want a bite at the pudding, yeah? Well, just 'cause you heard the copper singing don't mean yer invited to the table, like."

"That boy is a danger to you and all of London," Darke said, leaping to another wooden beam and watching the boy follow him with his gaze. "He's killed more than you can number. He is not the victim in this little kidnapping tale of yours...*you* are. Now, go before he gets impatient!"

"This beardsplitter may have already pulled at the mutton shunters," the pallid man said. "Carve the boy and we'll begin anew once the word becomes a mumble. Ain't no shackles in my figurin', so I ain't apt to stay."

"You can't kill him," Darke warned. "Abandon your folly now and leave this place with your lives."

"Don't listen to him, Mick," the frail man told the brute. "Stick the kid and I'll set fire to the lot. We'll scrub this mess and the one what robbed us of our coin, both."

"Ain't about to stick no kid, Weasel," the brute said, a bit perplexed by the young boy's peculiar smile. "The devil may already have me for all I done, but I ain't having that to sleep on. Not for all the gold in them heav'nly streets, I won't."

"Meater!" the pallid man shouted, giving the brute a shove. "Been smoking the lubberwort again, ya quisby? Right! Leave it to the muck snipe to do the deed you can't find the stomach for, eh? Move aside then, ya bitch-born, pigeon-livered ratbag, an' let dear Weasel give ol' Scratch a thrill for his mis'ry. I'll end this boy and the rakefire in the rafters all while dreamin' of some dirty puzzle down at the docks for my reward."

"Keep your eyes on the *boy*, fool!" Darke shouted. "He's more dangerous than you can even—"

Faster than Darke's eyes could follow, the boy broke free of his bindings and ripped the throat from the pallid man. The brutish man was next, drained of blood before his comrade's carcass hit the floor.

The traveler leapt from the rafters to position himself between the boy and the other four men who turned to flee. The boy was upon him in the blink of an eye, but Darke had come prepared. A simple cross around his neck repelled the boy like a force field, sending the little beast skittering away into the darkness of the warehouse.

"Go," Darke told the other, though in truth they had already begun to abandon him. "Tell others what you have seen here. Warn them of what is waiting for them in the darkness!"

A low growl came from somewhere deep within the warehouse. The boy was not pleased with being denied his prey and was determined—cross or no cross—to make the mysterious stranger regret interfering.

"Come out, Timothy," Darke said, scanning the warehouse with his goggles. "There's no hiding from your destiny. I've simply come to bring it to you."

"My destiny?" the boy cackled. "My destiny is blood and viscera, conquest and dominion, power and supremacy!"

The boy was a blur. Were it not for the protection of

the cross around his neck, Darke's throat would have been ripped open like a well-wrapped gift on Christmas morning. The boy, however, proved to be as clever as he was fast. The swipe had been made with the iron crow, which caught Darke's chain and sent it and the cross sliding into the darkness and out of his reach.

"My destiny seems to be getting the better of yours," the boy hissed.

"Your destiny is about to hurt once I get my hands on you. The name is Darke, by the way. I'll be handing your ass to you this evening."

"Brave words from a mortal," the boy taunted. "Hot wind and feeble hands, no doubt, but a claret to slake my thirst, nonetheless."

"Hmm. Of the two of us, which is *hiding*?"

"*Rrrrrrargh!*"

The boy's speed was impossible to gauge with Darke's all-too-human eyes, causing a momentary chill of panic to rattle his spine. He had been wholly unaware of his own left hand, signing in a language unknown to him. The boy's teeth found his throat but could not penetrate his skin. Frustrated, the boy tried to bite his arm as Darke struggled to get a solid grip on him. Once more, the lad's fangs found no purchase in the traveler's flesh. Confused, the vampire leapt away and scrambled into the darkness. Yet, the boy was hardly alone in his confusion.

"Quickly!" Darke heard in the back of his mind, like the forgotten lyric of a song which sprang to life once more upon hearing the tune. "That spell only purchased you a few moments. Use them wisely."

"Stop spellcasting with *my* hands, wizard," Darke

grumbled. "It's…disconcerting."

When no reply came, Darke drew his weapon—a little something from his own era he thought might prove useful.

"What are you?" the boy asked from the shadows. "Hunter?"

"No," Darke said. "I'm a friend. Sadly, you aren't mine. Not yet, anyway."

"You speak in riddles."

"Let's just say I have a unique perspective and leave it at that, yeah?"

A wall of stacked wooden crates came tumbling toward Darke, which would have brought a tidal wave of pain had the Great Library's agent not been fast and agile enough to dive out of its path. Scanning above with his goggles, he saw the boy scrambling across the stacks and making his way toward the door by which Darke and the others had entered.

"Hurry, fool!" Darke heard echo through his thoughts, but he couldn't be sure whether the insult came from his own frustration or from the wizard who had taken up residence in his psyche.

The boy was too fast, and he knew it. There was little hope of beating the vampire to the door, and Darke didn't relish the notion of chasing the creature through all of London.

"Damn it!" he muttered as he ran. "You owe me, Azael. Do something! Do something before he—*nyaargh!*"

The pain was overwhelming, shutting down all his senses and leaving his body twitching on the floor. As Darke's vision faded toward darkness, he saw the boy's silhouette against the moonlight streaming through the doorway.

Though he heard the stranger's scream pierce the darkness of the warehouse, the boy did not stop. The kidnappers were so afraid of what they had witnessed, he could smell it in the air. He would follow that scent to them and have his supper after all, dining on their blood and the rot of their souls. Only three more steps to freedom. Three more steps to the hunt. Three more steps to show the one who sired him that he was so much more than a pampered prince who couldn't hunt for himself.

The kidnappers were a blessing, the prey circling about the predator without sense enough to fear his teeth. He meant to prove his worth with their offal. He meant to quell any notion that he had not earned his place of power in the scheme of things. Three more steps and he would make that notion a reality.

The door slammed so quickly and loudly it startled even him. He had no time to slow his approach, so he hit the door and shattered like a clipper on the rocks. The pain was immense though his bones immediately began knitting back together. As he cursed in frustration, the stranger approached, his hands aglow with arcane power.

"Quick little devil, aren't you?" he asked. "Faster than poor Darke could manage. You must be quite the threat for him to let *me* out of the box."

"What are you?" the boy asked.

"Trouble, generally speaking," he said with a smile. "For you, it seems, a painful reminder that even power such as yours has its limits."

"What do you want from me?"

"Not a thing," the wizard said in Darke's voice. "My companion, however, has great plans. Fear not, boy. They are for your betterment…and no less than the salvation of this world. Now, it's nighty-night for you, lest I be forced to put a bit of *effort* into hurting you."

A few motions of Darke's hand rendered the vampire boy unconscious.

ONCE THE FOG LIFTED FROM DARKE'S MIND, HE was welcomed back to the waking world by young Dylan. Another man, whom Darke took to be the hunter, Cooke, was busy wrapping the unconscious vampire in chains.

"You okay, D?" Dylan asked. "Mr. Personality and I rushed here as soon as our boat docked and found the two of you lying here limp as…well, limp things. Sorry. That…didn't come out as cool as I had hoped."

"No worries," Darke said, taking his protégé's offered hand to get back on his feet. His head, however, proved less ready than his legs, and he swooned for a moment.

"Easy, D. Seems like you got your head scrambled a bit in the tussle."

"No," Darke said. "It wasn't the fight that did this to me. It was *him*. The wizard."

"You mean, he—I thought you two were like some sort of amalgam in stories with magic and the like."

"That's typically true, but here—for whatever reason— it was business as usual. I was "steering" so to speak, and the wizard was little more than a backseat driver."

"Except?"

"Except he motioned for a spell with my hands. Even as I was fighting the creature, he…worked to protect me."

"That doesn't seem like such a bad thing," Dylan said.

"Sure. If you discount the whole part where he was assuming control of my faculties without permission. It's peachy."

"Sarcasm duly noted. Still doesn't explain how you ended up on the floor unconscious."

"That part was my doing," Darke admitted. "I wasn't sure how close you would be or if you'd arrive in time, not to mention I preferred not to have you running headlong into a vampire who had already killed two grown men, so I offered the wizard a shot at the driver's seat to stop him."

Dylan glanced back at the unconscious vampire.

"Looks like he did just that. I guess once the work was done, he gave you back the reins."

"Either that or maintaining control required too much effort," Darke said. "Doesn't seem like the devil to easily give up control. Whatever the case, he's quiet now and I'm grateful."

"Did you check this man for bite marks?" the hunter asked, leaving the unconscious and heavily chained boy on the ground. "You can't be too careful. The infection works rapidly and, once infected, the devils always spread."

"No bites *here*," Darke said, offering his hand. "I'm Darke. I've read a lot about you, Mr. Cooke."

"Read about, eh?" the hunter replied. "You sound like the boy."

"I *am* the boy and, yet, not," Darke said with a sly smile, "but don't bother wrapping your head around that one. It has little bearing on the story you now find yourself in."

"So long as there's gold to be had and vampires to kill," Cooke said, "I'll roll with the punches thrown my way. The boy said you'd explain the nature of this—what'd he call it? Assignment?—once we arrived. I'd like you to get on with it, if you don't mind, mister. Ain't exactly known for my patience, and it's been taxed plenty since I met this here boy."

"I'm leaving you with plenty of instructions and more than enough gold to see them through," Darke said, pulling an envelope from his trouser pocket. "Take him to this address. You'll be able to stay there unseen and uninterrupted by the forces who might seek to recapture the boy. Your payment and instructions are there as well as the key to restoring a soul to your new charge here."

"That's madness," the hunter scoffed. "Ain't no way for one of these devils to be human again."

"He didn't say that," Dylan replied. "He said you could restore his soul. He'll still be a vampire. He'll still be dangerous. But, after you train him, he'll become a weapon you can point at the enemy."

"A weapon who will outlive you," Darke added. "One who will finally, many years from now…once all the pieces are on the game board, put an end to the darkness seeking to end your world."

"You can make him ready for what he must do," Dylan said, "and whom he must face."

"And, once his soul has been restored, you can remind him what it means to be human. Remind him what it was that they took from him. He'll be your greatest work,"

Darke said. "Possibly even your friend."

"I sincerely doubt it," Cooke said.

"Please do. I always love it when good men are surprised by hope. And it's coming for you, Mr. Cooke. Whether or not you choose to embrace it, of course, is entirely up to you."

"And the two of you? What will you be doing while I'm running your errands for you?"

"We've, uh, got quite a bit on our plate at the moment, Mr. Cooke," Dylan offered. "But one or both of us will be back at some point. We'll check in."

"And when the time comes for young Timothy here to make his move to restore this world," Darke said, "I'll be back to help see it through."

"For now, though, we've got to leave," Dylan said. "Take care, Mr. Cooke. Thank you for believing me enough to follow me all the way to England."

"I did it for the gold," Cooke said.

"I'm not sure I believe that," Dylan said. "I think you did it for Esmerelda. I think you'll see this through for her, as well."

Cooke smiled weakly.

"Until we return," Darke said, placing a hand on Cooke's shoulder, "keep the embers of hope burning in your heart. One day soon, grace will fan them into a flame warm enough to see you through to the end."

Darke and his young apprentice left the hunter and the monster there in the darkened warehouse and, through a side door to a fishmonger's shoppe, returned to the Great Library where a spooked raven seemed quite happy to see them safe and home at last.

IN THE ORCHARD

TINA THOUGHT IT BEST TO BURY HER SISTER, Cheryl, in the apple orchard she had cherished so much in life. She found a spot of grass between two of the larger Ruby Jons and used her father's pickaxe to break up the hard soil. It was cool out but pleasant enough and, in spite of her dire task, she found herself humming "Ain't Too Proud To Beg", and missing, at once, her sister's harmony. After loosening an appropriate amount of earth, she abandoned the pickaxe for a shovel and dug out the large hole which would soon be her sister's eternal resting place. The moment proved more bittersweet than she had imagined.

She and Cheryl had never been particularly close. Even from a young age, they had competed for their father's affection. Cheryl was exactly 87 seconds older than Tina but had always acted more like her mother than a sibling. Tina, thus, was always considered the baby of the family, requiring a great deal of supervision. Supervision turned out to be Cheryl's specialty, so much so that the fact that they were identical twins was all but forgotten by the rest of the family.

Daniel Kinsella, their father, was a difficult man; opinionated, obstinate and old-fashioned to a fault, but he loved Cheryl better than the rest and made no effort to hide it. It had driven Susan, their older sister, into the arms of a reefer-mad jazz man from Detroit. Their mother, Olivia, had taken the easy way out, opting for a special car ride in the sealed-off garage. For the last few years, Cheryl and Tina had been the only ones left to suffer through Daniel's antics, though little Tina had always taken the brunt of it.

As she climbed out of the grave, the slight breeze gave her goose bumps and yanked her thoughts back to the present. She surveyed the fresh wound in the earth. It wasn't deep enough. She knew it, but the time had grown short. Besides, the only thing which truly mattered was that Cheryl would be laid to rest by someone who loved her, in a place where they had always found some degree of peace.

Tina took a deep breath, taking in the scent of apple blossoms and, from the hedge which separated the orchard from the rest of her father's land, sweet, pale honeysuckle. Somewhere to the west, beyond the hills demarcating the westernmost boundary of the Kinsella Farm, coyotes called out to each other, planning whatever coyotes might plan. Their call was faint, but high and throaty—a sharp contrast to the deeper thrum of the mason bees flitting from flower to flower.

Tina turned back toward the grave and whispered encouragement to herself. She had rehearsed the words she meant to say, the short eulogy which would serve as her last goodbye to Cheryl, but she was hesitant to say them. Once she did, the moment would be over, lost to the past like any other. It was a private moment between sisters. No one else would understand, nor would they be strong enough to bear the responsibility. Part of her wanted the moment to last.

She looked to the stars, searching briefly for Orion. The lithe hunter had always been her sister's favorite constellation. It seemed only fitting that he should bear witness to her interment. A tear escaped into the lower lash of Tina's right eye, suspended there as she took another deep breath. She could hardly believe that she would never see her sister smile again—never again hear her laugh. She carefully leaned over the Radio Flyer and lifted Cheryl out, struggling to maneuver the unwieldy body into the grave. She climbed out again and looked down at the flesh and blood reflection of herself. She cleared her throat and let the tears warm her cheeks.

After glancing up again, to make sure Orion was still her witness, Tina spoke the few words she had prepared earlier in the day.

"Cheryl, you and I have shared so much. All of our lives, what's mine has been yours."

She wiped her eyes on the back of her sweater and took a moment to steady her nerves.

"Tomorrow, I'll turn fourteen," she said.

Tina looked down at her sister again and smiled.

"But *you* won't...you hateful bitch."

Tina took the shovel and began refilling the makeshift grave. It was easy to ignore Cheryl's pleading squeals, muffled as they were by the gag Tina had wedged firmly in her mouth. She hadn't located any rope to bind her sister's hands but found her father's electrical tape to be a decent substitution. On her back in the ground's open maw, Cheryl could do nothing but kick and moan as her sister continued to pile the dirt on.

It took another half-hour for Tina to finish the job and load her tools back in the wagon, and ten more minutes to walk the long way out of the orchard and back home. On the way, she worked herself into hysterics. After all, she still had to sell her father on the idea that Cheryl had run away from home.

TOLLY

MY NAME IS NEVAEH WHEATON, AND I HAVE been an investigative journalist for 17 years. In that time, I've built a reputation for being relentless in my pursuit of the truth. My ferocity earned me several prestigious awards and opportunities most young journalists would have killed for. I never cared. I was never hunting fame or fortune. I never gave a single damn about being a network anchor or sitting on a CNN panel. I wanted the story. I wanted the truth. Over the years, I've chased after stories that put me directly in the path of danger. It has never stopped me. The truth is my beacon. It calls to me night and day, and I run after it until all the strength has left my legs and my lungs are devoid of air. It's who I am. It's how I was built.

Seven months ago, a fire destroyed a small garage in Duburk and its chief mechanic, one Arthur McLowry, nearly died trying to free his employee, Sahir Ustad, from beneath a Buick Encore that had snagged his coveralls. McLowry managed to free Ustad but collapsed from the smoke inhalation after sending his employee running for the exit. The Duburk fire brigade—an all-volunteer outfit filled with inexperienced day jobbers—did their level best to battle the blaze and get to McLowry, but the smoke was thick and black from the burning tires, and those young men were too mindful of their wives and their babies to risk the unknown.

Sahir Ustad, screaming from the street for someone to save his boss, tried to rush back into darkness himself but was pulled away, kicking and screaming, by the police gathered to block off the two-lane street. When I interviewed him a few days later, Ustad said he had truly believed his boss would perish in the flames. No one would risk the toxic cloud or the intense heat. He said that "in the heart of his heart" he was already in mourning.

But then, something strange happened—the moment which set me on the path to this discovery. From the side of the blazing garage, a half-dead Arthur McLowry limped into view. He was as black as a raisin, covered in particulates and ash, but he was alive. The local ABC affiliate interviewed McLowry the next day from his room at St. Thomas and he claimed not to remember the events of the fire after freeing his employee from the grip of a determined Buick. He only remembered groggily coughing soot from his lungs as the stranger who had administered CPR slipped away. He never even saw the man's face. I watched the interview from my usual perch in my favorite pub. I was hooked. I wanted to know who rescued McLowry and why, in the age of Instagram and Twitter, the hero wasn't grabbing for his fifteen minutes of fame.

I visited the area and spoke with several witnesses to

the fire, but none remembered seeing the stranger or his rescue of Arthur McLowry. When you've been in the game as long as I have, though, you aren't lacking for ideas. I stopped into the corner convenience store and asked if they had security cameras facing that general direction. As it turned out, store security wasn't much of a concern, so there was no footage to be had. The bicycle shop across the street proved to be a different story. They had three cameras, but only one of them gave me a decent angle on McLowry's garage. I slipped the manager of the shop—a hipster neckbeard named Toby—a couple of Jacksons and he booted up the footage I needed. The resolution was low, and the footage lacked color, but as we watched the fire blaze, a man could be seen running behind the garage and, a few minutes later, slipping away and out of frame.

Duburk, for all its small-town charm, is considered by most to be the armpit of Westfall County. Every other building along Main Street is empty, a hollow artifact of some bygone era. Crossland Avenue runs parallel to Main and is nearly as barren. McLowry's garage—inaccurately named Quick Fix, according to the large neon sign overlooking its charred remains—occupied a lot on Fallburg Lane, the cross street connecting Main and Crossland. The footage from the bike shop suggested that our bashful hero had left the scene of the fire and headed west toward Main, which gave me no small amount of hope. At the corner of Main and Fallburg sat the New Alliance Credit Union and its walk-up ATM, which would mean cameras *galore*.

The bank footage, procured by my editor, Pete Hallsy,

gave me a solid photo of our mystery man. At that point, I could've run his photo to a detective friend of mine in Phoenix but instead, I opted for a reverse image search on a platform so famous for its search engine that we all use their brand name as a verb. I couldn't have known, when I tapped 'enter' on my keyboard, the mystery I was about to step into. I fell into a rabbit hole of research in which each new answer uncovered three more questions. I spent roughly six weeks playing Sherlock Holmes amid covering every other story my editor dropped in my lap. And once I had more questions than answers—when each new piece of the puzzle *refused* to form a single image—I drove to Wimberley, Duburk's more charming and east-ernmost neighbor, to meet with the pastor of Wimber-ley's First Methodist Church, one Anatole Renata.

I had called Reverend Renata under the pretense of writing a story on small town America and religion, spe-cifically in regard to poll numbers suggesting that even the more rural parts of the United States are turning away from faith. Renata seemed hesitant to meet with me, but I assured him—okay, *sure*, I lied through my pearly whites—that he would not be on record. I was only try-ing to gauge the temperature of the clergy and how such trends impact the day-to-day life of their churches. He agreed to meet with me during his lunch hour if I didn't mind conducting our interview in the park.

"I never meet with women in my office unless my wife or one of the ladies on staff can sit in," Renata had explained, "and they are all in Memphis, Tennessee this week for a women's retreat. So, if you don't mind watch-ing an old man eat a salad, you can join me in the park and ask whatever you'd like."

Larue Park was as quaint and quiet as you would imagine. The gazebo at its center needed repair, but the grounds were verdant, and every park bench and picnic table was less than two years old. Wimberley was long past its prime, but people clearly still gave a damn. If they didn't, the Wright Drug and Discount Store would've been swallowed up long ago by a Walgreens or a CVS, and Winston's Soda Shoppe and Ice Cream Parlor would sit empty, a monument to brighter days and simpler times.

I found Anatole Renata right where he said he'd be, at the only picnic table situated in the shade of the large basswood just to the west of the gazebo, tucking into a Tupperware bowl of simply dressed greens topped with a poached salmon filet. He smiled warmly as I approached and stood to offer his hand.

"You must be Ms. Wheaton," he said.

"Thank you for agreeing to meet with me, Reverend Renata," I said, shaking his hand. I was immediately surprised by how rough it felt. I wouldn't expect a man his age to moisturize, of course, but his hand felt like sandpaper, as coarse as his eyes were soft and kind.

"Please," he said, motioning for me to sit. "Reverend is such a *formal* thing. I'm a servant. As you are, I would imagine, in your own way. We serve the people of our communities as we search for truth."

"I don't guess I thought of it that way," I admitted.

"The world around us is always trying to sell us on the notion that we are the center of the cosmos," he said. "It's all about *me*. It's all about *you*. The rest can go hang. It's a rare thing, then, when people commit their lives to the service of others."

"I'm not sure my job is as altruistic as you make it seem," I told him. "My bosses like to write big headlines. I like to get paid. No one is selfless when it comes to selling papers. Especially now that it's a dying medium."

"Don't sell yourself short, Ms. Wheaton. Too many people are content to assume the truth. Those good at your chosen pursuit—and I'm sure you are—pursue the facts of a matter without bias or prejudice until such time as the truth is evident to all."

"I wish it was always so simple," I said, reaching into my messenger bag and removing the file I had managed to compile over a month and a half of investigating the good reverend.

"Oh, I'm not under the impression what you do is easy, Ms. Wheaton. I'd imagine it can be quite difficult. Your work uncovering the human trafficking ring you traced back to the truck stop in Martinville was astonishing. That investigation alone must have put you in harm's way more than once, but you continued your pursuit, and there are undoubtedly a number of women who owe their lives to you and your article."

He continued eating his salad as if he hadn't just revealed the fact that he had done a bit of research on me.

"I only put the story together," I said, scanning his face. I couldn't tell yet whether he was on to me or not. "The state police and FBI did all the heavy lifting."

"Seems a bit strange, doesn't it?"

"What does?"

"Your superiors sending an award-winning journalist of your caliber to a little town like Wimberley to write a puff piece about religion in Middle America," he said. "I'd think a young woman of your well-earned reputation could pick any assignment she wanted, and this...well, it doesn't seem like your kind of story at all, does it? Unless, of course, you're working on something *else*."

I smiled. How could I not? I had underestimated the man, and he schooled me something good.

"Seems like you might have a bit of an investigative streak yourself, Reverend."

"My friends call me Tolly," he said, flaking the salmon with the tines of his plastic fork. "It's a silly derivative of my name, but I've never minded it."

"Fair enough," I said as I placed the file folder on the table between us. I didn't open it, though. I wanted to let him talk first.

"As for being an investigator," he said, "you must understand I've lived in Wimberley for going on twenty years, Ms. Wheaton, and I've never been the interest of even the local paper, let alone a big outfit like the Herald. I may not be the sharpest pin in the cushion, but your phone call didn't pass the smell test. So, I did a little digging and discovered what an amazing journalist you are. You are, if I may be so bold, quite the revelation. Not to take anything away from St. John, of course."

"I'm curious why—Tolly was it?"

"Yes, ma'am."

"I'm curious why you didn't cancel the interview."

He picked at his salad and took another bite or two as he constructed his answer. I waited patiently. You don't do my job for long without learning to read the moment. My gut said Renata wasn't thinking of a way to dodge my question. He was soul searching.

"I suppose," he finally said, dabbing at the corners of his mouth with a paper napkin, "that when you've lived long enough, life begins to feel like it no longer holds many surprises."

He pushed the remainder of his salad to one side and offered a kind smile.

"Are you a praying woman, Ms. Wheaton?"

"Not anymore," I admitted. "I was raised in church—Missionary Baptist, mostly—but, once I moved away from home, well, I guess I didn't have much *need* of it. No offense, Tolly."

"None taken," he said. "I think even the most devout of us has *seasons* of doubt. Some seasons last longer than others. But I've often found that even the least religious among us find themselves offering up a prayer now and again."

"I suppose in times of crisis, we all tend to hope a higher power is paying attention," I said. "Why do you ask?"

"No reason, really," he said. "But I sometimes see patterns in the world—the ebbing and flowing of design and purpose—and I've learned to trust my instincts. Right now, they're telling me that you felt the need to mislead me. Perhaps you thought I would deny you the interview if I knew your true purpose. Perhaps I would have. Who can say, really, what a person will do in any given moment?"

I opened the file folder between us and pushed it toward him. He reached into the inner breast pocket of his sport coat and retrieved a pair of reading glasses before inspecting the photographs and newspaper articles I had collated. If he was surprised by the contents of the folder, it didn't show. He seemed entirely unconcerned.

He closed the folder and slid it back to me. After removing his glasses and placing them back in the pocket from which he had retrieved them, he offered me a kind smile.

"I'm curious, Ms. Wheaton, as to what you believe you've found."

"I was hoping you would tell *me*," I said. "As you can imagine, I've seen a lot on this job. I've tackled my fair share of mysteries, but this…well, it doesn't add up."

The minister smiled at that the way a parent humors his (or her) toddler's attempt at a joke.

"Forgive me. That's always struck me as an odd expression," he explained.

"How so?"

"Math and science have their place, Ms. Wheaton," he said, digging around in his coat pockets for a moment before producing a pipe and a small pouch of tobacco. "They are, of course, *incredible* tools—useful and a common grace for anyone willing to explore them. But life is filled with more mystery than mere science or mathematics can contain. Wouldn't you agree?"

I have been around long enough to be wary of chasing a conversation down rabbit trails, but something about Renata put me at ease. Wherever he was going was not an attempt to avoid the subject I had laid before him but instead, a scenic route intended to provide the foundation upon which we would build the rest of our discussion. So, I climbed aboard his train of thought and rode on toward an eventual horizon.

"I'm a journalist," I said. "I like facts. Feelings matter, too, of course, but facts carry more weight. Math is all about the solution. When done correctly, the right answer is always achieved. And science—"

"Let's stop at math for now," Renata said. "You said you believe math to be all about the solution. That's incorrect. Math originates with the problem. It busies itself with uncovering the solution—that much is true—but without the problem, there is no need for the solution. John's two balloons and Jenny's two balloons are not a problem in need of solving until someone comes along to ask, 'How many balloons did they have all together?' The problem *prompts* the formula, the formula leads to the answer. It's all quite lovely and mechanical."

Let's say, though, that young John was born into a wealthy family and is used to getting fifteen balloons each time the carnival comes to town. And Jenny, born into a poor family, has never had balloons before in her young life. Likely, John feels quite poor of balloons and Jenny rich beyond what she has ever known. Factually and mathematically, yes, there are four balloons altogether. But the worth of those balloons has an *extrinsic* value beyond their minimal *intrinsic* worth. The factual, mathematical answer is only correct in a certain sense. It is, however, a limited sense."

"I understand what you are saying," I bluffed, "but I'm not sure what this has to do with the questions that brought me here."

"Now, take science," Renata continued, stuffing tobacco into the chamber of his pipe. "I've not met an atheist yet who didn't bend the knee to the great monolith of science. They value it above all things, not the least of which are their own experiences. And science is a fine tool and a grand pursuit. I had a grandson once who studied the sciences. Did quite well for himself if I recall. But science *cannot* answer all of our questions, Ms. Wheaton."

"You don't believe in science, Reverend Renata?" I asked. "I know that people of faith sometimes shun—"

"Before you insult me, Ms. Wheaton, it might be best to let me get to my point."

I motioned for him to continue.

"Science is a wonderful tool, but it is *only* a tool. A stethoscope is also a useful tool. Used properly, it can detect a faulty heart, an infected lung, and any number of other things. It cannot, however, detect Venus or predict the weather. It cannot respond to a radio signal, nor can it encourage someone broken in spirit. It is limited, you see, in its usefulness. It is a fine tool for the work it does, but it does not do *all* the work. Am I making any sense here, Ms. Wheaton?"

"I suppose," I said, reluctant to give him too much ground.

"Think of it this way: we've been given a great many tools with which to experience and learn about creation. Science is merely one of them. But relying on it as your only method of understanding the world around us is like using only the red crayon to draw a portrait. You may create a fantastic image which closely resembles its subject, but you're setting aside a whole box of other bright and vivid colors that would bring greater depth to the picture."

"Okay," I said, still mulling over his words. "Now, tell me what any of that has to do with the file I showed you."

"Everything, Ms. Wheaton. It has *everything* to do with it."

He took a moment to light his pipe, the ritual not unlike the more sacred rituals a man of the cloth is called upon to perform. It lent him an air of dignity and wisdom. He didn't need the loan.

"You've placed before me a mystery," he said, "that you have come to unravel. Through your lens of 2+2=4, you will never understand the great truth behind this mystery. Science could never reveal it to you, nor can you boil down the truth of it to some simplistic form that science *can* tackle. Whatever your background in faith may have been, you—and so many others, so please do not think I'm leveling this charge solely at you, Ms. Wheaton—lack the imagination to see beyond the natural into what lies beyond it."

"So, tell me," I said, spreading the photos and documents from the file across the picnic table between us, "what explains *this*?"

"I'm curious as to how you found me," Renata said. "I can only assume it has something to do with the Quick Fix over in Duburk."

"That fire would've claimed a life had you not intervened," I told him. "I found it curious a hero like you wouldn't at least check on the man whose life he saved."

"I didn't need to. Mr. McLowry made the news for three nights straight and seemed to be in good health each time they interviewed him."

"But your disappearance was a mystery," I told him,

"so I did some tracking. I finally got a look at you on an ATM camera. Didn't get much of a look at your face, but I did get something better: your license plate number."

"And, from there, a deep dive into madness."

"That's one way to look at it," I said. "I was planning on meeting with you even then. I was impressed with what I assumed was your humility. But it occurred to me that perhaps the aversion to attention I was crediting to you as humility might be grounded in something less honorable."

"I was either a hero or a villain, eh?" Renata asked. "Is your thinking always so binary, Ms. Wheaton?"

"Not at all, Tolly. I only wanted to get at the truth."

"You say so *now*, Ms. Wheaton. We'll see if you still stand on that ground once I've answered your questions."

"Once I had the license plate, I was able to find out who you are and where you work. Even found a good picture on your church's website," I said. "I had a buddy of mine—who will remain anonymous since his favors for me would likely end his employment—run facial recognition. The alphabet agencies had nothing. You weren't a criminal. That confounded me a bit, I admit it. But, I didn't quit. I broadened the search to the entirety of the internet. The first photo I came across was this one."

I handed him a black and white photograph of a march down State Street in Chicago. It was taken March 25, 1967. Led by Dr. Martin Luther King Jr., some 5,000 participants marched to the Coliseum where Dr. King would address the crowd in protest of the Vietnam War.

"I remember this day," Tolly said. "Dr. King had been quiet about the war for some time—more pressing matters, you know—but he had finally decided to take a stand, and I decided to march with him. He was a charismatic fellow, that man. I didn't always see eye to eye with his theology, but I admired his indomitable spirit."

He handed the picture back to me.

"You wouldn't be here, I think, if this was all you found, Ms. Wheaton. Please continue. This is all a bit like *This Is Your Life*, I think. Of course, you're far too young to remember that program."

He was correct. I wouldn't get the reference until long after the interview, when I looked it up. I handed him another photo. It was taken in May of 1946 by a photographer working for The National Tribune. It showed men from the Brotherhood of Railway Trainmen standing in solidarity. They were on strike for higher wages, a move which left thousands of travelers stranded. The strike would last only four days and come to an end when President Truman intervened. Amid the group of a dozen or so soot-covered trainmen, stood Anatole Renata. He appeared no younger but certainly no older than he did as he perused the copy of that old photograph.

"George Malkin," Tolly said, "was a friend of mine in those days. He'd go on to become a businessman. Owned his own cobbler shop, if I recall. He'd learned the trade from his father. But in '46, both of us were working the lines. It was back-breaking work, but we saw a lot of the country, and I made some fine friends on those rails. When our union decided to join the strike, I went along. I didn't care about the money as much as the job, but I didn't want George and the fellows like him to be mistreated. The conditions weren't the best, and standing with them was the *least* I could do. The strike lasted only a few days before Truman stepped in and threatened to have the military run the lines. George stayed on the job for another few months before departing for dreams of greater riches."

"And you?" I asked.

"I stayed on another year or so," Tolly said, "and then left the country. I went overseas and didn't come back to the states for nearly 20 years."

"You say that as if it makes sense, Reverend Ren— um, Tolly. But here you sit, looking as if you haven't aged a day since this photograph was taken."

He smiled at me. It was disarming.

"I'm going to go out on a limb, Ms. Wheaton, and guess you have a photo in your file considerably older than 1946. What do you say, for both our sakes, you skip ahead to *that* one?"

I produced the item which had driven me to Tolly's door. A copy of a cyanotype image from Paris. It was hand-dated 'Spring, 1872' by the photographer. It showed a couple standing on the bridge over the River Seine. They were clearly in love.

As Tolly studied the cyanotype, a tear escaped his left eye and traveled along the side of his nose only to cling to the side of his nostril. He brushed it away with the sleeve of his gray wool coat.

"Her name was Simonne," he said. "She was a shaft of light into the blackness of doubt I had allowed into my soul. She reminded me of God's grace and restored hope with her love and devotion. She pulled me out of despair and, in spite of me, became my wife."

"In 1872," I said, to make sure he understood exactly what he was admitting.

"1873, actually. April, if I recall correctly. Her parents were quite supportive, but they preferred a long engagement."

"You see why I'm having a hard time with this, right?" I asked. "You're sitting here, and you can't be more than, what, mid-50s?"

"You tell me," he said, puffing on his pipe. He seemed amused with himself.

"I have photos here going back more than a hundred years, Tolly, and you look the same in all of them. A few pounds up, a few pounds down, but…you're the same guy. Clearly, something strange is going on. There has to be an answer."

"Oh, there certainly is."

"So, I search for relatives. I figure, hey, maybe he comes from a family with extraordinarily strong genes, you know? Maybe you had distant relatives who could pass for your twin. It didn't sound plausible to me, but I had to find some kind of answer. That's when I discovered Anatole Renata has only existed—and, by that, I mean in any official capacity—for the last 40 years. There are no birth records. No family tree for me to climb up or down. Nothing."

"So, you kept asking yourself questions," Tolly said.

"That's what we do," I said. "Journalists, I mean. We keep asking questions until we get to the answers. We dig and poke and prod and eventually—if our persistence outlives the subject's resistance—we come away with the truth."

"This is where you and I find our common ground," Tolly said. "We are seekers of the truth. You have *your* set of tools and I have *mine*. The goal is similar: to understand something we did not before…to uncover a mystery hidden in the commonplace."

"You see, then, why I could not resist coming to you once I had seen the evidence I've collected in this file," I said. "I couldn't walk away from something this—"

"Ridiculous?"

"Intriguing," I corrected. "I know there's a solution to this conundrum. Something solid. Something my readers will buy, but I'll be damned if I can see it. Oh, sorry about the language, Tolly. I didn't think."

"No apology necessary, Ms. Wheaton. Though, I would offer a correction if you don't mind."

"Feel free."

"You said you'd be damned if you can see the solution. I think, rather, you're damned if you *don't*. But I suppose we won't know the will or won't of it all until I've told you what you came to hear."

"So, please, Tolly…enlighten me."

Renata took a few puffs of his pipe as he considered how to craft his explanation. It was then I remembered the digital recorder in my purse and retrieved it.

"Would you mind if I record you? I should've asked before."

"Not at all," Tolly said. "I assume such a thing is stock and trade for people in your field."

I pressed the record button. Renata rubbed his chin for a moment and removed the pipe from his mouth.

"When I was a boy," he said, "I didn't have many

friends. My family was poor, and I spent my childhood doing all I could to help put food on the table. I had barely made it to adulthood when my father passed away. As the man of the house, I helped provide for my mother and my sisters, though I admit I did not carry that weight without a stumble or two. When my mother passed away, I was suddenly all my sisters had. They depended on me…not only to provide for us, but to protect them. We were a conquered people, you see. Our enemies occupied our cities. It was a frightening world, but we created our own sense of normalcy and survived the day to day. As I became more successful, we were able to help those around us in need. My sisters—even as youngsters—had the holy gift of hospitality. They always knew the needs of our neighbors and did their best to intervene."

"You mentioned an occupation," I said. "Are we talking Nazi-occupied France, or—"

"All your questions will be answered, I assure you, Ms. Wheaton."

"I'm sorry for interrupting. Please, do go on."

"My sisters and I had settled into our routine. We missed our parents, of course, but we were surviving well enough and had even managed to eke out a bit of joy now and again. And, one day when I least expected it, I met the man who would come to be my truest friend."

"George Malkin?"

"Oh, no. George came into my life much later, Ms. Wheaton. Much, *much* later."

"I'm sorry. Go on."

"It's hard for me to recall what I was doing when I first heard the stories."

"Stories?"

"My friend's reputation preceded him, you see. I was born a Jew, Ms. Wheaton, and though my people were often as maligned and mistreated in those days as they are today, I was faithful in my pursuit of Yahweh. I heard rumblings in the Temple of a young teacher whose knowledge of the Torah was beyond anything they had ever heard. The older men, of course, didn't care much for upstarts, but the young men spoke in whispers, questioning whether this man was a heretic or a prophet."

I didn't think much about those things, to be honest. I was far too busy with keeping food on the table and the wrong suitors away from my sisters. In the market one day, though, I met my friend. He was buying oil and salt and found himself a bit short. He was prepared to put the oil back when my older sister offered to cover the shortage. He thanked her, and they began to talk. Being the man of the house, I stepped in. Even in those days, you didn't simply let some stranger chat with your sister. You interjected and sized him up."

He smiled at the memory.

"It's hard to say what inspires friendship, but ours was instantaneous. Before we left the marketplace, I had invited him for dinner. My sisters loved him as easily as I did. And I don't mean to say they had any *romantic* interest in him. I had not brought him home to play matchmaker and they knew that. They also understood, as they got to know him, that he was a bit beyond such things. There was a loneliness about him which suited him, and a wife would only slow him down."

"Career-minded," I offered.

"Something like that," Tolly said, his eyes searching mine for something. In retrospect, I think perhaps he was disappointed that I hadn't yet figured him out.

"My friend, as it turned out, was a rabbi. In point of fact, he was the same rabbi I had heard so much about. For the life of me, I could not see why he was such a controversial figure. He had such a gentleness about him that I couldn't imagine anyone seeing him as a threat or a heretic. His knowledge of the Torah, and the way he could speak of it with such authority was mesmerizing and inspiring."

Before the night was over, my sisters had invited him back. He tried to politely decline as he had several men who traveled with him and didn't want them to feel as if he was ditching them for a free meal. I assured him we had plenty for all of them and would be pleased to offer them our hospitality as well."

"I'm guessing your friendship didn't go over well with some of the more conservative members of your synagogue," I said.

"No one paid much attention to it, honestly. Not then, at least. My friend wasn't as well-known at the time. He traveled a lot, so his reputation was different from place to place. My sisters and I always greeted him with food and celebration, though. He and his friends were welcome guests each and every time they passed through."

Knowing him changed us, Ms. Wheaton. He was *transformative*. When he spoke to us it was as if he saw our greater selves—the men and women Yahweh had always meant for us to be—and spoke directly to them and not to the broken, messy selves we were in the moment. He spoke of God not as some distant king or emperor, but as a kind, loving father and a husband willing to sacrifice all he held dear for his bride. And, from that point on, as I listened to the Torah being proclaimed in the Temple, it became impossible not to see its truth and mystery through a new lens."

"Is this how a Jewish man became a Methodist minister?" I asked.

"I'm getting there."

As Reverend Renata spoke, I paid strict attention to his mannerisms. Police officers with a few years under their belts will tell you they develop an instinct for the truth. Liars, even the best ones—the ones who craft lies so closely tied to the truth even they lose sight of what is real and what isn't—have ticks and tells which give them away. Investigative journalists tend to develop that skill, too. We have a finely tuned "bullshit meter" to paraphrase my editor. I'm telling you this because it is important to note that, at no point in the entirety of Tolly's tale, did I feel like I was being tricked, lied to, or scammed. He spoke with utter sincerity. I now believe that it was because he had grown tired of his secret and needed someone else to shoulder the burden. He hoped that I would ultimately be that someone and free him of that weight.

"My dear friend and teacher had been away for some time," Tolly said, "when I became quite sick. The girls wanted to get word to him. They felt that, because God shined so greatly upon him, his presence might bring healing and restoration to their sick brother. We had all heard the stories, of course, but had never seen such a thing for ourselves. As sick as I was, I ordered them to leave him out of it. His teachings had caused enough friction that people were calling for his arrest…as if he was going to lead some governmental revolt. Such a thing was *never* his goal, of course, but you know how people can be, Ms. Wheaton. Give them a scrap of misinformation to hang their hats on and fan the flames with enough rhetoric and fear-mongering, and you can whip them into a violent frenzy easily enough. We still see the same sort of nonsense today."

"All too often," I agreed. "How long were you ill, Tolly?"

"I couldn't tell you," he replied. "I was in and out of consciousness for most of it. I had a fever that wouldn't break, and my body would seize and shake from tremors."

"Your sisters didn't take you to a hospital?"

"We didn't have access to the sort of sophisticated medical help we have access to now, I'm sad to say. It was more of a 'watch, wait, and pray' situation. How long the relentless fever had me in its grip, though, I cannot say. I can only tell you that, once the situation became so grave that they could no longer find any room for hope, my sisters ignored my wishes and sent for my friend."

Again, Tolly paused and searched my eyes.

"What are you looking for in there, Tolly?"

"Recognition, I suppose. But I think the math is getting in your way."

"The math?"

"No cell phones in those days," Tolly continued, as if he hadn't left my question hanging in the air. "No telegrams, either. So, my sisters sent a messenger to tell the rabbi that I was knocking—quite insistently by that point—at death's heavy door, and they truly believed he could make a difference in the whole situation if he would only come running."

"And did he?"

"No, no. He was an extremely busy man and did not believe the situation to be as dire as my sisters made it seem. He would come visit later, though, once his work was finished."

"I'm sure you were glad to see him," I said.

"Not exactly," Tolly said, taking a short puff from his pipe. "By the time he arrived, I had been dead for four days."

Over the years, I've heard a great many things slip past the lips of the men and women I have interviewed. I've been inspired, frightened to my core by a sociopath's confession, filled with laughter at a child's innocence and simple wisdom, and humbled by the scope of humanity. Never before that moment with Tolly had I ever found myself speechless. Whatever destination I had assumed his story would drive us to, I suddenly found myself in some alien terrain. The look on my face must have been entirely ridiculous, yet Tolly just puffed away on his pipe and gave me a moment or two to process before he continued.

"Martha, my older sister, ran out to meet my friend on the road. She—"

"You…y-you're telling me that…that you are—"

"Lazarus? Yes, Ms. Wheaton."

"And your friend was?"

"Jesus. Do keep up, Ms. Wheaton."

He smiled at me so warmly that I found myself with

little to say. I didn't believe him, of course, but I was so enthralled by the madness of it all that I wanted to hear everything.

"Martha ran to meet him on the road and said she believed that if he had only been there *before* I died, things might have turned out quite differently. But she also said something that was a giant leap for her. Martha, God love her, was always the cautious sort, you see? She loved Jesus and opened her home to him, of course, and always treated him with the sort of respect any of us would have shown a rabbi. But it was our younger sister, Mary, who had always come to faith more easily and readily than Martha and me. But, seeing him there, she said her spirit opened her mouth and spoke *for* her. She told him she believed, even in that dark moment four days after my death, that God would hear him and grant whatever he might ask. If you had known Martha, Ms. Wheaton, you would understand how great a confession of faith it was for her. Little doubt my friend was moved by her trust."

From there, of course, you likely know the narrative presented in scripture. It's as accurate a telling of those events as I could repeat for you."

"Um, lapsed Baptist here," I said, raising my hand as if asking an elementary teacher to explain my homework assignment. "Can we pretend I *don't* remember much about that story?"

Tolly smiled at me kindly and continued. I saw no judgment in his kind eyes.

"Many around us believed Jesus to be the Christ, the Messiah spoken of by the prophets. To me, he was nothing more or less than my very best friend. Oh, I knew he was something special—a holier man than any I had ever known—but I had wrongly assumed that the Son of Man would come as some conquering warrior. Someone to set us free from Roman captivity. Martha, though, for all her busybody ways, had come to the truth of it. Jesus was far more than a simple teacher. More than just a man. In her grief, she laid it all out there. She confessed what she truly believed: that, although all evidence suggested I was long past the point of intervention, Jesus could still deliver. It turned out, of course, she was right. Jesus told her that *he*, himself, was the resurrection. That *he* was life. That even death would submit to his authority. And, God love her, she believed him."

He stopped for a moment and searched my eyes again. "Go ahead, Ms. Wheaton. Ask your question."

"Do you remember what happened?"

"Not really, no. All I remember is a feeling I had: the sensation of waiting for something or someone. Not the bored sort of waiting one does as the DMV, mind you, but an expectant waiting. I was trapped in a moment, and all the moment contained was the sort of joyous and anxious exuberance of a young child when he first opens his eyes on Christmas morning. *Wherever* I was, Ms. Wheaton, it was a waiting room. There were no sights to see. There was only the expectation of seeing my friend again."

"And then?" I asked.

"And then…I heard him call out to me: 'Lazarus?'— the way any friend might say your name when they've spotted you from across the room. But his voice spoke to me beyond a much larger void. 'Lazarus?' He called again, and I wanted to shout out, 'I am here, my friend!' In all this time, I have not forgotten the *feeling* of his voice. I do not think I was in my body, Ms. Wheaton. I do not think I retained any sort of physical form at all. I was nothing but spirit. And yet, even in my formless state, I felt his words reaching out to me and tugging gently, the way an archaeologist might carefully remove a fossil from the earth. 'Come forth,' he said, and by God I did. My eyes opened to the cloth they had wrapped me in and I could barely move. But he called, and I came. And when he asked those gathered to remove the wrappings, I saw a sight I had never seen before."

"What?" I asked, leaning so far across the picnic table that, to any onlookers, it might have seemed flirtatious.

"There were tears in his eyes," Tolly said. "Not tears of joy for my return, mind you. These were the remnants of his sorrow. The toll of his great humility. The price of him becoming like us, Ms. Wheaton. Part of the triune God come to us as a man and bearing the weight of all our human frailty and suffering. That he would take upon himself such sorrow over the likes of me…well, I would never doubt him or his love again."

"If I may," I said, my mind spinning like a tilt-a-whirl, "can we…uh, what I mean to say is, can you confirm in plain English that you are saying what it sounds to me like you are saying?"

"I'm saying I am Lazarus, brother of Martha and Mary, citizen of Bethany, friend to Jesus of Nazareth," Tolly said as calmly as if he was talking about the weather. "I was sick and died, and he raised me from the dead."

"And you never died again?" I asked. "Or does your death never *stick*?"

He laughed at that, the sort of belly laugh which becomes infectious. I found myself uncomfortably chuckling along in spite of the fact that I felt that one—if not both—of us had lost their mind.

"I only died once," he said after his laughter subsided. "To be perfectly frank, Ms. Wheaton, I'm not sure *why* I never died again. I've developed a theory or two, of course, but I suppose I won't know for certain until my friend and I are reunited at the end of things."

"What sort of theories?"

"The one most compelling to me is simply that Death was frightened away from me," he replied. "She had her hooks in me something solid before he pried me loose. You can imagine such a thing would be unsettling for her. Her power surely seemed invincible until someone with *greater* authority came along. Maybe she simply doesn't want to risk a confrontation. After all, Ms. Wheaton, Death knows her place in all this. We all know how the story *ultimately* ends. Death will be vanquished and powerless. Perhaps, to her, I'm an ugly reminder of her fate."

I needed to think. To process. I gathered all the photos and news clippings and stuffed them back into the folder. Renata remained silent, watching me with a keen eye and puffing thoughtfully on his pipe like Gandalf the Gray amused by a bumbling hobbit.

"You don't believe me," he said.

"I'm not sure what I believe, Tolly. The story I came here to uncover was already...well, I don't even have a word for it. Not impossible. At least, I didn't *think* so. I assumed there was an answer I couldn't see."

"Surely you didn't see *this* coming," he said, wearing a

hint of a smirk.

"I met a man some years ago," I said, "who helped me out of a rough spot. He stepped into my dangerous world and managed to save my life from some pretty evil men and women my investigation had managed to piss off. You remind me of him a bit, Tolly. There's something about you which seems otherworldly to me. He didn't stick around long but, like you, he seemed to think my eyes were closed tight to the unexplained wonders of the world. I never thought it was true, but now—"

"Now you are confronted with the miraculous and aren't sure how to make it fit into the framework you've built for yourself," Tolly said. "Either I'm a liar, a lunatic, or I'm telling the truth. Your framework leaves no room for my story to be the truth, but your instincts argue against me being a pathological liar or having some sort of mental illness. You trust your instincts and you trust your framework…and suddenly you are confronted with something that has them at odds. Am I close?"

I nodded, distracted momentarily by a large tow truck driving past the park entrance pulling behind it another tow truck. Not something one sees often. The scent of Renata's pipe tobacco drew me back to his eyes and his words.

"I don't think you are a liar," I said. "Crazy? I'm not qualified to make that kind of diagnosis."

"Fair enough."

"I believe that *you* believe what you are telling me. Furthermore, I believe there is something strange going on with you, Tolly. Something I can't seem to work out. There's a part of me that, as hard as it is to fathom, believes you are…unaging. Perhaps not immortal, but demonstrably more long-lived than the oldest living people who tend to make the local news cycles as personal interest stories. I don't know how it's possible or why you're the one with this gift, but…well, here you are. But asking me to believe you are who you say you are is—"

"A bridge too far?"

"Well, yes. I mean…I believe that Jesus was a person. I believe he walked the earth and taught peace and forgiveness. I even believe the core values of his teachings are valuable to us as a society. But, Tolly, you're asking me to believe he was truly what they say he was."

"What *he* said he was," Tolly corrected. "He doesn't let you off the hook so easily. He said he was the Son of Man, a term we reserved for the long-awaited messiah. We didn't lift him up as some false deity, Ms. Wheaton. We only proclaimed what we saw and heard from him. And, believe me, I understand your hesitation and doubt. I do. People doubted the truth of what had happened to me even then. It didn't matter how many people had witnessed the thing. It didn't matter that he performed signs and miracles wherever he went. It wouldn't matter today, either, you see. Those with ears to hear and eyes to see, do. Those waiting for the numbers to add up or the science to confirm, do not. He did those things in front of them, and some still didn't believe. Why would *you* all these years later? No, no. It isn't a spectacle that motivates faith. It's God himself who motivates it…gives you a touch of faith enough for small, great things."

"You are asking a lot of me, Tolly," I said, shoving the file back into my bag. "I don't know what I came here hoping to find, but I'm fairly certain this wasn't it."

"You said you came here for the truth, Ms. Wheaton. If you'll recall, I said you might not still be standing on that ground after you heard what I had to say."

"How can I?"

"Is it so difficult? If math and science do not answer your questions, Ms. Wheaton, what are you left with? Math can tell you one man plus one woman plus a life-long commitment equals a marriage. Science can tell you what falling in love does to you physiologically and what parts of your brain spring to life during sex, but where does that love *come* from? Why is it important? Is it merely some biological imperative and, if so, why do couples who don't want children still fall in love, marry, and have sex? You see, Ms. Wheaton, we instinctively know that there is more to life and creation around us than what we can touch, see, and understand. We lie to ourselves, of course, because we dislike the notion of having someone else to answer to. We much prefer to be our *own* little gods in our own little worlds answering to no one—our own final authority. It makes it easier to cheat, divorce, swindle, and sacrifice everything at the altar of self if all that matters, in the end, is what feels good and what is right for each of us as individuals. And every bit of our self-focus drives us further and further away from seeking deeper truths…from seeing the hand of God at work in the muck and the mess of mankind."

"What you are asking me to believe—"

"The truth?"

"—is beyond rationality," I said. "I don't have a problem with you keeping your religion, Reverend Renata. But

I do not believe in miracles or the supernatural."

"You're suddenly quite formal," he replied. "And strangely *rigid* for a truth-seeker. Perhaps you are not the one I had hoped you would be."

"What does that even mean? The one what?"

"I have carried this truth for a great many years, Ms. Wheaton," he said, pointing at me with the lip of his pipe. "I had hoped to unburden myself to someone trustworthy. Someone for whom the truth would be...sacrosanct if not sacred. It appears I ask too much of you."

I don't recall replying. I don't recall much of anything, to be honest. Not the drive home. Not burning the file I had compiled on Renata. Not even the cause of the tears which woke me in the night. The next day, not fully understanding why, I drove back to Wimberley. I didn't bother calling. I found Tolly on the front steps of his church waiting for me.

I sat next to him not knowing what to say. The silence was deafening as I watched him fill his pipe and light it. I retrieved the digital recorder in my purse and pressed the record button.

"I wondered if I would ever see you again, Ms. Wheaton," he said at last, "or if I was a bigger fool than I had previously believed. Perhaps I had misplaced my faith in you."

"You may have," I admitted.

"Nonsense. You came back. That's all the proof I need to believe my faith was rewarded."

"For argument's sake, let's say I believe you, Tolly. If I were to imagine every single thing you told me yesterday was true—"

"Yes?"

"I need to know what happened *after*. I need to know how you got from there to here."

"You know a lot of it already," he said. "Some of the highlights were in your file."

"I don't mean the details of where you went and what aliases you used. I need to know how someone deals with being resurrected. I need to know when you realized you weren't going to die. I need to know—"

"Yes?"

"If you have regrets."

"Hmm. I see."

Tiny puffs of smoke billowed from his pipe as if it was a cloud factory for all the Whos in Whoville.

"The witnesses didn't feel any need to keep quiet about it," he finally said. "The word of my death and resurrection spread throughout Bethany and beyond. Jesus stayed with us a short while before he continued on his way. His disciples, though they marveled at all he had done, feared the forces rallied against him would use my resurrection as some sort of proof that he was a devil or something. I was sad to see him go, of course, but I feared his arrest. As you know, however, nothing would have prevented it."

"Did you ever see him again?"

"Yes. On the day of his crucifixion."

"You were there?"

Tolly's eyes never left mine, but his thoughts drifted far away.

"Once word of his arrest was made public, I tried to find his disciples, not realizing that most had scattered to the wind fearing their own arrests. I stood in the crowds lining the road to Golgotha. I saw him carrying his—"

Renata did not strike me as a man who was often emotional, yet the look on his face suggested that he needed a moment to compose himself. I said nothing.

"He was carrying his cross. Had I not been a close friend, I might not have recognized him. He was beaten and bruised beyond anything I have seen since. Not even in war, Ms. Wheaton, have I beheld something so brutal and unjust. And, when they hung him on that torturous device which has become, for believers, a symbol of our hope—the sign of a *finished* work—I stood there among the many and watched him bleed and die. The image of it still haunts my dreams now and again. How could it not?"

"And three days later?" I asked.

"Oh, I felt it even before I heard the news. His body wasn't there, they said. Someone had stolen him in the night. It all seemed quite mysterious to most of them, no doubt. But not to me. From the deep depths of my mourning, I felt his return. It was as if all creation had been holding its breath for three days when, suddenly, it was allowed to breathe again. I never got to see him, though. He appeared to his disciples, and a great many people saw him throughout the area over the course of the forty days which followed…but he was gone before I could get to him. If I have a regret, Ms. Wheaton, it is that."

"And when did you realize you wouldn't die?"

"It wasn't exactly an epiphany," Tolly said. "As time passed, I watched the people around me getting older, but I never did. Martha eventually passed away, and Mary and I were left to mourn. Then, Mary passed away and I was left alone to mourn. I became all too aware of the whispers. People were asking questions and looking at me strangely…as if they hadn't done so already."

"Small town gossip," I said. "A plague not unknown to the folks here in Wimberley, I'd imagine."

"Well, aside from my congregants, folks here have never had much reason to consider me. Your newspaper article would change all that, of course, but I trust you'll do with it what you think is best."

"Once you realized your condition, for lack of a better term, what did you do?"

"I sought counsel from those who walked with him. We weren't so organized in those days, of course, and the apostles had begun to travel in separate circles to expand the message of his life, death, and resurrection beyond the ground he had walked. They were witnesses with firsthand accounts of how he turned everything they thought they knew upside down. It was an exciting and dangerous time for all of us, but—one by one—they welcomed me as a brother. Unfortunately, none of them had any answers for me. If our friend had raised me with some larger plan in mind than underscoring the truth of who and what he was, he had never shared it with the likes of James and John.

I don't know how familiar you are with the fates of the apostles, Ms. Wheaton, but things ended badly for most of them. Some were martyred, some imprisoned…each and every one of them a living sacrifice for the glory of the God they served. They were not the smartest men, nor the bravest, but by the power of the Holy Spirit they were emboldened to carry the Gospel as far and wide as they could. Upon their deaths, others took up the call, and the story of my friend and his grace spread out to the four corners of the world."

"And you?" I asked.

He turned his eyes out toward the street and beyond, to the park where he and I had met the day before. The smoke from his pipe briefly clouded his soft features, but there was something in his warm, brown eyes that made it seem as if he was looking beyond the moment to an earlier time. Perhaps not remembering it so much as watching it play out like a vivid movie lighting a darkened theater.

"With the death of the last of them, I felt alone and adrift. What few remaining friends I had were old and not long for the world, so I asked one final favor of them: that they mourn me in public places and speak of me as though I had finally passed away."

"You faked your death?"

Tolly nodded.

"It was cowardly," he said, "but I was frightened and alone. I felt the need to leave the world I knew behind before anyone else could leave *me*. So, I traveled. When my money was gone, I begged for food. I worked for a while and was a slave for a while. Over the centuries, I made fortunes and lost them. I spent seasons in solitude and seasons enmeshed in the lives around me. My loneliness, however, followed wherever I went. I journeyed throughout Asia and Ethiopia. I told no one who I really was. By that point, who would have believed me?"

"You didn't marry?"

"No. Not for a few centuries. In spite of my great loneliness, I felt it would be awful to marry and have children only to outlive them all. Even if I shared my secret, they would think I was mad. I also considered that my undying nature might be passed to my children. What would it mean in the grand scheme of things? As wicked as man's heart can be, what might a race of immortal men unleash upon the world? I decided it was best not to find out."

"But you're married now," I said. "And you married Simonne. You must have changed your mind at some point."

"Of course, I did," Tolly laughed. "I am as weak a man as any you have ever met, Ms. Wheaton. Eventually the pain of my solitude outweighed my fear of the consequences, and I stopped hiding myself from the possibility of marriage. Over the years, I have loved many families. I've raised children and grandchildren. And I've watched them die."

He tapped his pipe on the step, shaking loose the smoldering remnants of tobacco in the bowl. He placed the pipe in his pocket and took a slow, deep breath.

The day was warm though not oppressively so, and the birds in the trees were joyfully singing back and forth to one another whatever stories the birds share. A cool breeze lifted the tobacco ashes from the steps and carried them down the street like a murmuration of starlings. I watched them go and looked back to find Tolly weeping.

"There is sorrow in every passing," he said after a moment. "Sometimes, death is grace. Sometimes, it is expected. I've found, though, that it always feels a bit unfair. I've spent too many days to count weeping over my children and theirs."

"I can't imagine what that must be like for you," I said.

"It's a cycle, you see? I love and lose and hide away. I've removed myself from being an active participant in the world more times than I can count. But, always, the seclusion prompts me to reengage. I love again. I lose again. I hide again. It is endless and horrible and beautiful and sad and joyful and cruel and gracious and…it is who I am."

I took his hand in mine. To this day, I still don't know why. I cannot tell you I *believed* his story in that moment, but I believed his sorrow. I felt it radiating from him as tangibly as the kindness and hospitality I had felt before.

"Did you ever lose faith?"

"In Christ? No, dear. Not in him. In the purpose of me? In the plan? Of course. How could I not? I am a frail human being and just as prone to wander into self-focus as any man who has ever lived. So, yes, I had my seasons of doubt. Seasons when faith took a backseat to self. Seasons when I questioned my place in it all. Maybe I had merely been caught in the hysteria around him and bought a ticket for the ride."

"I hear a 'but' in there."

He pulled a handkerchief from his pocket to wipe the tears from his eyes.

"No matter how far I drifted," he said, "I couldn't escape the tender sound of his voice. No matter what name I hid myself under, I could still hear him calling, 'Lazarus!' And as I had one day so long ago in Bethany, I answered his call. I've come to realize that I might never know *why*, Ms. Wheaton. I may never understand what has happened to me or its grander purpose, but…I *trust* him.

And just as I had felt that sense of waiting I spoke of, the sweet expectation that I would see him again, I feel I am waiting once more. Caught in the in-between. Whether or not I live until his return, I trust I will see him again face-to-face. And that's enough for me. It took me hundreds of years to get to this point, but it's enough. With that realization I decided that, although I had missed my chance to travel with the apostles and spread the story of the messiah to the hurting world, I could at least share it with those around me. I could be a simple minister in a small-town church. I could point men, women, and children to the truth and they, too, could be called from the grave of their day-to-day existence and into a new life."

"Why tell *me* all this?" I asked. I knew, of course, that I had come to him for answers, but the truth was that it would have been easier for him to lie to me or try to convince me of something I would be more willing to believe. Instead, Tolly had told me the least convincing story I had ever heard with all the conviction of a small child telling you what they want for their birthday. There was a realness—for lack of a better word—to Anatole Renata that I could not deny no matter how I felt about religion and the supernatural.

"You found me out," he said, giving my hand a squeeze. "You were a Godsend, Ms. Wheaton, in that you gave me a reason to stop hiding. When I received your phone call the other day, I remained utterly unconvinced by your stated motivation. So, I prayed."

"For what exactly?"

"For *you* exactly," he said with a kind smile. "That you would be someone I could trust. That you would hear me and not run away thinking I was a lunatic. That at long last, I could be myself with someone again without fear. Whether or not you believe me, Ms. Wheaton, you have given me a great and wonderful gift. I pray God will bless you a thousand-fold for your kindness to me. And since I am now free of this weight I have carried, I pray God will grant me rest. I have grown weary of this place and—"

"And you miss your friend," I finished for him.

"Yes. I long to hear his voice again without the veil between us. But, if I *must* tarry until his return, I will do so as his servant…assuming, of course, the publication of your story does not take that from me. But I trust you, Ms. Wheaton, to do what you think is best."

I smiled at him. I'd be lying to say a small part of me didn't worry that I was being taken for a sucker.

"I don't have any intention of sharing your story, Tolly. Whatever is or isn't true about you, I believe you're a good man. I may not ever have the sort of faith it would take to believe everything you've told me, but I think I have a bit of faith in *you*. And that's enough for me."

"But what of the mystery, Ms. Wheaton? What of the eternal search for truth? The need for answers?"

I considered his questions for a moment and stopped my recorder.

"I didn't get much sleep last night, Tolly. Our conversation stayed with me and turned my brain into Swiss cheese. But I came back this morning because I realized, whatever the truth might be, that some things are better left as a mystery. Not every question needs answering. I came back because I wanted to *hear* your story, not because I wanted to tell it."

"My prayers were answered, then," he said. "God has sent me a friend to know me as I am."

"Will you stay here?" I asked him. "Or will you disappear into a new identity?"

"I plan to stay put," he said. "How else would you be able to find me when you feel like talking?"

I smiled at the suggestion. I had no intention of becoming his friend. Yet, several times a month, I found myself sitting across from him in Larue Park, eating lunch and talking about his long life and my considerably shorter one. And eleven months later, when I received a call from his wife, Helen, I dropped everything and drove to Wimberley to meet her at the small community hospital which seemed, at least to my eyes, not to have upgraded their facilities since the mid-1970s. Helen explained that Tolly had collapsed on the steps of his church, clutching his chest. She had rushed him to the hospital immediately, but the damage to his heart was catastrophic. They had managed to keep him alive but, so far as they could tell, they had only briefly forestalled the inevitable.

"He asked for you," Helen said as she embraced me. "You've become such a dear friend, Nevaeh. I've tried to encourage him and keep him fighting, but...I think my Tolly knows his time is short."

I walked back to Tolly's room to find him attached to thoroughly modern equipment in spite of their outdated surroundings. I was no doctor, but I had been around long enough to understand some of the readings. It wasn't good. His eyes were closed but, when I took his hand, they fluttered open and homed in on me. It likely took what little strength he had left to muster a smile, but he did. And I wept.

"Save those sweet tears," he said, his voice ragged and weak. "This day is a prayer answered."

I shook my head. I wanted to say something—anything—to make it better. I felt powerless.

"I don't want you to go," I said, mentally chiding myself for my selfishness.

"I know. But you, my child, have given me such a lovely gift. You listened. You gave me a chance to be myself again. For you to have taken my secret upon yourself was grace to me. I have been thankful for you, Ms. Wheaton, since the moment we met."

I kissed his forehead, baptizing it with my tears.

"When you see your friend again, Lazarus, put in a good word for me?"

He smiled at me weakly.

"I will."

Helen came back to the room and we stood there together, each of us holding one of Tolly's hands. His children and grandchildren were on their way from other parts of the country, but they wouldn't quite make it on time.

On a peaceful autumn day, my friend, Reverend Anatole Renata, finally left this hard earth behind. I wept for him just as Jesus had so many years before.

AFTERWORD

I TOOK THE FIRST STEPS TOWARD SHADOW PLAYS in January of 2009. I had the ridiculous notion that I would write a new poem or bit of short fiction each and every day for an entire year. Right out of the gate, it was a much more daunting task than I had considered, but I managed to stick with it until mid-April at which point I burst into flames, cursed myself for a fool, and died a thousand painful deaths before my wife smacked me on the head for being overly dramatic.

Like a phoenix rising from the ashes, I recovered from my metaphorical demise and quickly put the poetry to work for me. The bulk of it, along with some newer pieces, found themselves in 2011's *I Am a Broken House*. The fiction, however, was set aside in favor of fresh pursuits, namely *Tales of the Evermore Volume One* and its sequel, both YA Fantasy tales in which I built a world and characters I plan to revisit many more times. In fact, a few of those characters returned in this very book.

Once *Tales of the Evermore Volume Two* was finished,

Afterword

I honestly didn't have the first clue as to what my next project might be. I still had two completed manuscripts which needed editing, a graphic novel I wanted to tackle, and a project I was cowriting with a friend that was only half-finished. Any of those could have been next.

Enter "The Cinder Man."

While writing the manuscript for *Tales One* (forgive me for shortening those lengthy titles,) I began a Patreon campaign as a way to let readers into my process. There are different tiers of support, of course, and different rewards for those tiers, but it was important that everyone who supported me, at even the lowest tier, would get some exclusive fiction—a story for their eyes only. Last year, that story was "The Cinder Man."

It's hard to explain how my mind works when I write. I can only tell you that writing "The Cinder Man" sparked a desire in me to tackle a few more short stories. It also reminded me that I still had fiction stretching back to my mad experiment in 2009 that had been shelved while I focused on my novels. So, I did a bit of digging and took a trip through the sort of stories I was writing all those years ago. I found humor, horror, romance, fantasy, and adventure.

I began to picture how they might all come together in a new collection, a collage of short fiction to bridge the chasm between who I was then and who I am now. It was an exciting enough consideration that I began to get anxious about writing some new tales, a few of which had been percolating in my noodle for some time.

I had the notion for a time travel story that took place entirely in a small diner, and another about a kidnapping gone awry. The character called Darke, previously a denizen of my fantasy tales, found his way into two more short stories, interacting first with a would-be mass murderer and, later, with a young vampire I borrowed from that graphic novel I keep threatening to write. I imagined a young man who followed easy street straight into hell on repeat and a disturbed young woman receiving phone calls from The Beast.

Strangely, my spiritual side found its way into the tale of a young man who spies Death sitting on a park bench, and through the story of a Methodist minister who happens to be much, much older than he appears. As someone whose writing is not likely to ever be labelled "Christian fiction," it felt a bit awkward for me to be so transparent about my faith, but those stories felt important to me, so I fought past my cowardice to be faithful to the Muse.

By far, the story I fretted over the most was the tale of a mother discussing with her daughter the impact of racism on the young girl's life. Though I am blessed to have connections to the black community, I know full well this middle-aged white man might not be anyone's first choice to tackle such a subject. Thankfully, the black mothers in my sphere, whose children journey through life alongside my own, were willing to read the finished work and provide their input. A tone-deaf story would've done the subject matter a grave injustice. These moms trusted my heart and leaned in to lend me their wisdom and their blessing. For that, I am truly humbled.

Now, here *you* are, dear reader, holding at last the work which, in some form or another, I've been working toward for nearly a decade. You are, as always, the final judge of my work. You alone decide whether or not it was worth my effort. As for me, I rather enjoyed my time with these characters, from bloody little Hubert to damaged David Kinneman, from Ed the raven to the late Reverend Anatole Renata. Each of them has shown me a bit of heaven or a bit of hell. Each has given me a portion of their story to tell. It is my fervent hope that you have enjoyed reading them as much as I have enjoyed writing them.

J. Patrick Lemarr

P.S. More than anything, we writers covet feedback from our readers. If you would be so kind as to take a moment to leave a review via Amazon or anywhere you feel readers would come across it, I would be ever so grateful. Reviews often prompt new readers to take the plunge and provide for me a lens through which I can see what worked and didn't work for my readers. As always, your kindness and time is greatly appreciated.

 J. PATRICK LEMARR, author, poet, and educator, lives in Texas with his wife, Heidi, and his three children. He currently works as a stay-at-home dad for the younger two kids, spending many of his off hours crafting his latest works of poetry and fiction.

Lemarr's Patreon campaign allows fans the opportunity to fund new works and receive rewards in exchange for their support. From update videos and exclusive short stories to advance releases and t-shirts, Patreon offers a unique way to participate in the author's journey and work.

SUPPORT J. PATRICK LEMARR'S PATREON TODAY!
WWW.PATREON.COM/JPATRICKLEMARR

 www.jpatricklemarr.com

 facebook.com/theofficialjpatricklemarr

 @jpatricklemarr

Other works from J. PATRICK LEMARR:

I Am a Broken House

Underneath (eBook exclusive)

Tales of the Evermore Volume One

Tales of the Evermore Volume Two

www.ingramcontent.com/pod-product-compliance
Lightning Source LLC
Chambersburg PA
CBHW070725280626
47159CB00023B/2699